To Dottie
From Mom

One Day a Stranger

One Day a Stranger

By

BETTY SWINFORD

* * *
* * *
* * *

MOODY PRESS
CHICAGO

Library of Congress Catalog Card Number: 71-123160

Printed in the United States of America

1

He stood in the doorway of his tent, head cocked as though listening intently for some sound on this Nubian night other than the strange flow of language, the raucous laughter, the weird Egyptian music, the staccato snap and bristling crackle of the fire. But there were no other sounds. Nor would there be until his mission here was over. Except for the occasional trips into Cairo to keep in touch with the Department of Egyptology and pick up supplies, this desert was his life. Paul Coltren and the tattered crew of dirty workmen, some of whom would undoubtedly cut his throat for a nickle and make off with any discovery he might make—if it could be transported.

He could trust Ahmed, his foreman. Blackened like an overtoasted marshmallow, Ahmed never bothered with thirst, burning sand, or broiling sunrays. All were alike to this long, lean man of the desert who had both lived in the desert and mastered it. For him it was not an enemy to be feared, as other men might fear, but an acquaintance which he treated with respect. He knew and understood its desolations, its devilish sandstorms that ripped and tore and destroyed; and he had learned to survive all its cunning devices and unexpected deviations. He had seen other men succumb to thirst and dehydration and swollen tongues, and even to death in the sand.

Ahmed was lanky, and when he walked he looked as if he might fall apart at any joint in his frame. He ambled along like a clown at a circus, like a marionette controlled totally by strings, like Ichabod Crane! He had thin black hairs sticking out of his chin like a schoolboy ready for his first shave. Paul secretly doubted that a razor had often touched the man's face. He was cleaner than the others and wore tan pants and shirt, his head continually swathed in a tattered white cloth and fixed in a crude turban. Yes, Ahmed could be trusted, for all his mixed-up traits.

Paul stepped outside into the soft shadows surrounding their camp. He only glanced at the crew of eight men who sat a little way from the fire that cast such strange masks over their bronzed faces. One was playing a high-pitched flute that gave off a sweet melancholy tune. Another man played an odd-shaped stringed instrument that jarred against the flute like an angry violin colliding with a French horn in an orchestra rehearsal. Yet, after listening for some time, it became not just a bearable sound but one that was almost beautiful. Perhaps here on the desert where there was no music and one had no choice, the ear could in time receive anything that resembled a melody. At any rate, with a few of the Arabs singing their strange songs in accompaniment to the instruments, it became quite satisfactory.

Some days singing was their life. Ahmed even led them in various chants while they worked at the excavation site. He claimed it made them produce better work and, besides that, it made the time go faster.

The American passed the tents and went into the desert a little way, feeling its throbbing loneliness, the emptiness of its arms, the futility of its death. And at last he paused, fully exposed now to the night and the white rays of moonlight. He stood with his hard hands hanging at his sides and allowed himself to be scrutinized completely by that white mist of light.

He wasn't a big man, Paul Coltren, but there was a square, determined set to his shoulders, and he carried himself tall and straight, sometimes almost stiff. His dark eyes bore the fire necessary for success, and they had the intensity of machine-gun fire. A clean, strong jawline spoke slightly of his Chippewa great-grandfather. His nose was thin and aquiline and severe, and his chin was set, firm, unchangeable. His countenance spoke neither of good looks nor bad. He was a man of severity who allowed little time for laughter. He was a man of fact, ruled by his head alone, a man of little emotion. He had a job to do and he wanted to succeed at it. He wasn't afraid of the liquid, searing heat by day nor the danger by night. He faced the desert, its thirst and its sand, as one would face an opponent in a ring. He wasn't afraid to live and he wasn't afraid to die. Only his eyes occasionally gave him away, for there lay within those fathomless depths some memory, some sadness, of which the man himself perhaps was not aware.

He grunted aloud, a sound that was really a choked-down chuckle. "Sure! You could have had that business office in the New York Department of Archeology. You could have." He pursed his tense lips, relaxed. "Sitting behind a desk made for a giant—carpet four inches thick—window overlooking a million misty neon lights—people. People laughing their silly laughs and living their little childish lives! Ha!" He lifted his face to the heavens, studied the Big Dipper like a sea captain charting his course before beginning a voyage overseas. "Their silly, meaningless little lives." The words bit and stung him like rankling canker sores in his mouth. "I wouldn't trade places with them for all the Rolls Royces and front-page prestige in the world." And this time he did laugh, the sound rolling up from deep within his stomach but ending as abruptly as it had begun.

He turned back on the endless sand track, a quiet ocean under the moon. Posing no threat, offering no resistance. Peaceful, alluring, restful.

Away in the distance, in a massive cliff of rugged sandstone, a jackal lifted its nose to the moon and sent forth one long, chilling wail. It almost blended with the mood of the singing from about the campfire. The answer to that eerie cry, however, was sounded after only a moment, and from a spot so near to Paul that it left his flesh tingling.

Paul's steps carried him on beyond his tent and past the rougher, coarser Arab tents to the dig. He smiled now to himself, and it was a smile of intense satisfaction. "You never know what will come out of the sands of Egypt!" He breathed in deeply, filling his chest, feeling the cold desert air in his lungs, and experiencing a deeper gratification yet. "Jackals. Hyenas. Scorpions!" He grimaced at the memory of the scorpion which had almost stung him a couple of nights back. *"Tombs!"* He threw back his sandy head and laughed without making a sound. "Old Egypt, you haven't given them all up yet!"

What a sensation, what heady significance to be on the very threshold of discovery! It was much the same feeling as riding the high ferris wheel for the first time back in Idaho. Their little town of Perrisburg had never seen a carnival until one balmy spring great trucks had come rolling in with such rides as he had never known to exist in all his ten years. He remembered the fear, the trembling of his muscles, the tingling of his nerves, the thrill of being swept high into the sky, and of wondering about coming down again and never wanting to.

Stooping, Paul lifted handfuls of sand and allowed it to flow through his fingers. What treasure did these sands hold for him? What all would they yield from the ages and ages beyond? How much would they give up? "What a life!" he murmured ever so softly. "No fancy carpeted offices for me, never! Who wants to sit around pushing computers, gathering and filing data for others, when he can be on the front lines himself?"

Carefully he reached forth exploratory fingers to touch the first few blocks that had been uncovered. "The beginning," he whispered, and the breeze moving from the north caught the words and erased them as easily as a hummingbird silently and secretly dropping down to sip nectar from a rose. "The doorway to a dream— All my aspirations springing into life!" He gulped down a breath of cold air, stood and looked up into the heavens again, as though they, too, belonged to him. "Success! That's what all of this spells out. Success."

He'd been struck down by poverty all his life. It was a fist jammed up tight against his face. One of the first quarters he'd ever had to spend on his own was for that ride on the ferris wheel. A deaf-mute farmer on a little farm in Idaho didn't have much in those days. Especially when his wife was old before her years and always needing a doctor.

Paul's teeth came together in a tight clench and he forced himself to change his thoughts. Deliberately he strode up the slight incline toward his tent. Away in front of him and to his right was a small oasis. He fancied he could hear the tight, thin rubbing of the palm branches silhouetted there against the star-spangled sky. Water at the oasis provided a splendid drinking supply for the occasional Bedouins who wandered that way and for the camel and his driver who passed by. And Paul Coltren also went to it for a fresh supply daily and then boiled it until it was safe for him to drink. A man could easily drink a gallon of water a day in the intense heat. Water in this land was life and strength and courage.

The music had nearly stopped and what was left was without life or energy. A few stringed notes here and there, a voice or two making a final effort at melody. Even that dropped away as Paul approached. Some of the men were drinking date wine.

Paul's gaze was sultry. He quietly drew his hands into fists. He could feel the fiber of his whole being take on a certain unexplainable tension toward his scrubby crew. Tattered, dirty clothing. Shoes without strings. A couple of the men were barefoot, their feet conditioned to the burning sand from long years of living with the blazing fireball that would rise exactly on time the next morning. Straggly hair stuck out of their turbans, hair probably eaten with lice and filth.

"Don't let them get drunk, Ahmed!" Paul shouted half in anger. "We have a lot of work scheduled for tomorrow!"

Ahmed rose and sauntered to him, baggy trousers trying to catch his narrow frame as he moved. The Arab stopped three feet from Paul, and the face under the white moon was one of complete innocence. His turban was set at a jaunty angle and his breath spoke of Egyptian cigarettes and thick coffee. Ahmed spoke fluid English.

"Mr. Coltren, most of these men have worked for me before, and they know when to stop drinking. I'll see that the others don't get too much." He gestured as one having a broken wrist. "You've been down to the dig?"

Paul relaxed. He always relaxed around Ahmed, for the Arab never got in a hurry and Paul doubted whether he had ever had one tense moment in his life. He remembered what his class had been told once in college by a professor of psychology.

"When you start to tense up and your mind gets too tired, that's the time to take a few minutes off and relax. Pretend you're a rag doll filled with sawdust and there's a small leak in your cloth exterior. Watch very carefully as the sawdust trickles out of your frame and you grow more and more relaxed—limp—with every small loss. Soon, when the sawdust has all leaked out, you'll find yourself completely relaxed."

The fellows had laughed about it after class and said the old guy had been in the school too long. But they tried it secretly and found some measure of truth in what the professor had told them.

So it was watching the Arab and his slow, definite, liquid movements. Paul wondered if the man was put together with loose rubber bands.

"I couldn't help looking just once more," Paul confessed with a smile. "I can see it already—marble columns—all kinds of artifacts—maybe a large boat!" He was caught up by his own enthusiasm. "Why, we may have the tomb of a king!"

He stopped speaking abruptly and the two men laughed briefly together. It was a night to laugh, even though both of them knew the very remote possibility of discovering anything very famous. It was true of course that there were famed Egyptians still unaccounted for, but that this should be a pharaoh or anyone famous was but fanciful imagination.

"But it *is* a tomb," Ahmed spoke softly, and to this Paul nodded heartily.

They looked at one another a moment longer, understanding one another and liking what they saw. Then Paul stepped back over the assorted pile of bulky supplies they had brought along—lumber, five-gallon cans, various saws, shovels, picks, and other implements—and went on to his tent.

Sitting down on the edge of his cot, he forced off his stubborn boots, placed his sun helmet on the small table by the Coleman lantern, and began to undress.

It was with a sense of disappointment that he looked over to the other cot. He wished fervently that Eddie Lambert was there with him as planned. But his co-worker had entered a hospital in Morocco, seriously ill with a ruptured appendix. The infection had been so critical that the man's life had been uncertain for a day and a night, but then the thread had tightened and the infection halted in its process of eating away the man's life. Eddie should be doing well by now and, unless there were any new complications, perhaps he would join Paul by the end of the month.

Paul had hated to come on alone, for Eddie was more experienced than he with work in Egypt. He understood the people and their customs. But there hadn't been another man available for the job, so Paul had come on alone.

He tumbled onto his cot, tucked the netting in securely about him for protection against scorpions and insects, and lay staring into the soft half-light. He envisioned the full uncovering of the tomb, for aerial evidence gave them full proof it was not just a portion of a wall. There would be the scaffolding to brace the structure, if needed, and the massive doorway, tall as though made for a dead giant! Strange-smelling air that belonged to another world and had managed to hide in the privacy of the tomb for long centuries. The chamber holding the mummies. Vases. Statues. Hieroglyphics.

He released an explosive breath, realized that his eyes were wide and strained, and closed them by force. Maybe he ought to try that rag doll bit tonight! But it was not necessary because exhaustion took him captive quite suddenly and he fell into deep slumber.

Somewhere, however, in that mysterious place between wakefulness and sleep there came a fleeting thought: *It's going to be smooth from here on out. Nothing can go wrong now. It's going to be great, and it's going to be a job well done for Paul Coltren!*

The stirring Egyptian music had ceased and the men had bedded down for the night. A jackal ventured close enough to sniff at the large pan which had held the crew's supper of rice and mutton. Its nose suddenly sent the pan clattering, the sound causing the animal to flee silently into the night. In the misty white veil of moonlight not a creature moved. Night had seemingly turned the land of antiquity into a land of death, its shroud of creamy sand covering everything.

And what about tomorrow? A majestic column, perhaps, waiting to see the world again? A piece of pottery, which was the archeologist's calendar of prehistory, a precious timepiece for this strange land? Maybe some hieroglyphics on the stones being uncovered?

The loneliness and peace of the night lay unbroken, a calm lake whose surface was too serene for skipping rocks or casting of nets or children splashing. The man passed more deeply into sleep. There could only be good in the future. A successful career. Money. Adventure. Skill. And he went deeper yet, a satisfied smile playing illusively about his lips.

2

*Paul was up at dawn and fully dressed. The clatter of pans out*side called attention to breakfast and the fact that the camp cook was well on his way to having the meal prepared. The aroma of food was not as offensive to Paul as it had been at first. In fact, he almost thought he could join the men for a meal. Only common sense stamped a sharp no in his thoughts. Lack of sanitation and their way of eating would only serve to bring on an attack of dysentery, and that was something Paul could do without. One such attack on a previous dig had been sufficient.

He could enjoy their coffee, however. Little danger there. He attacked his own supply of rations, bringing forth a can of ham and eggs, biscuits, dried fruit, and cheese.

"Just like downtown," he muttered aloud, "only not as tasty." He attacked the stubborn little can opener, peered down at the cold yellow eggs, and got a grip on himself. Then, picking up his helmet from the table, he went out into the brilliant sunshine that was already promising to broil the flesh by noon.

"Coffee, Mr. Coltren?" Without waiting for a reply, Ahmed took the empty cup from Paul's hand and poured the boiling liquid into it. Then he moved closer to the American, indicating that he really disdained the smell of sweat and filth and the ignorance of the other men. Ahmed sat down.

Paul hid his amusement, wondering if the Arab had ever taken time to examine his own body for distasteful odors. The American thoughtfully studied the chocolate-covered bubbles of foam on top of his coffee, but his mind was going actively ahead to the dig and there was a certain impatience that he was going to have to control.

Ahmed tugged his loose trouser legs up a little and brought up his knees, around which he wound his thin black arms. "Mr. Coltren, there's something I think you ought to know."

Paul shifted his dark eyes to the other man's face. "All right."

He pulled a large handkerchief from a back pocket and folded it into a sweatband, which he tied around his forehead. Then he perched the sun helmet on top of his sandy hair and waited. Ahmed usually took his time to tell something, all the better to use his dramatics, Paul thought, so the American had become accustomed to waiting for this strange, likeable Ichabod to move.

"Before daybreak this morning I went to the oasis for a water supply. A camel driver who had spent the night there was getting ready to leave while it was early. But," he said, staring reflectively into the distant reaches of sand, "we got into a conversation and he lingered on for about a half hour."

Ahmed fell silent, as though waiting for Paul to pick up the thin thread of conversation and continue the story.

"Well?" Paul asked patiently. At this point it was impossible to see even remotely what a camel driver at an isolated oasis could have to do with him.

"He had come from the Valley of the Kings, where some new excavation work is taking place. While passing through that area, he met a man by the name of George Arnold. This Arnold seemed to know his way around and the driver told me that he asked a lot of questions about this particular dig."

Paul's gaze flashed to Ahmed's penetrating black eyes. But he couldn't look at Ahmed's face long before seeing those black hairs protruding from his chin, so he turned back to the desert. Drawing his brows into a thought pattern, he inadvertently felt a tightness up around his chest and neck.

Now that his story was begun, Ahmed proceeded doggedly. "Arnold, the driver says, roams from Cairo to the Valley of the Kings, but it was this excavation that he asked about. Apparently he's looking for more than a perfume flask or a bit of pottery or half an alabaster face. Arnold isn't looking for souvenirs."

"You suspect he's a grave robber?" Paul asked quickly, setting aside his coffee cup with an abruptness that almost brought the loss of the thick sediment in the bottom. He'd save these today and let the sun dry them out and tonight around the campfire Mohammed would read them and tell Paul his fortune. Not that he believed it, of course, but it was a fascinating pastime. "And he thinks we have something good going for us here?"

"I believe so, Mr. Coltren." Ahmed had become a little more

excited than usual and his accent was becoming more noticeable. "The camel driver warned us to watch out for this man. He says Arnold speaks with a crooked tongue." The Arab grinned broadly in the American's direction. "That means he's a liar!"

Paul's teeth flashed against the bronze of his face for a moment. "I know what it means. Then you believe, Ahmed, that grave robbers are still on the prowl in Egypt?"

The Arab nodded his turbaned head firmly. "They have always been with us. They will always be."

Paul pulled his sun helmet forward, adjusted it against the sweatband, and rose to his feet. He stood at six feet and weighed a solid one hundred seventy. "All right, friend, we'll keep our eyes open for one Mr. Arnold. Let's get to work, all right?"

All the workmen had gone to the dig except two, and Ahmed prodded them with a sharp command in their native tongue. It came like a snaking whiplash from a master foreman and seemed utterly out of keeping with Ahmed's easygoing personality.

The heat had settled for the day, rising up to meet them from the sandy floor of Egypt and beaming down upon them from an alien sky. Searing, blistering heat that was relentless in its dealings with mankind in this desert wasteland. A trickle of perspiration passed from Paul's neck and ran down onto his chest, being absorbed at last in the fibrous material of his khaki shirt. Within minutes the whole back of his shirt was dark brown, a clean, neat pattern marked by perspiration.

He made a mental note that he was nearly out of water too. That meant a trip to the oasis at the earliest moment. But water and heat were both forgotten for the moment as Paul dropped to his knees to brush away the sand that was caked between newly uncovered blocks of stone.

The area around this wall was growing every hour as the workmen walked in and out of the dig with bucketfuls of sand on their shoulders. Primitive work methods still prevailed in much of the country; but since they proved to be steady and effective, it seemed ridiculous to try and force a change. Besides, no earth-moving equipment could ever do this work. The crew worked as mechanically as though power-driven. Carrying buckets that were handleless and some that were lopsided, the men scooped up sand in these vessels, hoisted them to their shoulders, and carried them out of the dig to empty them. Over and over, over and over, hour after hour.

Their faces showed no evidence of pain or struggle. In fact, they cracked jokes among themselves and sometimes sang for hours. Paul thought of all the statues he had studied in the Egyptian Museum in Cairo and the expressions of peace upon the stone faces. Maybe this was a kind of carry-over from their ancestors. Anyway, this particular crew was easygoing and, for the most part, agreeable. Paul was profoundly grateful for that.

To the ears of the American, the picks and shovels moved in perfect rhythm. Almost he could close his eyes and be listening to the Philharmonic. Whisperings of sound, then definite fortissimos, reaching for a crescendo so vast, so great, that it left the heart aglow with feelings of awe and overwhelming joy and inspiration. Thrilling! And this was greater than that, this grand concert of sound and feeling, this glorious music given forth from skillful precision, tawny arms, and sweating faces. And Ahmed, versatile enough to act not only as foreman but as choir director, stood swinging his arms fiercely. After a moment it began, the singsong chant that rose and fell with the dull thud of the pick and the more "bru-*ish*-ing" sound of the shovel.

"Salli ala elnabi!" Over and again. "Pray for the prophet. Pray for the prophet!"

He wondered if the workers of the pharaohs had perhaps chanted this way as they had built the great pyramids of Giza and the Step Pyramid of Saqqara. In their loose-fitting nightshirt-type garments and turbans, had they chanted to help them work and to keep up their spirits? What a sight it must have been in those days, hoisting and struggling with blocks that weighed about two and a half tons each—heaving, sweating, steadying, straining—

Paul stifled the desire to wrest the shovel away from the man in front of him and begin digging like he meant business. But he was not conditioned for such physical labor under a grueling fire bomb like the heavens held today. Nor was that his job. More and more, however, he was convinced that this would not be the tomb of a commoner. The slight formation showing up under the sand from the aerial photographs indicated a large tomb, perhaps an important one. And so, summoning a degree of patience that was contrary to his nature, Paul waited, his heart throbbing with challenge and anticipation every time a new block was uncovered.

Once, around noon, he thought he heard the distant sound of an engine. A jeep, perhaps. The name *George Arnold* leaped immediately to his thoughts, but he quickly turned it aside. No one with bad intentions would venture that close during daylight hours. Besides, Paul seriously doubted whether Arnold had any real designs on this dig.

Ahmed appeared out of nowhere, gesturing loosely with an arm. "A jeep passed not more than a mile away," he offered.

Paul nodded. "I heard it." He took a long gulp from his canteen and spit out the last mouthful. Having an insulated holder did little good in this land, for the water always became hot before noon. "Some idiot out for a bit of adventure," he returned after a moment. "Probably spotted that oasis and headed in fast."

"It was an American-made jeep," Ahmed said slowly, his dark eyes straining away in the distance.

Paul slapped his friend on the shoulder. "Forget it, Ahmed. You're real sharp, but Arnold—whoever he really is and whatever it is he might want—would never come around in the daylight." Paul wiped the perspiration from his forehead and neck and pushed the handkerchief back into his back pocket. "I'll take a look around when I go for water tonight. Though chances are, jeep and all will be gone by then. Right now, what do you say we knock off for lunch?"

"I'll buy that," Ahmed grinned, somewhat proud of himself for picking up bits of American slang.

Paul watched the men gather around a common bowl of sour camel's milk, swarthy hands reaching into the bowl with hunks of bread to soak up the milk. Watching made it a lot easier to dive into his own ration of cold beef, fruitcake that was musty-tasting, cheese, and peaches. From the small packet of coffee, Paul made himself a cup of the black brew.

"When I go to Cairo," he vowed, "I'm buying myself some real food. This stuff is all right now and then, but two weeks in a row is enough for me!" And, sitting down on a canvas campstool, he envisioned an inch-thick T-bone, broiled to juicy brown perfection, baked potato with mountains of sour cream, tossed salad of real vegetables—crisply raw and savory—and several cups of really good coffee. The only drawback was knowing where to go in Cairo to discover such a feast.

He downed the last drop of coffee, discarded the last few bites of fruitcake and cheese, and returned to the dig. He'd knelt so many times to examine the blocks that sand was pressed into the very threads of his trousers, leaving square patches of light tan against the khaki. Now, kneeling again, he saw for the first time that quarry marks were beginning to appear on several of the blocks. He looked even closer, his eyes aflame and his beaked nose throwing a strange shadow. This was for real! Markings left behind by the workmen of the dead—yet strangely living—past.

"Ahmed! Come take a look."

The Arab came quickly, the very personification of that rag doll. The American wondered that a man like Ahmed, having gone to an American school and acquired at least something in the skill of Egyptology, had not also learned something in the school of poise.

"Quarry marks," the sun-blackened man said quietly. "We're on our way, Mr. Coltren."

"Any idea what it says?"

The Arab shook his head slowly. "Probably something like *endurance* or *courageous gang*. They often gave themselves such names because the work was so hard."

Paul nodded. Anyway, he'd be photographing it, so they'd find out later just what it did say. He looked up and away across the desert sands, his penetrating eyes picking up and discounting the great, sparkling lake in the distance. Heat waves could do a lot of things.

Ahmed grinned, his teeth showing up dark brown from coffee stains. "You're feeling a bit impatient. So am I." He studied the sky briefly. "The day will be over too quickly. But," he added optimistically, "there's always tomorrow."

Paul looked skeptical. "Yes. Tomorrow." He unscrewed the cap of his canteen, only to discover that it contained but a few drops of water. It was four o'clock. He'd be heading for the oasis by six anyway. No sense sitting around for twenty minutes boiling a cupful of Ahmed's water.

"Go ahead," Ahmed urged, sensing the other man's mood. "By the time you come back you'll see a lot more accomplished than if you stand around waiting. I'll take care of things." He looked at the sky again, as though that dull, cloudless mirror told him everything he needed to know. "It'll be time to quit work in a couple of hours anyway."

The American nodded without answering. He strode away from the excavation and threw an empty five-gallon water can into his jeep. Then, without looking back, he started out over the dunes to the oasis a mile and a half away. His throat felt parched. Every day he went through this now. He'd get the feeling that he'd mastered the heat and thirst, only to find himself dried out by mid-afternoon. And then, even in spite of taking a long drink, his throat would grow raspy and sore. By nightfall it would begin to clear and by morning it was gone, only to return again that afternoon.

Visions of everything from icy root beer to iced tea passed before his eyes. He decided that iced tea would definitely have to be added to that meal in Cairo.

The jeep swung over the last dune and was headed for the nest of palm trees when Paul was suddenly aware that a change had been made at the oasis. Two tents stood near each other just under the shadow of the first palm tree, and a jeep station wagon sat nearby. They gave Paul the feeling that he was intruding.

"I knew I heard a jeep this morning," he murmured aloud, "but —tents! Makes it look so permanent."

Paul parked his vehicle with some hesitation. He'd been coming here freely for two weeks, bathing, lounging, getting water. He grimaced, pulling his lips tightly across his teeth. Then, taking a firm grip on his water can, he got out of the jeep. A cameleer, visible through the palm trees watering his camels, gave Paul courage to stride past the tents.

He tried hard not to look. At least he tried not to be obvious about it. Better to look across to the ruins of that ancient palace with its majestic porch and massive, marblelike columns reaching toward heaven like silent sentinels. But, in doing so, he could also see the camping stove, the great water jug, various skillets—*real eggs!*

He allowed his eyes to move slowly until they rested upon the doorway of the first tent. But a sound from within set him walking hastily on, making his way to that pool of crystal water nestled in the shade of a palm. It never ceased to amaze him that such an oasis could spring up here in these burning sands, fed by some hidden and mysterious spring. Welcome relief for hot, tired Bedouin—

He broke off abruptly, startled, Someone was singing! Paul swung his gaze in all directions, but all his eyes encountered was the dusty cameleer who was on his way out of the oasis. One of his animals roared loudly, as though in protest of leaving such a haven behind.

The voice came again, closer and more distinct this time. Paul waited, listening.

"One day a Stranger, a wondrous Stranger, came walking down by blue Galilee! None other spoke like this gracious Stranger—none spoke such wonderful words as He. . . ."*

Paul rose to his full height. His dark eyes narrowed and he felt a surge of an emotion related vaguely to that of rebellion pass through his innermost being. Still he waited.

"And this same Jesus still has the power—to save the lost and sick to—"

The song ended abruptly. A girl emerged from the trees and an unexpected flash of sunlight turned her hair to burnished gold. Lovely. Dazzling. But, upon seeing a stranger, her facial expression—previously one of joy and inner radiance—changed to chagrin and confusion, and her eyes became intensely blue.

"Oh, I—I'm sorry," she managed. "I thought I was alone here."

Paul, first strangely angry, now became simply frustrated. He summoned a smile that was without mirth. "Surely you aren't the wife of that cameleer yonder?"

She flushed so that he thought for a moment she was angry. An instant later, however, she smiled too and her countenance was as it was before. "Surely I'm not." She started to pass by him. "Excuse me, please."

He was blocking her pathway unintentionally. Now that she was in the shadow, he saw her clearly for the first time. The soft lines of her face, the blue, blue of her eyes, and the look of intense joy behind her eyes. He wondered if she laughed a lot.

Her hair was not as blonde as he had at first imagined. Rather, it was the color of wheat under the white brilliance of a full moon, ripe and waiting for harvest. Her lips were full with a touch of color and she stood very sure and straight. She was a young woman of purpose, of determination, of inner strength. Paul wondered who her companion might be, and if she realized her very dangerous position here in a world of men. Ruthless, hungry men who sometimes lived as long as four months without ever seeing a woman, let alone a striking young—

The roar of the camel smashed his thoughts and sent them flying into fragments. He recovered himself and moved aside. "I'm sorry, I didn't realize— Here, let me carry that pail of water for you. I can assure you that I'm quite safe." He smiled at her look of dubiousness. "My name is Paul Coltren and I'm an American like yourself." He glanced at her and away. "You *are* American, aren't you? And I'm an archeologist from New York. My dig is about a mile and a half away." He picked up the pail of water and gave her a mock bow. "Now, it's your turn."

She stared at him doubtfully a moment longer before bursting into laughter. "All right, Mr. Coltren. My name is Carolyn Foster and my father is doing—or will be doing—some agricultural experiments here at the oasis. And," she added thoughtfully, "I'm still not sure I trust you."

He rubbed his angular jaw. "I look better without a two-day stubble." Paul wondered at himself. He hadn't felt light inside like this in more months than he could count. Certainly he wasn't given to banter! His face withdrew back into a shadow of severity as he set down the pail near the tent. "You don't intend to drink this, I hope?"

"No. We brought distilled water along for drinking. But I thought, if I boil this, I can safely use it for washing pans and even for making coffee." Her voice was low, warm without being the least bit intimate, and when she moved it was impersonal yet with accurate liquid movements. She was a dash of color and melody and brightness in this forsaken brown land.

Paul knew he ought to get his own water supply and leave, but he stood irresolutely near the tent. "What exactly does your father plan to do here?"

She spread her slim white hands. "See what he can grow here, that's about it."

Paul laughed. "You make it sound so simple!" He was still facing her, liking her direct gaze and the way she stood in that unstudied pose that came clearly from an easy, uninhibited nature.

Carolyn cocked her head. "Actually, it isn't that simple at all. But Dr. Boyer from London declares that all such desert experiments involve the use of salty water, and such salt is often found under the desert in water. Such is the case in the Negev in Israel where Dad just completed extremely successful experiments. Dad believes he can produce vegetables, cereals, and fodder right here!"

Paul's dark eyes were almost smiling, though his mouth remained firm. He studied the girl intently, really not so much interested in her father's experiments as he was in hearing Carolyn's soft lilting voice.

Finally he shrugged and nodded at her. "Well, it sounds great. I guess if any place in the world needs food products, it's Egypt. I hope you have a lot of success." He tilted back his helmet slightly and gestured toward the vast reaches of sand to his left. "Only thing is, won't the sand continually shift enough to cover whatever is grown?"

She gave a slight toss of her fair hair. "When fertilizers are mixed into the sand and irrigation is brought in, the sand won't be likely to shift. And when areas are farmed, it won't be just small plots but thousands of acres at a time, so that whatever damage is done by the sand shifting will be along the fringes."

Paul readjusted his helmet. "Well! I've been taking up your time, Miss Foster. I hope you don't mind too much. In fact," he said, pausing hesitantly, "I'd like very much to come back sometime and show you the ruins of that old temple over there. It's been quite a place in its time. And maybe you and your father would come look at my dig one day too?"

"That does sound nice, Mr. Coltren. I'm sure Dad would like seeing both the temple and your dig."

Paul was abashed, but he quietly regathered his thoughts. He stood very tall, very bronzed. Looking around at the various camping supplies and allowing his eyes to linger on the cold, silent coffeepot on the camping stove, he went on doggedly. "Maybe you'll even invite me for a cup of coffee sometime." The inflection in his voice said, "Like tonight," but Carolyn, if she had noticed, dispelled any such idea.

"I have a lot of unpacking to do. You see, I *don't* want to be shipped off for home, so I've got to prove my worth." She hesitated, smiled shortly and nodded. "But, of course, Mr. Coltren, we'll have you *sometime*. Dad and I will eventually arrive at that place where just speaking to another American will be glorious! Meanwhile, thank you for carrying my water for me." And the young woman disappeared into the tent.

Paul's mouth twisted to one side and he felt the stirring of new anger. Then, deliberately shrugging as though to throw off some unwanted weight, he went to the pool, dipped deeply with his can, and returned to the jeep. He even put his deflated ego so far under as to throw back his head and laugh on the way from the oasis. Certainly he didn't need a female companion to sidetrack him from his work.

"Carolyn." He tasted her name slowly. It was a nice name. It flowed. "Carolyn."

A frown brought his dark brows in close. His teeth were hard together. The song. Why had she been singing such a song? A sensation, short-lived but akin to frustration, stung him.

He pulled the mask of severity easily into position. He would become disenchanted over Carolyn before she ever touched his life at all. That was the safe way. And once again his brown eyes became cold business. The skin stretching from his eyes to his chin even took on a look of tautness, though searching fingers did reach up to stroke the sandy stubble that covered his face. It was in this strange mood of irritability and half anger that Paul arrived back at the dig.

3

The Arabs were working steadily when Paul arrived. He heard them chanting their endless song before he got there. It was a rather weary, meaningless sound that hung motionless on the great empty canopy of sky over desert.

The men swarmed about the dig as bees around the hive on the farm back in Idaho. In and out, up and down the incline, carrying bucket after bucket of sand. Some of the so-called buckets were simply old tires cut in two, forming a kind of deep vehicle for carrying the sand. Every shovelful was sifted carefully before it ever left the excavation site, lest a fragment of pottery or some other valuable remnant be lost.

Paul cut the ignition and sat with his chin on one fist. The walls looked good, solid, clean. The workmen had skillfully worked around the adjoining wall, so that now there was a definite corner on the structure. Those who were not carrying sand and were more skilled in the labor were working carefully with knives, brushes, picks, and shovels, each picking out a sound of its own and combining all into a kind of desert melody.

Ahmed, having spied the American's return, came toward the jeep quickly. He paused breathlessly beside the jeep.

Paul grinned briefly. "It's coming along fine. The doorway should begin to show before too long. Two or three days from now, I should judge."

The Arab nodded soberly as he caught a loose strand of his white turban and tucked it expertly into place. "Do we have visitors at the oasis?"

Paul swung his long legs from the doorway of the jeep. "Sure enough! Americans! How about that, Ahmed, can you take it?"

Ahmed's piercing eyes strayed toward the invisible palm trees. "What is their business?"

Paul put his strong bony hand on the other man's shoulder and shook it firmly. "Now, don't go getting suspicious of everyone. Mr. Foster is an innocent benefactor. He's an agriculturist, and he's trying to see what will grow on this desert."

Ahmed pulled his mouth downward and nodded. "Well! That kind of business we can use." He grinned sheepishly. "It's Americans like Arnold that worry me."

Paul sighed, lifting his brows high. "So right, my friend." He picked up the five-gallon water can by its side handles and swung it upward and through the door. But the bottom of the can caught on the flange where the door fastened and the can fell forward, with the lid dislodging and water splashing Paul from the waist down.

Ahmed twisted his face to one side and shrugged. "Another trip for water, eh? Well, as you would say, that's life!"

Paul swore under his breath, but it turned quickly into a moan. "Yeah, that's life, Ahmed. I can't say I'm for it!"

He walked away with deliberate steps, his boots carrying him toward the dig. At least his canteen was full, so he wouldn't have to make another trip until nightfall.

His lips were pressed into an invisible line, and there was a look of hardness in his eyes. He had no desire to have another encounter with Carolyn Foster. Sure. Sure, it had seemed nice there for a moment to have a girl around. But, being absolutely rational, he didn't want or need her. The desert was no place for a woman anyway. Why hadn't she remained at home in the States?

One day a Stranger, a wondrous Stranger, came walking down by blue Galilee. None other spoke like . . . and this same Jesus still has the power—

A cynical look came to mingle with the hardness. If a girl had *had* to come to this barren land, why couldn't it have been one like he'd known back in New York? A girl with neon lights in her eyes instead of stars, one who knew her way around and liked to play and have fun. One who liked to play the game of life a little dangerously, even. But, then, a girl like that would never leave the lights and the music for a desert like this anyway.

He stifled the foolish sense of anticipation that had leaped within his heart at the realization that he must return to the oasis tonight. An anticipation that belied all he had just told himself.

"She's not my type," he softly muttered. "She's definitely not my type."

Eagerness for the work rebounded quickly within his heart as he stooped to survey the newly uncovered blocks. And a new, unusual marking alerted him just at ground level. He traced it gently with a forefinger. This was not the marking of a quarry gang; this was a personal marking. He'd bank anything on it!

His long, lean frame came quickly to a standing position, but he was back examining the mark almost instantly. His nostrils flared with excitement, and his long brown hands reached out again. This time he picked up a brush and with tender strokes dislodged some crusted sand. "Ahmed! How about taking a look at this?"

The Arab rounded the corner and knelt beside him.

"What do you think?" Paul and the other man gazed briefly into one another's eyes, so intently as to penetrate the soul. Then their eyes fell once again upon this strange new marking.

The Arab spoke wonderingly. "It's clearly a different marking from the others." A deeper accent sounded in his voice now, as it commonly did when he was excited. "The cartouche, perhaps, of the one buried here. Perhaps not. Time—" Ahmed rose and looked thoughtfully toward the rugged, almost forbidding cliffs in the distance. Somewhere in that general direction lay the Valley of the Kings, that remarkable place where so many tombs had been uncovered, many of them already looted but nonetheless valuable and where new discoveries were still being made today. The intensity of Ahmed's black eyes said he was hoping secretly that this tomb would be such a valuable one. "Time will eventually tell us all her secrets," he mused softly.

Paul could not keep from giving the foreman a wry smile. Ahmed was a many-faceted man. Not one thing about him seemed in keeping with the next. Totally uncoordinated in every way, yet perfectly coordinated. Quick. Intelligent. A perceptive thinker. But—a dreamer, too, this desert dweller. Easygoing, but stubborn as old Job, the mule that had plowed miles of furrows for Paul's deaf-mute father.

"Well!" Paul breathed deeply. He felt something like a detective having found his first real clue, the clue that would in time solve the mystery. He turned now to Ahmed, the dreamer, and awakened him gently from his reverie. "Isn't it true, Ahmed, that many times in ancient Egypt the son or successor would finish the father's work?"

"That's true," Ahmed replied, then added with a cunning smile, "and many times much praise and glory would be added of which the father was not worthy."

"Build up the family name," Paul said, his voice edged with sarcasm. "Would you believe they do the same thing in my country? You should hear the amazing obituaries I've heard read over downright scoundrels!" He glanced at Ahmed, saw that the man did not really understand what he was saying anyhow, though he was trying desperately to put on a mask of bright intelligence. Paul waved a hand. "Forget it! I'm going for my camera."

It was a quarter to six and there was plenty of sunlight for pictures. Besides, Paul was restless. Every nerve seemed to be crying out for diversion. Crazy, ridiculous, that's what it was! He was on the verge of his first discovery in the land of Egypt, and he felt like he'd explode if he— Where *did* he put that camera? Let's see—he'd had to hide it from the curious workmen. Oh, sure! He pulled out a wooden box from under his bed and began pulling out rations. The camera was on the very bottom, a Polaroid 360.

The workmen stayed at the dig until a quarter till seven. Daylight hours were excellent and the searing heat left the desert men undaunted. While Paul's feet burned through the heavy leather soles of his boots, those workmen who strode through the sand barefoot seemed oblivious to the fact that the sand beneath them was like hot coals.

Paul returned to his tent only when the crew broke for the day. Looking over the various tins of rations with a feeling of disdain, he replaced them and shoved the crate back under his cot. Maybe later. Right now his stomach was too upset to cram food into it.

He set a small round mirror upon the table beside his cot and surveyed himself critically. "Beard's grown a foot," he muttered to himself. He dumped the water from his canteen into a washpan, making a mental note that one need not even heat water to shave in this climate. The only reason to boil it was to make it safe for drinking.

What a handicap, having a woman at the oasis! The way it had been up till now, Paul could come and go as he pleased, wander about, enjoy himself to the full. Now he'd have to endure skimpy baths in the heat of this tent.

He took a final sweep across his right jaw, felt it gingerly to be certain the blade had been sharp enough, and laid the razor aside. Maybe he ought to remove that sweatband. There! He did look somewhat better. Flinging the water from the pan out the tent door, Paul reached for his helmet and went outside.

"Sir!" It was Ahmed, rising from his squatting position like a limp pile of dirty clothing come to life. He approached the American. "A shave and clean clothes! All this, Mr. Coltren, just to go to the oasis for water?"

Paul's head lifted involuntarily and his dark eyes became suddenly contemptuous. "So? What does that mean, Ahmed?"

The Arab, not catching the inflection in either eye or voice, made a stab at mock seriousness. "Why, nothing, Mr. Coltren. Only, one of my men reported to me that he thought there was a beautiful girl at the oasis."

Paul's head lifted even more and his shoulders went square and stiff. "I wouldn't know whether Miss Foster is beautiful or not. I paid no attention. As for you, Ahmed, I suggest that you mind your own affairs."

Angrily Paul swung the water can into the jeep and slid onto the seat. A moment later he left a bewildered Ahmed looking after him. Paul didn't look back. He jammed the stick into second gear, and the vehicle hesitated and coughed for a moment.

OK, so now Ahmed knew that there was another side to his employer's nature! Only thing was, it left a man feeling so blamed foolish after such an explosion. Like a schoolboy caught writing bad words on the blackboard and then having to come back into the room and face everybody.

Night fell softly on the desert, leaving a rose-hued misty veil that hovered over the horizon and turned the sand to pale lavender. It lingered for minutes and was gently pulled back as stars popped into the sockets of night to deck the heavens with myriads of light.

The headlights of the jeep barely picked out the ancient pillars of the temple through the palm trees. Paul cut the ignition and sat for a moment in the cool darkness. The heady aroma of coffee, well brewed, floated on the night air, and the sound of a pan against the camping stove lent the oasis a "back home" atmosphere.

They'd had a cast-iron cooking stove on the farm that had burned both coal and wood. Early mornings, before dawn, had found Paul waking to just such a sound of a pan against the plates on that old stove. Usually it was a pan of oatmeal which had been as tastefully prepared as possible, then served with real cream, produced by the farm's one milking cow. His mother had always managed to make something extra delicious out of something ordinary. He'd loved her very much, his only link with a world of voices.

Sighing and thrusting aside his silent musings, Paul got out of the jeep and started past the Foster camp. Casually he glanced ahead to the Arab tent and hoped that the Fosters' guides were "protectors" also. The sound of trickling water came pleasantly from a point ahead, and a soft breeze stirred the fronds of the palm trees, tracing into their movements the delicate grace of a ballerina. This oasis was not waste or desolation. After a day in a searing sand pit, it was a paradise. Lovely to behold, a haven for a tired mind and body.

And, suddenly, there was Carolyn. Paul hesitated, made a small try at avoiding her, and finally stopped where he was, summoning his charm and self-confidence. He felt very tall, very masculine, beside her slimness.

"I seem to be barging right through your camp, Miss Foster. I'm sorry."

"We didn't buy this oasis, Mr. Coltren," she replied quickly, "and you did have a path worn to the water. Besides," she added, as though to put the man completely at ease, "now you can meet my father."

Paul smiled in spite of himself. A feeling of exhilaration left him tingling. He liked the clean sweep of her brows, the soft contour of her face, and the slight flip in her shoulder-length hair. He liked her in white jeans and tennis shoes and wanted to warn her about scorpions, but he didn't. He wondered if she realized how crude and uncouth the guides might be at times and hoped that no one would hurt her. Men came by the oasis for water frequently, and Carolyn was a most attractive feature.

"Mr. Coltren?"

Paul caught himself up. "Yes! You're Mr. Foster!" He extended his hand and hoped it hadn't been too obvious where his attention had been. "I'm glad to know you."

As their hands met, so did their eyes. Paul found himself looking into the face of a man of perhaps fifty-five. A Coleman lantern, fastened to a hook at the corner of the tent, threw the professor into clear relief and showed him to be a man of energy and purpose. He possessed clear gray eyes and straight white hair which was neatly parted down the middle, so thin that the scalp could be seen along the part.

Professor Foster had tenderness and dignity. His speech and movements alike were precision-like, and yet his handclasp was warm and strong. The twinkle in his eyes said he had a fountain of perpetual joy within his heart, and the hard yet gentle lines upon his pinkish face said he could be compassionate and kind.

Paul liked him immediately. Then both men realized that they hadn't even waited for Carolyn to introduce them and they laughed as at some private joke.

"Call me Jim," Mr. Foster said. "Come sit down for a cup of coffee," he urged.

"That aroma is hard to resist," Paul said, gulping a deep breath of delicious air. "But I know you both must be tired. And, actually, I never meant to return tonight. I came for water this afternoon. Then I upset it before getting out of the jeep." He hesitated. "Another time soon, perhaps?"

"Nonsense!" the professor snorted. "We won't take no for an answer. Do you have a third cup unpacked, Carolyn?"

"I do," she declared quickly, and Paul remembered her previous statement about having work to do that day and that perhaps she would invite him for a cup of coffee *sometime*. He felt a vague sense of satisfaction over being invited in spite of her.

Mr. Foster sat back in the canvas chair and crossed one bony ankle over the knee of his other leg. "Well, Mr. Coltren—or shall I make that Paul?—are there other Americans in your party?"

It was easy to be comfortable and relaxed in Jim Foster's presence. Paul had a hunch that he would be gracious alike to either Bedouin or dignitary. He made one feel that he was doing the older man a favor just by being there.

"Call me Paul, by all means," the archeologist encouraged. He took off his helmet, suddenly aware that he was still wearing it. It had become a part of him in past years, but now it felt good to have the chill night air drying out his hair again. "Besides, it's a little ridiculous to stand on formalities here," he added, a little giddy over strong fresh coffee and the presence of other Americans. He sipped the coffee slowly, allowing it to brace him and wipe the cobwebs from his brain.

"You asked if there are other Americans in my party. Yes and no. I left New York with a co-worker, Eddie Lambert, but he became ill in Morocco and I had to leave him behind with a badly ruptured appendix. He'll be joining me as soon as possible."

Jim Foster laced his thin fingers together and studied them thoughtfully. "You'll have to forgive my ignorance on the subject, Paul, but are you a free-lancer of some sort, or do you work under assignment?"

"I work for the New York Department of Archeology—studied at Princeton. The New York Department works closely with museums, other exploration parties and archeological foundations. At the moment we are working in cooperation with the Department of Egyptian Antiquities." He allowed his gaze to stray to Carolyn, studying the design in her orange and white blouse. Surely she didn't mean to try and stay this fresh looking all the time. Obviously she did not yet know of the boiling sun rays that bore down day after day after day, never letting up. Nor of the sand that the angry breeze would throw into her soft, sweeping hair. Nor of the weariness after the heat had managed to wring out all life and vitality.

"Is your work progressing well?" Jim asked, pretending not to notice Paul's apparent diversion.

The young man brought his gaze swiftly back into position upon Jim's face. "Much better than we expected! You'll have to come see our dig, Jim. Of course," he added with a brief smile, "after you have your own work underway." He held his cup for Carolyn to refill with the fragrant brew. "And what about your work, Jim? How will you begin? How do you know what to do first?"

Professor Foster contemplated silently before making any kind of reply. His linked fingers, laid flat together, pointed upward over his chin. "Some of it will be strictly trial and error," he said at last. "We'll construct a long board fence to use against the sand shifting, and we'll determine whether or not there are salt deposits underneath. I'm getting in a fairly good shipment of soil nutrients tomorrow. Nitrogen, vitamin B, potassium, and other minerals.

The need of some things will be ruled out, of course. Other nutrients will be demanded in large quantities. We'll know that by experiment."

"I suppose that's one reason why your work—and mine—is so fascinating."

A sound arose some twenty-five yards away. It began with a musical tinkling that was both strange and delightful. After a moment it was joined by other equally unusual sounds of music. Finally, to the ear accustomed to Egyptian music, a kind of melody came into being.

To Carolyn's inquiring gaze, Paul replied, "That first one was a sistrum. Rather an unusual instrument these days, even in Egypt where they were once played. A man in my crew even has a double flute which looks as if it came from the days of the pharaohs. He brings it out occasionally and plays it at night."

"That's amazing." Carolyn sat forward, listening to the music, weirdly beautiful in the unusual setting. "Do you suppose a person could pick up any such instruments in a curio shop?"

Paul shook his head. The perspiration had left his hair crisper than usual and a little unruly. He passed his hand over it absently. "I doubt if you could. At least, not the genuine article; museums have eaten them up. But you can buy a replica of almost anything *anywhere!* You'll see what I mean before you leave Egypt."

"Tell me, Jim," Paul asked, swinging around in his chair to face the other man directly, "why did you choose this particular desert to work in? Why not Arabia or the Sahara or some such place?"

Jim Foster brought his thin, veined hands to rest on the aluminum arms of his canvas chair. "Well, like you, Paul, I'm working under assignment. The US Department of Agriculture is interested in food programs in other countries, as you know, and Nasser is making land available to the people right now. Of course the land is no good to them, or to anyone, unless it can be made to produce. And then, too," he said with feeling, "there is such *need* here. The Jews have piped water into the arid regions of the Negev and it's producing wheat, citrus—why, I imagine they could make it produce anything they set their minds to!" He sobered quickly. "With Egypt, it's different. Poverty is present everywhere. The people are depressed by many things, hunger perhaps being the least of them."

"Depressed?" Paul laughed, the sound breaking forth like a bubble from the bottom of a lake, only to be immediately silenced. "Depressed? That makes it sound like they've got the blues. Come on, Jim, I can't agree with you on that score."

During the short silence that followed, each of the three persons was made aware of the music, sweet and melodious, that drifted on the cold breeze. *Why,* thought Paul, *even the tops of the stately palms are swaying with the music! Depression in that?*

"Not the blues, Paul," Jim asserted at last. "Although I see little laughter or real joy in their faces. But depressed—oppressed—by hunger, thirst, poverty, being driven by cravings they don't understand."

Paul pressed his lips and frowned, his sandy head tilted to one side. "Like what?" he pursued.

Jim's eyes were the most honest Paul had ever looked into. He almost had to swing his gaze aside, and it was with difficulty that he kept himself steady under the other man's deep searching.

"Like spiritual oppression, Paul. Spiritual hungerings and thirstings that some men never find in a lifetime and that others never apply, even though certain truths have been made plain since childhood. The light of God's truth went out long ago in this land, Paul, and when this takes place, wherever it be, oppression takes over. We've seen it in Mexico and Africa and other places."

Something inside of the archeologist suddenly stood up, something bitter and very angry, something that wanted to lash out, to fight back. He swallowed very carefully, blinked to clear his hot, dry eyes, and took up his coffee cup again to try and hide any feelings that might inadvertently be showing.

"Do you think," he asked when he could trust his voice again, "that solving the problem of physical hunger can also solve that problem?"

"Never," the professor declared emphatically. "But if my efforts here will help only a little, I'll be glad for it."

Paul clamped his jaw tightly shut and made no reply. Only the narrow slits of his eyes, burning like a bed of coals, spoke for him. The stillness was complete when the music died suddenly. Paul felt a quivering in his muscles and he sat tense and stern-faced, waiting for the moment and the mood to pass.

"More coffee, Paul?" Carolyn asked quietly, her tone suggesting that she knew his mood and would like to ease the situation for her father's sake. And Paul, not wishing to offend, for whatever cause, relaxed and forced himself to respond.

"No, thanks, Carolyn. The time's gotten away from me completely. Ahmed will think I've taken off for an evening in Cairo." He rose and stood for a moment with his hard brown hands gripping the back of his chair. "Coffee was delicious. Thanks." He gestured. "Oh, say, how would the two of you like to walk over with me to get the water so that I can show you the remains of the temple beyond the palms?"

Jim got to his feet and extended his hand. He was straight and tall and, while he was characterized by a certain gentleness, there was strong command for respect. Jim Foster was not a man who could be deceived or walked on, for he was also a man of perspective and strength. Paul liked him immensely.

Carolyn's wide-spaced eyes were alight with eagerness. "Do you feel up to the walk, Dad? I'd like very much to see the temple and hear its story."

Jim gestured with a hand. "I'm a little tired. But you go on—tell me about it when you come back." The professor poured himself another cup of coffee and sat back down. If he had been even momentarily perturbed over the attitude of the archeologist, which Paul seriously doubted, it certainly had not been evident.

They walked the distance slowly, Paul matching his naturally long gait to Carolyn's shorter strides. There was no need for him to use a light even when they approached the steps leading up to the columns of what was once a spacious temple. Moonlight sprayed the oasis and turned the treetops to silver. A breeze whispered its secrets about them in soft little giggles and then suddenly became silent, as though its privacy had been abruptly invaded by alien forces.

Paul looked at Carolyn and felt an odd chill race up his spine. She wasn't beautiful, but she was pretty. Striking. Feminine even in jeans. Her wheat-colored hair, barely shoulder-length, swept gently with the renewed stirring of wind. She trembled in the chill night.

"You see the columns, Carolyn?" Ridiculous question! She was looking right at them. One could scarcely see the steps without seeing the columns also! "They're very much like the great columns of the Luxor Temple in that they're formed like papyrus buds. I think the greater beauty is the hieroglyphics that cover these particular columns; but for all that, they're pretty much unimpressive because no one has found out why they're here or who they were built for."

"I think the place is lovely," she cried softly. "Think what it must have been when it was new! Can you imagine Samson getting hold of such massive pillars and bringing down a whole temple upon the people?"

"I cannot," Paul replied coldly.

His voice caught her off guard and she spoke again without looking at him. "Paul? You didn't agree with my father on spiritual issues at all." It was neither a question nor an accusation. It was merely a statement.

Paul braced one foot on a higher step. He felt that he was also bracing himself on the inside. He had no desire to speak of political or religious views. Especially the latter.

"Well, you're right about that, Carolyn." There was a restlessness in his voice that mounted to impatience, like the storms that used to strike their little Idaho farm. A strange restlessness would fall upon the countryside and the cow would bawl and the mule would hang its head. And finally the tossing wind of impatience, until at last the storm would break.

"Do you not accept God's Word as fact?" she explored carefully.

He spoke with measured words. "I believe," he said firmly, "that the Bible is a book of impoverished myths, and I believe that those who read it and place faith in it *are fools!"*

Carolyn's breath caught sharply and a look of hurt came into her eyes. "You sound like someone else I talked with once. She said that so-called Christians were weak little plants taken from a hothouse before the time of maturity and placed in a world that's reeling to and fro."

"And making little impression on that world, I might add."

"Do you mind, Paul, if I ask why you feel so strongly?"

"You can ask." His lips were so tight that they bared his teeth. "But I can't answer." He turned and took her arm to guide her down the steps. The enchantment of the night had fled, the moonlight was senseless, and the desert about them was but a desolate sea of nothingness. Even the remains of the ancient temple had totally lost their charm. “Let’s go.”

She followed him wonderingly. “All right, Paul.”

He got the water in silence and in silence returned it to his jeep. Reentering the tent, he picked up his sun helmet. “Good night, Jim.” He turned briefly. “Carolyn.”

“Good night, Paul.”

The young American started the jeep, revved the engine a couple of times, and felt the tire treads conquer the sand. His head spun and his heart was beating a kind of staccato. Somewhere—somewhere deep within—something had been disturbed. But what it was, Paul could not—or would not—say.

4

One day a Stranger.

Paul sat bolt upright and became all but hopelessly entangled in the mosquito netting. For a moment his face contorted with anger; and then with deliberate care he forced himself to be calm. Gently his long fingers smoothed back the netting and he got up from his cot.

There! He was going to have a good day. And he was not going to the oasis. Not if he perished from thirst or his body rotted with filth and perspiration. He would send Ahmed after water. And most certainly he was not going to awaken again with that—*that song* going through his mind.

"Salli ala elnabi! Salli ala elnabi!"

Pray for the prophet! Pray for the prophet! That meant Ahmed and the workmen were on their way to the dig. Peering out the tent doorway, Paul glimpsed the men in khaki. Walking with awkward grace among them were other men who clung to the old-type Arab dress—the long, nightshirt-type covering. Their shadows fell behind them over the sand, their heads appearing large and irregular because of their turbanlike headdress.

Apparently a happy group, these. Certainly didn't look oppressed. They had their wine and their songs last night and—Funny, but all the people Professor Foster—Jim—had mentioned as being oppressed had to have their strong drink. Could it be that it was a kind of innocent defense against the very oppression they suffered?

"Well, if that's true," Paul told himself through tight lips, "it's because of so much sickness and poverty. Period!"

He gave his belt a jerk that put it in the wrong notch, so he had to do it all over again. Leaving his shirt open at the throat, he reached for his sun helmet. Might as well put some water on to boil. He'd come back in about twenty minutes and turn off the heat. Dratted water supply, anyhow. Next time he was in a town where they had distilled water, he was sure going to put in a supply!

The thought of breakfast didn't set well this morning, but he did open a box of powdered milk and made a glass of chocolate before going out to join the other men.

The sun was hanging in a cloudless sky and a hot, dry wind was blowing in from the north, scorching the already sunbaked sand. Ahmed saw the American coming and carefully turned the other way to avoid meeting him face to face.

Paul hesitated. He must have treated Ahmed rather badly last night. And he certainly had no desire to make an enemy of his foreman. Squaring his shoulders, Paul got ready to make another apology. Seemed like that was all he did lately. Humph! One would think that apologies did not come from calloused hearts, for apology had the earmarks of contrition. Paul took a deep breath, buttoned his shirt cuffs, and went directly to the Arab.

"About last night, Ahmed— I must have been a real bear."

The dark face turned slowly but the eyes, always before filled with friendliness and warmth, were unsure. He looked at Paul for a long time, but the wide mouth did not part to reply.

Paul fumbled, wanting to set things right. "The—the girl. She really *is* lovely, Ahmed. I don't know why I got so angry last night when you implied I was going to the oasis to see her." He grinned sheepishly. "And I *did* see her, you know. I had coffee with them—the Fosters, that is—"

By now the Arab was smiling and there was a merry twinkle in his black eyes. "Mr. Coltren, you don't have to explain to me. We all have our moments."

And, with that, he lifted his arm and gave a mighty yell. One by one the men drifted into song. It was a melody that asked God for happiness and good luck. The words stressed that no one present should be forgetful that there is one Almighty who feeds both bird and fish, and that He is mindful of everything He has created. And Paul, catching a word here and there, turned away and closed his mind to the song.

The digging continued without interruption. Both Paul and Ahmed hoped for other blocks showing a clearer emblem of the man whose cartouche they had found the day before. But nothing else came to light. One entire side of the tomb, however, was uncovered and a trench six feet wide had been dug. To keep the sand from drifting back in, and to support the blocks, the men started a firm framework to support the side of the tomb.

So the day passed. And the next. By day Paul worked as he had never worked, driving himself as hard as possible. By the dark of the Nubian nights, he stood gazing toward the oasis, wondering and trying not to wonder, what the Americans were doing. Quenching the desire to visit them. Desperately wanting their friendship; telling himself that it could never be. He had disgraced himself that first night. His actions had been unforgivable. Besides, he didn't want to be preached at. And, leaving it there, Paul would throw himself onto his cot and hope for sleep.

The work progressed smoothly. And on the fourth day after Paul's visit to the oasis, a workman looked up with an elaborate gesture and let loose a steady flood of Arabic.

Paul looked to Ahmed for the answer. The foreman grinned and shouted to Paul. *"Steps!* Kamal has found some steps!"

Paul's boots left a flurry of golden sand in their wake. He rushed forward eagerly, fell to his knees and began scooping sand with his hands. The wind and sand had conspired together to cover this tomb for eternity, but they hadn't been able to do it!

Paul stifled the impulse to dig in feverishly now. The steps started some fifty feet away in the front of the tomb. It was obvious that they were leading down to the door of the tomb, which would appear soon now. Kamal had stumbled upon the steps by sheer accident; so now most of the work was concentrated on the bank of sand where the steps were appearing, one wide step at a time. The men continued to sift every bucketful of sand before it was hauled away by the steady march of workmen.

"Allah has blessed us with success today, Mr. Coltren!" Ahmed was poised on the hill of sand, one leg extended downhill like a crane standing one-legged in a shallow swamp. He was wearing a grin that split his face in two. "It will be easier from now on."

"It's a beautiful sight!" Paul agreed heartily. "From the width and depth of the steps, I'd say we can uncover them without too much time involvement." His nostrils flared with his swift intake of air. "That door is the sight I'm waiting for!"

"I agree with you," the Arab laughed. "I've heard many rumors about a big discovery in Gaza. I'd like something like that myself for a change!"

Paul and Ahmed would have worked on far past the time when the misty veil of shadows fell over the land; but the crew was tired, and so with great reluctance they quit work for the night. Paul lingered for a moment, casting his eyes over the queer assortment of buckets, brushes, spades, picks, lumber and other paraphernalia. But the deep feeling for the work had lessened with the conflict of his own heart.

". . . and this same Jesus still has the power to save the lost and. . . ."

Paul's frame jerked to its full height, and his mouth and chin tightened until there was a hard line under his lower lip. His eyes blazed and his hands knotted into fists. *That song!* Why couldn't he get it out of his mind? Why did it haunt him so? It was nothing to him, had no part in him! Steeling himself to even a greater degree, he turned and walked quickly away from the dig, as though in doing so he could walk away from any memory of the song also.

Still in this tense condition, Paul opened a can of rations and forced down mouthfuls of meat and vegetables which he thought he might lose later on. Apparently his stomach was taut and disagreeable too, to the point of repelling both food and drink.

Turning his mind completely to his work, the American bathed in a sparse amount of water and went to join the men for coffee. When the date wine was passed around, Paul hesitated. Drinking was something he had never taken up, but—

The light of God's truth went out a long time ago, and when this takes place, wherever it be, oppression takes over. Jim Foster's words!

He rose to his feet abruptly, almost upsetting an Egyptian in his haste. He certainly was not oppressed, and if this was the reason for drinking, then he wasn't interested!

Paul whipped the screen of his tent shut behind him and zipped it angrily. He threw himself onto his cot and lay staring at the canvas ceiling. For once he wished the men would sing—or play. But they did neither. Tired from a long day's work, they, too, tumbled into their tents, sleeping on goat hides and straw. They appeared to be but masses of filthy rags tumbled here and there, shapeless things with human faces and sun-blackened hands.

Surprisingly, Paul went to sleep quickly, worn out by his own tense feelings and the conflict of his own heart. None but the Arab foreman heard the usual and unusual night sounds, some inner sensitivity making him quietly alert.

He heard the sound of a camel a long way off, its mighty roar causing the night to tremble. And he heard the twin cries of the jackals away in the crags. Once he shivered, this man of the desert wastes, so used to alternating heat and cold. Finally, unable to succumb to the beckoning hand of sleep, Ahmed rose and went outside. Like a smoothly gliding panther, he moved toward the excavation.

Sometime between midnight and one o'clock he slipped into Paul's tent and shook the American gently. "Mr. Coltren, wake up. Sh! Don't make any noise!"

Paul first started out of a sound sleep, then sat up slowly, feeling toward the Arab. "Ahmed? What is it? What's the matter?"

The other man's whisper came harshly in the stillness. "There is someone at the dig. A man."

Paul swung his legs over the side of his cot. He shook his head rapidly back and forth a few times. Subconsciously he was glad he'd fallen asleep fully dressed. "Come on! I'm with you!"

Ahmed paused, breathless. "I'll get my rifle! Wait!"

Wait, nothing! Paul thought. *I'll get him before it's too late!* And his long legs carried him quickly down the slope toward the dig. There he paused, dark eyes probing the moonlight for sign of the man in question. For a moment he thought Ahmed had been wrong, then suddenly there was a stealthy movement below. A shadow broke over the sand, a shadow that came silently around the corner of the wall and moved toward the newly discovered steps. The man moved carefully, surely.

With an ease that was inbred from years of hunting the woods about the farm for cottontails and deer, Paul stepped onto the path used constantly by the crew for hauling out sand, and started down the slope. His body was low and forward, his breathing silent and studied.

The man before Paul Coltren had his back turned and he, too, had stooped forward, obviously studying the steps and the whole area. Paul moved up close enough to touch the other man before exploding his bombshell.

"Mr. Arnold, I presume?" He was shocked at his own calm,

for his heart was pounding a little too hard and his body was tensed to spring.

In a spontaneous whirl that left even Paul wondering, the other man was facing him. For one naked moment Paul saw his opponent clearly. A medium-sized man perhaps five feet eight in height and weighing in at one seventy. In that instant Paul knew that George Arnold was not a fighting man, at least not physically, because the man's body appeared to be more flabby than muscular. His loose-fitting shirt obviously was covering a protruding potbelly. At the same moment Paul sensed he was a man who would fight to the bitter end, using any means available, to gain his own ends.

Arnold had bushy hair and brows, and his eyes were fairly close to his big knuckled-looking nose. He needed a shave desperately, but apparently his mustache, bushy like his brows, was a permanent fixture. There was such hate and coldness in his eyes that another man besides Paul might have shuddered.

As Arnold fumbled to open a switchblade, Paul grabbed his shirtfront with one hand and smashed him in the face with the other. The blow had all the appearance of lifting Arnold from the ground. For a moment he writhed, holding his jaw and groaning aloud. But the next he was reaching for the fallen knife. A heavy boot came down hard on his wrist and Paul took the switchblade out of Arnold's limp fingers.

Ahmed had appeared above the slope, hopping about excitedly, not being certain which course of action to take. He couldn't fire because the chances of hitting Paul were too great. Besides, things seemed to be going in the American's favor anyhow. And finally Ahmed pushed the safety on and stood watching in great admiration.

Paul stood back, watched Arnold stumble to his feet, and plowed into his stomach when the man was halfway up. Another blow to the jaw sent Arnold face down on the sand again, and this time he cried out in pain as the sand flew into his eyes.

Paul grabbed him from behind and hauled him to his feet. He stood a foot and a half from him, still keeping his grip. Arnold coughed and sputtered, wiping at his injured eyes.

"Now *get out!*" Paul ground out savagely. "And let me tell you something that will keep you healthy. You ever show up here again and I'll give my foreman orders to shoot you on sight!" He shoved the beaten man up the path. "Hurry up and get out of here!"

Half blind with sand, George Arnold stumbled away from the dig and finally became a blur under the star-studded heavens. A long time later Paul and Ahmed heard the engine of a jeep roar into existence, and then it, too, slowly became a phantom of sound in the far distance.

"That was quite an exhibition, Mr. Coltren," Ahmed said quietly. "I was proud to have you as my boss."

Paul grinned as he rubbed his bruised hands. "Thank you. It's the first fight I ever walked away from without receiving a single blow." He contemplated silently as they walked back toward the tents together. "I don't think Arnold knows much about fighting except with knives and broken bottles. He's that kind of a fighter." Paul brought forth the switchblade and flicked the tiny button that snapped it open and locked it automatically in position. "Take a look at what he pulled on me. Pretty nice, huh?"

Ahmed looked at it in admiration.

Paul closed it and thrust it toward the Arab. "Take it, Ahmed. No, I mean it, I don't need it."

"You mean it, Mr. Coltren?" Ahmed took it wonderingly, paused to open it again and stroked the blade lovingly. "I like it very much. Thank you, Mr. Coltren."

"What do you think of this guy Arnold?" Paul asked before departing for his own tent again. "Is he some skulking hyena just waiting around to get in on our discovery? Hoping to grab a few artifacts, if there are any?"

Ahmed nodded firmly. "He's that kind. Too lazy or too stupid to make his own finds—probably just an amateur archeologist anyway. So he hangs around new excavation sites, watching the progress and waiting to, as you say, pick up a few things for himself. Curio shops pay good prices for genuine artifacts, and many of them ask no questions."

"Yeah. I see what you mean." Paul tugged at his lower lip thoughtfully. "OK, Ahmed, see you in the—well, would you believe a few hours from now?" he asked. "And you heard what I said. If he comes around again, you've got your rifle." With that, Paul nodded toward the other man and went back to bed.

5

*When Paul wakened the following morning his thoughts im*mediately flashed back to the night before. There was a growing awareness that his hands were sore, especially his knuckles, and that the flesh was becoming dark beneath the tan. He'd walloped Arnold a couple of good ones, all right. A half smile appeared on one side of his mouth as he wondered how the other man was feeling right now.

Throwing back the netting from his cot, he poked around in his supplies for a packet of instant coffee. A good strong cup of coffee might be in order before he did another thing. As he went outside to heat water, however, he realized that the crew was already heading for the dig. Downing his breakfast in haste, Paul started after them. Nocturnal fracas or not, he wasn't going to be found slack in his work.

The crew was still working with renewed energy later that morning when a jeep station wagon pulled up. So engrossed was Paul, however, in the wide steps being uncovered, that he wasn't aware of it until a shadow fell over the ground where he was standing.

"Jim!" Paul gave the older man a quick flashing smile and put out his hand. An instant later his smile vanished and the shadow of a frown spread across his forehead. "Hello, Carolyn."

"We've missed you," the gray-haired man said warmly.

Barely had the words left the man's lips when the working crew caught sight of the lovely girl. Almost as one man, they stared at her.

Paul stood quietly for a moment, his face more severe in the half shadow of his sun helmet. And then his dark eyes mellowed and he smiled gently at Carolyn. "Don't let them embarrass you. They mean it all for a compliment. It's just their way."

Carolyn only came to Paul's shoulder, and she looked up at him with eyes that were full of sunshine. "I know. It's all right."

The feeling in Paul's heart was gone as abruptly as it had come. He felt a frank admiration for Carolyn Foster. He gazed down at her with a smile.

Ahmed watched the Americans somewhat surreptitiously. He made no move toward them, but that he was impressed could not be denied by his expression.

"I wish I could offer you a tall glass of lemonade," Paul said, lifting one eyebrow and shrugging. "But I can't. I can offer you a fairly good cup of coffee though."

Jim put out a hand and Paul marveled that the older man did not tan but simply retained the pinkish flesh that had perhaps grown a shade darker. "Thanks just the same, Paul. Actually, we dropped over to ask you for dinner tonight. I make a mean plate of spaghetti, and who knows but what we might be the ones to call forth some lemonade. From a can, of course, but the flavor's pretty good."

"Sounds like a winner!" Paul responded. "God knows I can stand a change in diet! Thanks a lot." *God knows.* A figure of speech; he hoped the Fosters knew that and wouldn't make a big thing out of it.

"I don't know how it is for you," Jim ventured with the frank warm smile of a statesman addressing his audience, "but we've been comforted by the simple fact that another American is so close to us."

Paul cocked his head and the shadow of his aquiline nose was thrown against his helmet. "I confess I've been a little lonely here at times, too. I'm glad you came today."

Jim nodded toward the dig. "Looks like a lot of activity going on over there."

Paul gestured. "Come take a look. You too, Carolyn. We have reason for genuine excitement." The archeologist did not mention last night's mishap, but he tossed the idea of telling them around in his mind. He had no desire to frighten them; but on the other hand he didn't want Arnold nosing around the oasis, especially with Carolyn there. He'd have to weigh the matter.

Five broad, thick steps led steadily downward into the sand which was being slowly but surely hauled out. Soon all parts would fit together. The steps would lead down to the level of the wall, the door would appear and then the dream of his career would open to them all.

"How did you find all this?" Jim questioned. "Surely not by starting to dig at random?" And he laughed.

"By aerial photographs. Three thousand years, roughly, of sand had covered it tightly, sealing it from the world forever." Paul gave them a rueful grin. "It seemed! But there was a sandstorm that hit this area this past spring, and again the desert shifted and took on certain changes. When things had settled down, the Department of Egyptian Antiquities began photographing. They found irregular lines beneath the sand and thought them sound enough to bear investigation. So—" He spread his hands expressively, noticed the discoloration that had begun, and thrust them quickly into his pockets. "Here I am. And here, I trust, Eddie will join me very soon."

"What fascinating work!" Jim breathed.

Paul wondered again at this man's knack of placing so much eagerness and enthusiasm into another's work when he was surely so taken up with his own affairs. Paul had the strange sensation again that he was doing Jim a favor by just talking to him and telling him about the work. It was by sheer force of will that Paul switched the trend of conversation.

"I could talk about archeology from dawn till nightfall," he said. "But what about your work, Jim? How's it coming along?"

Jim took off his hat to wipe the sweat from his forehead and Paul saw that the other man had indeed acquired another coat of pink. It was darker than at first, so that his hair looked whiter. And there was a neat half-inch ribbon of white flesh that ran along the top of his forehead where it was protected by his sun helmet.

"It's much too early. I have some small plots fenced off and have a small irrigation system going. I've used various types of fertilizers and minerals, and I've planted some wheat and corn and some vegetables, just for experimental purposes."

"I'm anxious to see what you've done," Paul offered, but he found it impossible to get the same eagerness into his words for Jim's work that Jim came by so naturally and so honestly for his.

Carolyn had remained silent. She stood with her fingers laced together, utterly engrossed by the work at the dig. She was wearing a rose-hued skirt today with a matching print blouse, and she looked as though she might take off any moment to join the ragged, admiring workmen hauling sand away from the steps.

Paul studied her unconsciously. He knew so very little about her. He'd never searched out the depths of her eyes, blue as the canopy of heaven that arched the desert from horizon to horizon. He had never, not once, touched her, but he had to admit that such a thought left him tingling. Her skin, unlike her father's, was taking on a beautiful tan and she was strictly feminine in spite of any way she might choose to dress. But what she was really like, Paul had not the remotest idea.

Somehow, in some inexplicable way, she brought pain to his heart. That he longed, deeply within, to be in her presence was certain. That he loathed her presence was just as sure, and Paul decided that it was impossible to correlate these two things, so he stopped trying.

If thou wouldest prolong friendship in a house to which thou hast admittance, as master, or as brother, or as friend, into whatsoever place thou enterest, beware of approaching the women, Paul thought to himself.

Carolyn turned her face slightly, in bewilderment, pulled by his steady gaze. "You're smiling at me, Paul. What is it?"

He caught himself up hurriedly, stifling the desire to laugh. "I was just thinking of an old Egyptian proverb, that's all."

6

Paul felt better after the Fosters left. Looking forward to their invitation to dinner filled him with a kind of eagerness that was related to joy. Perhaps he'd needed to get away from the dig more than he had realized. Or perhaps it was the anticipation of being with those of his own kind. He wasn't sure which it was, but he did know that he felt more relaxed than he had in days. There were no furrows denting the smooth brown of his forehead and no brooding in his eyes. Even his hands took notes and worked in a fashion befitting an archeologist instead of being tense and shaky.

When sunset began to cast its spell over the desert, and the bluffs in the distance seemed to hang in a red-purple light, Paul bathed and then changed the blades in his razor. He must be assured of a clean shave tonight. Then, with a feeling almost of guilt, he patted his face with Oriental Jade after-shave lotion.

Ahmed had never mentioned the pretty girl who had come to the dig with her father this morning. But now the Arab lifted his bony black face and sniffed as Paul emerged from the tent.

"The perfume of angels!" he uttered softly, his eyes dreamy and half closed.

"OK, Ahmed," Paul said soberly, approaching his foreman, "I didn't spill the bottle. In fact, I was quite conservative. But tell me," he went on, edging closer to the other man, "is it *that* strong?"

Ahmed tugged gently at the few straggly hairs protruding from his own chin and laughed heartily. "No, Mr. Coltren, it's just so obvious out here where nothing ever smells good!" He dropped his voice to a growl. "Sometime, if I ever take a razor to my face, would—" He glanced surreptitiously toward his crew and his voice went into a whisper. "Would you let me have a drop of that?"

Great peals of silent laughter rose up inside of Paul and his frame shook spasmodically for a moment. The hardness went from the man's eyes and genuine humor took its place. He reached out a hand and touched Ahmed's shoulder. "Man, I'll go further than that. I'll loan you my razor!"

One impressed Arab was left standing looking after the jeep, right hand still tugging at those hairs, contemplating whether he ought to just pluck them out now so he could have a drop or two of that fragrant after-shave lotion.

The exotic aroma of garlic, oregano, and bubbling fresh coffee hung heavy on the air as Paul parked the jeep and walked toward the Foster camp. "I could have come blindfolded," he told Carolyn, who was testing the spaghetti at the stove. "But I thought it was your father who was the spaghetti-maker here."

The young woman turned, her face flushed from the heat of the stove. "He makes the sauce," she explained. "I just cook the spaghetti. That's the easy part." She laughed softly. "Although he's a little fussy even about that. Has to be just right, not cooked too long or too short."

"Cooking's an art I've never mastered," Paul confessed. "But, if you'll pardon my saying so, I've heard that men often make better cooks than women."

She poured two cups of coffee and sat down opposite him at the metal table. "Isn't that funny! I've heard the same thing. And do you know what? It doesn't even bother me!"

He found his voice blending into her laughter and wondered why it was so easy to laugh and relax around this woman. Since that first night was over and past, it seemed easy to be natural, not to put on, but to be what he was. That's the way it had to be.

Jim was still tracing a comb through his thinning white hair as he came to join Paul and Carolyn. "Say, Paul, wouldn't you like to come to Cairo for a day sometime next week?"

The archeologist ran a hand over his hair which was rapidly turning a shade darker in the desert country. "That's a tempting proposition, Jim. After spending several weeks here, I do feel a need to get away even for a few hours. And I've been visualizing a big steak somewhere in Cairo with real iced tea and—"

Jim waved a hand and sat down. "I know just the place!" he said enthusiastically.

Paul shook his head quickly. "But I can't do it. I couldn't possibly leave the work at this point. Maybe a little later."

Jim wagged his head. "I know. Actually, I can't get away this week myself." He ducked to brush an ant from his leg and the part in his hair stood out like a neat white scar. "Maybe by the time we can get away, you'll be able to go too."

"I'll sure pigeonhole it for further consideration!" Paul affirmed.

Carolyn busied herself by piling spaghetti on the plates, but it was her father, tasting and contemplating silently one last time, who dipped the sauce onto the spaghetti.

"We even have garlic toast!" Carolyn said with a flourish. "But no green tossed salad with oil and vinegar. Sorry."

Paul joined in the dramatics momentarily by pretending to be disturbed. Then, with great ado, he settled his napkin over his khaki trousers and reached for his fork. But here he quickly sobered again. Jim would want to pray. Here, too, Paul would pretend and join in the act. So, sighing inwardly, he bowed his head and waited.

After the prayer was offered, Paul again reached for his fork. Hearing Carolyn's intake of breath, he looked over at her curiously. "What is it?"

"Your hand, Paul! What happened?"

Paul hesitated, frowned, and finally put on a faint smile. Now that she had noticed, there was nothing to hide. He thrust forth the other hand, where discoloration had also begun. Both hands were dark blue just under the flesh where the first knuckles began, running almost the full length of his fingers. Tomorrow they'd probably be black and then slowly they'd turn green. It would be most difficult to hide the marks indefinitely.

"Well, I guess it's just as well you saw it, Carolyn. I'd pondered it anyway, telling you, for your own good."

Jim replaced his coffee cup by his plate. The twinkle in his eye was gone and he looked more serious than Paul had seen him.

"For *our good?"* he asked.

Paul heaved a vast sigh. "Did you ever hear of a grave robber? Seems I have my own personal grave robber. A fellow—it would be hard to call him a man—by the name of George Arnold has been hanging around my dig waiting for us to uncover something of value. My foreman and I had heard about him, but last night or early this morning he made a personal appearance. Ahmed caught sight of him in the excavation and came to tell me, and—well, you can see that we tangled rather badly."

Jim glanced at his daughter and there was a trace of worry on his thin, pink face. When he spoke at last, his voice was low and a bit strained. "I take it that this Arnold wasn't exactly in good shape when he left your dig?"

There was no mistaking the tone of authority and of victory in Paul's words. "I assure you that he left my place in pretty bad shape, and without his switchblade too, which was a deadly looking instrument."

Jim expressed himself with a half-groan, half-murmur. "And do you think he'll come back?"

Paul shrugged. "I hope not. But only time will prove whether or not he's had enough. Anyway," he added, spreading his hands wide, "now that you know, you can be extra careful. If you have a good guide, why not let him know so he can keep alert too?"

Jim nodded in agreement. "That's a fine idea, Paul, I'm glad you told me about it."

If George Arnold, or the idea of George Arnold, and his uncertain rovings caused Carolyn a moment's anxiety, she did not show it. She would be the kind of girl who would listen, take stock of any situation that could develop, and be on guard.

"How are the steps coming along, Paul?" Carolyn asked after a time.

"They're coming!" he replied emphatically. "We're all excited over our progress with the steps. They lead to doors, you know, and that's what we're after." He put his fork down. "We just hope that the tomb hasn't been looted like so many have."

She sat forward, her soft hair falling about her shoulders. "What about hieroglyphics?" she asked. "All tombs have them, don't they?"

"All that I've ever heard about." Paul took a moment to comment to Jim about the savory spaghetti sauce before pursuing the subject of hieroglyphics. "I can't read them well at all," he confessed to the girl across the table. "And Ahmed's certainly not a pro at Egyptology! In fact, the circle of really good Egyptologists is extremely narrow." He fingered his coffee cup and made a mental note that Jim had forgotten about the lemonade.

"About all I know is that, in picture writing, for example, the human and animal figures always face *into* the way of reading. This holds true whether it be from left to right or right to left, or even first one way and then the other." He paused, narrowing his eyes thoughtfully. "And I know a little something of the symbols."

"Symbols?"

"Yes," Paul answered quickly. "For example, the mythical phoenix bird is the symbol of resurrection. The eye is the symbol of Horus, one of the Egyptians' gods. Remember, the ancient Egyptians worshiped anything and, it would appear, *every*thing. The sun-god, animals, creeping things—the holy family of which Horus was a member. It's a confused matter, actually, trying to keep their ancient religions straight. There were so many."

Carolyn's countenance was unsmiling, but her eyes spoke of a hunger for more knowledge of the country. "Well, take the holy family, Paul. What—or who—were they?"

Paul frowned. They had moved away from the table now to the more comfortable chairs with canvas backs. His brown fingers, linked loosely together, suddenly tightened. He laughed shortly, changed his position slightly, and began hesitantly to speak. "Well, the holy family was more or less the universal object of worship. Osiris, Isis, Horus—father, mother, son. Osiris, it is said, married Isis and they ruled the world. Incidentally, they were both grandchildren of the sun-god Ra. Impressive, huh?"

Carolyn looked momentarily disappointed, but it didn't last. She sat forward with renewed eagerness. "And—that's *not* the end, is it? Surely there must be more than that?"

"Cornered!" Paul cried, smiling. "How is it that I always get cornered when I come here? Always having to apologize for something or other and—"

"You're hedging," Carolyn bantered back at him.

Paul swallowed with difficulty. He felt as if he was walking into a trap, but if he backed out now it would not only be obvious but rude as well. A look of sternness fell over his face and the skin became tight over his jawbones. "All right. Let me expound further," he said dramatically and wondered at his ability for lightness. "Osiris had a brother named Seth who became jealous and murdered him, then cut up his brother's body and hid the pieces all over Egypt. Isis determined to find all the pieces and put them together again, which she did! He even came back to life, only it was a life in the next world, where he, Osiris, became the god of the dead, the great judge of souls. People prayed to Isis and Horus.

Horus was the son of Isis and the dead judge. He finally defeated Seth and won back his father's throne. They believed that everyone who died went to meet the great judge, but they had to pass certain tests before they could enter into the pleasures of the afterlife. The tests were supposed to have been written on papyrus, collected and called 'The Book of the Dead.' " Paul pressed his lips firmly and sighed. "And *that,* Carolyn, is the story of the holy family."

"How awful!"

"Awful? I thought you were impressed."

Carolyn seemed to be looking into another world. "I shouldn't be surprised," she murmured, "for it's so since the beginning of time." She leaned forward, deeply intense, her blue eyes mirroring a fathomless kind of sadness. Her hair fell over her right eye and she was too absorbed to push it aside.

"What are you thinking?" Paul probed gently.

"I'm thinking of Satan's deception." Her voice was low, serious, concerned. "Deception," she repeated. "Not whole lies. Half lies. Brother killing brother. The great judge of souls. Myths, all of it, yet based upon solid truth. And people believed the half made up lies and went to hell without Christ."

For the first time Paul found himself gazing into the eyes of the girl near him. As he gazed and saw into her very soul, he could not turn away, though he wanted to desperately. And, gazing, he encountered not only compassion but love, tenderness, yearning over the souls of men and women. And quickly now Paul turned away and sought again the refuge of his hardened heart.

"Many people base their beliefs upon myths," he replied simply, remembering what he had called the Bible that first night. "But doesn't it seem very strange that no one ever seems to know it."

The implication was there, cut through with cold sarcasm. Paul sat outwardly calm, but there was no calm within his heart. He waited with throbbing pulses for either Carolyn or Jim to step forward on spiritual issues and declare what they believed.

When Jim spoke, his voice was like the surface of an unruffled sea. "Paul? Does your very intellect not tell you about God?"

Paul's hands dropped apart and some dull, aching memory came into his eyes. "I believe in God," he replied slowly. He fished for the key to his jeep. "Professor, your spaghetti was delicious." Paul gave the older man a mock bow, but the feeling for lightness was gone. "But tomorrow is another day, so I'd better hit the sack."

To the archeologist's surprise, Carolyn was standing too, and there was fire in her eyes. Her hands were folded in front of her and one eyebrow was poised as though for flight. Only her voice remained cool and controlled. "So you're going to run away again? You can enter into conversation on any subject except where the spiritual is concerned? Paul, why? Why are you running from it?"

"Carolyn!" It was a gentle rebuke from her father. "If Paul doesn't want to discuss the spiritual, we hardly have the right to force him."

Paul looked somewhat grim, but he came back deliberately and sat down. "It's all right, Jim. If Carolyn wants to preach at me, I guess maybe I ought to let her have her say."

Contrition leaped into Carolyn's eyes, but it was not a contrition unmixed with a determination to do what she felt was right. "Paul, I don't preach at anyone. I guess you'll just have to believe that. But you're your own natural self with us." She brought a camping stool close and sat down near the men. "Paul, let us be normal with you too. This is a part of our very lives. Christ is a part of us, don't you see? We're not 'putting on' anything; we just want to be natural."

Paul did not answer for a few minutes. He bowed his head thoughtfully. "You're right, of course, Carolyn. I've acted like a child, I know. And you do have a right, both you and your father, to be at ease in my presence. I wouldn't want either of you to be uncomfortable because of me." He glanced at his watch. "But now it is late and I'm not trying to run away. Thanks for everything. And, Jim, keep in touch about that trip to Cairo."

7

The days moved smoothly after that night with the Fosters. The relationship that existed between them was pleasantly unruffled and afforded all three persons rare moments of relaxation and confidence. The conflict within Paul's own heart had subsided also and he felt lighter than he had in a long while.

The steps at the dig continued to work steadily downward. A few of them were cracked and broken and had to be carefully repaired along the way, but others of them were solid and even. They had been formed of large gray granite blocks, brought to this remote spot from an unknown quarry and carefully placed to form the steps. Paul concluded, concerning the decline, that there had been a wide, deep valley at the excavation site at one time, and that through the years violent sandstorms had filled it in. Therefore, the steps led downward and would eventually end at the door of the tomb.

Another cartouche had appeared on one of the blocks facing the steps, totaling three such markings. The last two, after being cleaned with knives and brushes, were almost as clear as the day they were made; but whose they were remained a mystery to both Paul and Ahmed. Each marking was photographed and filed away with notes and other data.

The workmen had caught the excitement in their breasts, so that at times it was almost impossible to make them quit work. They had the feeling that with every bucketful of sand hauled up and out of the dig something significant was bound to spring forth. Paul wondered at their black calloused feet, bare against the sand, and how their skinny, hard bodies held together in the heat.

And still the work continued. As the blocks were uncovered, each one was tenderly cared for. Sand, lodged in the crevices for long-forgotten centuries, was carefully dislodged with knives and brushes. So far both blocks and steps were made of granite. Bit by bit the walls were coming into sharp relief. With the removal of vast quantities of sand, it was really beginning to look like a real building emerging from the dunes. It was like a grave giving up its dead.

There was no thought of making the desired trip to Cairo at the present time. Even when Jim mentioned it again days later, Paul put him off. Maybe next week, but certainly not now. Occasionally Paul joined the Fosters for evening coffee, an event that stimulated him, yet sent a strange ache into his heart. His fight was gone now, having turned to a quiet resignation. Neither Jim nor Carolyn ever pushed in the direction of the spiritual. But, as Carolyn had declared, she had to be herself, so she and her father never wrapped up their spiritual cloaks and hid them in a drawer when Paul came to the oasis.

One day when the men were actively engaged in carrying away sand, Kamal held up his hand toward Ahmed and let loose with a cry of surprise. His further cry was a rapid speech in Arabic which the American could not understand but nevertheless realized to be something worthwhile.

Paul dashed forward to see for himself. "A pillar! Take a look, Ahmed!'

The Arab scooped away a dozen handfuls of sand. A column eighteen inches in diameter came slowly to light.

Ahmed squinted. "Supports for a porch. And about—" He glanced back of him. "—twenty feet from the corner." He dug into his baggy trousers for his tape. "So twenty feet—or whatever it turns out to be—from the other corner should be another one. I'm surprised, Mr. Coltren."

"I am too," confessed the American. "Yet, some of these old boys liked to do things up impressively for their own deaths."

"And the door," Ahmed estimated, "will be about five feet inside this column."

Paul nodded. "About so, Ahmed." He scooped away some of the sand, carefully feeling into the burning furnace with his fingers. Gently he stroked the pillar. "That's solid granite, like the rest of it, Ahmed." Paul took the end of the measuring tape, held it against the wall, only a portion of which was in evidence beyond the pillar. "Column stands eight feet from the wall." He sighed outwardly. "Certainly looks like we've got to move half the desert yet!"

Ahmed grunted. "You Americans get so impatient!"

Paul scrutinized the Arab, paradoxically noted for both energy and lack of speed. Instead of adding a retort, however, Paul shrugged and gave the other man a slow grin. "Yeah. You're right, Ahmed. But that's the way we are."

Ahmed's large mouth fell into a grin. "Not even an argument?"

"'Uh-uh. Not today. Hey, take hold of the other end of this, will you?"

The afternoon was occupied with photography, making notes and hovering near the workmen. But when work ended that night the column was still only half unearthed. That this was the scene of a mysterious and somewhat bizarre resurrection, however, could not be denied.

Paul stood overlooking the site for some time after dusk fell, but he didn't stand there alone for more than ten minutes until he was aware that another man was standing nearby, sharing his thoughts, reading into them.

"There isn't anything for Arnold to carry away yet," Ahmed muttered in a deep growl. "Later, yes. But he can't get inside that place now, not without a door. Don't worry, Mr. Coltren."

The archeologist turned to Ahmed, took note of the fact that some of those long worrisome hairs had disappeared from his chin and gave his foreman a real grin. They both knew that the time was drawing close for Paul to shell out a few drops of after-shave lotion, and the American wondered if an onion had ever been sprinkled with cologne and been made to smell like orange blossoms.

It was a week later before the door appeared. The steps were cleared, though some repair work was going to be necessary on four more of them. They had brought the crew to the entire front of the tomb, which measured twenty feet tall and sixty feet wide. The blocks with which the tomb had been erected were a massive four by six feet and each one would have weighed in at about one and a half tons.

The pillar to the left of the door was made of a solid piece of stone and designed with various emblems and symbols which were mainly related to the gods of Egypt. The pillar to the right of the great door had been broken, however, and the upper few feet had toppled to the ground. So had a portion of the great stones that had been placed across the columns to form the porch. The one column bore the weight of a great slab of granite which extended beyond the pillar and reached for its other support. Halfway there, though, it too had broken, evidently when the pillar had fallen.

"It's *still* impressive!" Paul said aloud to himself. "A noble's grave undoubtedly, and one who wasn't too awestruck by his own importance." He stood on the steps looking down on the scene. Perspiration beaded his face and ran in rapid little trickles down his back and chest, so that his shirt bore great dark sweat patches. A little impatiently, the man took his sweatband in his fingers and rubbed it down over his forehead before readjusting its position on his forehead.

Only one wall had been braced with a scaffold. It was looking good! And now the door had appeared, a mere outline at the moment, this giant slab of stone set into a doorway that was fifteen feet tall. And on the other side— *What?* A tomb filled with mummies? Or—disappointedly, one that had been looted a thousand years before?

Striding forward, a man with a purpose, Paul knelt before the stone facade and worked with a special knife blade to dislodge the encrusted sand that almost hid the outline of the door from view. The men all worked very slowly now and with a show of exceeding carefulness.

Ahmed gazed at Paul through liquid black eyes. "Well, Mr. Coltren, we are almost there." And, turning, he spoke the same thought to his men, who immediately fell into a song that exalted Paul and his successful exploits in Egypt. They sang of what they hoped to find within the confines of this tomb, its mummies and museum pieces and golden statues.

Paul rose to his feet, set the helmet back at a jaunty angle, and rested his fists upon the sides of his belt. "Now, Ahmed, it's time to take all measure of precaution against our friend Arnold. Night guards. The whole bit. OK?"

"I'll see to it, Mr. Coltren."

"Do the men know about Arnold?"

Ahmed glanced toward the crew, some of them winding slowly out of the excavation site to empty their buckets.

"Only Kamal. He'll make a good guard and we both have rifles."

The Arab hesitated. "Actually, some of the men are stupid. They'd make a big issue of Mr. Arnold, and their knowing might make matters worse. Don't worry. Kamal and I can take care of things."

Paul nodded soberly. "We'll have to keep a guard, all right. Maybe put some lanterns around the front. Once we get inside and know exactly what we've got—" Paul's brown eyes narrowed. "Of course, that's what Arnold is wanting to know also."

Ahmed clucked his tongue. "If I were Mr. Arnold, I think I'd use the brain given to me by Allah and stay away from this place."

"Yeah." The American raised his brows. "But you're not Arnold."

The Egyptians, as was their rule so far as hospitality was concerned, asked Paul again to eat with them. He was tired enough to be tempted and to chance the illness that could follow, but the aroma of their food held him at bay. He could easily have taken their dates and wheat cakes, but the thought of eating *rayib* and *melukhiya*—curdled goat's milk and a greasy spinachlike vegetable—nearly choked him.

There was a peculiar longing in his heart tonight for the peace of the Fosters' camp. And again his heart was aroused, almost disturbingly so, at the thought of being with them. They made him desperately uneasy. At the same time he was perfectly at ease with them. There was no drawing toward Carolyn as a woman—absolutely none—and yet he found himself lonely when he was away from her. Paul could not unite any of these feelings.

The following day was one of the most intense concentration Paul remembered. The work centered entirely about the door. The archeologist almost forgot the dry, burning air that seared his lungs and the sand that burned his feet through the heavy soles of his boots. He was unmindful of the sweat pouring off his body in rivers, and of the burning thirst and the smelly bodies. There was a common cause to pursue, and their work went smoothly in harmony.

The door was cleared. The crevices were cleaned with a knife blade with two exceptions. One was at the middle of the door on top and the other was at the bottom, also in the middle. Paul's long thin knife blade swung up and clicked sharply against stone.

"Works on a pivot," Paul reasoned aloud to his foreman who had come to the same conclusion. "And it's strong, Ahmed. Let's give it a try."

Eight men put their shoulders to it, pushing it with a force that was steady and smooth. For, even if it did have all the earmarks of being as strong as the day it was set in position, one could never tell with something this old, and an abrupt force could be catastrophic.

The massive door ground against particles of sand, protested because of its age, but finally budged. Five, six, seven—twelve inches! It stood ajar twelve inches, a wide-open invitation, a beckoning hand, the answer to an illusive dream.

Now the more skilled workmen went to work again, testing and examining to be sure that the structure was as sound as it appeared. Satisfied, Kamal spoke with Ahmed in Arabic for some moments, then stepped back and gestured.

Paul stepped nearer the opening, and the rush of air thousands of years old streamed up against his face, forcing him back. Almost simultaneously was the powder-fine dust, as river silt, that moved toward the opening, having been disturbed by the motion of opening the door. Paul grabbed the sweatband from his forehead and placed its folds over his nose, motioning for Ahmed to protect his breathing in the same manner. That dust could choke a man to death if he weren't careful.

They moved slowly, thrusting into the background the desire to rush swiftly inside and see just what they had on their hands. Paul's camera had been around his neck all day, but he didn't remove the lens covers until he and Ahmed had moved cautiously inside that forbidding door.

Colors as bright and beautiful as when they were painted leaped out at them from all sides and peered down at them from the domed ceiling. Symbols, emblems, hieroglyphics, faces both animal and human in enchanting forms and colors. Paul made sure the band was snugly over his nose and then removed the lens cap from his camera. It was clearly evident that the pictures were telling a story, so he started shooting—in sequence, he hoped. One after another, Paul got his shots, thrust them into his shirt pocket for the time being, and kept going.

It was going just great! A couple— Paul noticed that Ahmed had bent to pick up something, started to caution him against touching anything, yet he felt surprise that the Arab had not known. But, before he could utter a word, a slight rumbling sound came from the front right side of the tomb.

Paul looked up to see bits of dirt and sand rolling from the ceiling near the door. "Ahmed!" he cried sharply. "Get out! *Hurry!*"

Ahmed went flapping through the doorway, head extended before his body, like a chicken taking headlong flight from the chopping block.

Paul shot after him, wondering as he ran if he was to be loosed from the shackles of dust on this day of all days. A ton of block, sand, and rubble came crashing through the open doorway just as Paul plunged into the sunshine, choking and coughing. He felt thankful to be alive, and a touch on his pocket said that he had his pictures, even though his camera was doubtlessly crushed like a toy accordion between those blocks.

Bleak despair took hold of him for a moment. He looked for Ahmed and found the other man watching the tomb silently. He wasn't even quaking.

"Well, we don't have to worry about grave robbers, Mr. Coltren. Not for a while."

"I'd rather worry about them than for this to have happened," he replied grimly. "But I did get pictures."

Ahmed brought up one hand. "I got something too. It was lying on the floor, which was very peculiar. It's jasper, I believe."

Paul accepted the object. "It's jasper, all right. A cylinder—capped at both ends." He turned the cylinder over and over in his long hands. Eighteen inches in length and as big around as his wrist, it represented both a mystery and a wonder. The first object they had found. One capped end was chipped as though it had been dropped. Paul was still rather angry that Ahmed would pick anything up, but at the same time he had to admit he was glad to get the cylinder. And it certainly was strange that it had been on the floor.

"How long do you figure it will take to get that door back in shape?"

Ahmed deliberated. "Four, five days. Maybe even longer. I don't think the damage is really as bad as it appears."

Paul admired the polished red-brown cylinder silently. It was a moment before he spoke. "We'll see what's in this, Ahmed. Could be I'll be wanting to make that trip into Cairo while there's time—

especially if there's anything of worth in these pictures. Shall we go take a look?"

The Arab shook his turbaned head. "I'd better stay right here. You go ahead and study the pictures and I'll see them later."

"Right!" Paul gave a quick toss of his head and turned to trot up the sandy slope to his tent.

Elation gripped him. He didn't know which he was most eager for—to see the pictures or to find out what was inside that cylinder. He made himself a cup of tea with tepid water and sat down by the table under the awning of his tent. Meticulously he brought out the pictures and spread them on the small table, then lined them up in perfect order. The brilliance surprised him again as they lay facing him. All the pictures were mingled with symbols of various gods, for they had been such a part of ancient Egyptian life and their thoughts of the afterlife. Therefore, it was the natural thing to have them intermingled with thoughts of death.

As Paul studied the pictures and began making notes on them, a slow, bizarre thought began to linger on the outskirts of his mind. In one picture the phoenix bird, symbol of the resurrection, stood out clearly. It seemed ready to take a male figure on a sky ride in a solar boat painted there for that very reason.

Eagerly and with pounding heart, Paul cropped the pictures and replaced them on the table. To take away one picture from its proper place would have brought disorder and confusion to the whole. Slowly, incredibly, they came together.

Paul stood to his feet, brows knit, palms flat on the table. "It's impossible! *Impossible!"* He cried it to the lonely desert and to the hot breeze, protesting, pleading. "It can't be!" He walked up and down, returned and studied the pictures for some hidden clue that would tell him he was wrong. He didn't find it. "It can't be—*his* tomb!"

8

Paul felt dazed, bewildered. He got up and began to walk in slow circles around the small table. Stopping, he stared at the pictures again. It couldn't be! It was impossible, unthinkable. Now all sorts of ideas plunged into his brain until it became a veritable whirlpool of suggestions and possibilities.

He sat down again, forehead wrinkled. Elation, incredulity, dismay, victory took hold of him, and he was tossed from one to the other so swiftly that he felt weak and desperately shaken. Suppose —suppose—it was so—

He picked up one photo at a time and looked at its back, for he had numbered them as he had taken them. They were in proper order, all right, and to remove but one or two threw the whole picture off. Over and over he examined the pictures. If what he saw before his eyes should be true, a story had come to light that would shock the world. A strange light came into Paul's dark eyes. He was lifted up to dizzying heights on the wings of discovery. But the next instant he was dashed brutally against the rocks of fear and despair.

Gathering all the pictures together, he stood irresolutely, running his fingers feverishly through his crisp hair, absently smoothing it into place. An idea was slowly being given birth in his mind.

"I have to be sure," he said aloud. *"I have to know!"* He gathered both pictures and jasper cylinder and went into the tent. No one, not Ahmed, or the Department of Egyptian Antiquities, or his office in the States, must know what he had found. Oh, sure, he knew he wouldn't exactly be following a code of ethics. But this was too big, too important, too shocking. So great that he dared not trust even the ones he worked for. If the thing were true, it would destroy; and if it were not—well, there was no use in hurting people until they had to be hurt. It was too explosive to risk, that's all. He must wait. He had to be sure. Meanwhile there must be someone who could point him to a trusted Egyptologist. Who, or where, he could not say, however. Nor did he know where to begin looking.

Carefully Paul picked out three particular pictures and tucked them under his driver's license in his wallet. Now the scene was distorted. Ahmed would not remember the missing ones, for he had been much too busy with the cylinder to notice other details.

Paul worked with the cylinder until Ahmed came into his tent at sundown with two small cracked cups of Arabic coffee. Together they worked to loosen the finely polished cap. When it gave, it seemed quite simple, after all, and the men took it close to the light to peer into it. There was a quickening of heartbeats and breathing, and Paul replaced the cap immediately.

"Papyrus!" Ahmed cried softly, eyes lighted by an inner elation.

"Yes. Probably in fragments, but absolutely invaluable at this point." And to himself he added, *Whoever I find to read these hieroglyphics can also study the papyrus. But where will I ever find such a man?*

The men pored over the pictures until far into the night, but never once did Paul mention that there were pictures missing which he had secreted on his person.

Finally, hair tangled from too many finger brushings, Paul took a deep, shuddering breath and rose from the table.

"Yeah, I think I will take that run into Cairo, Ahmed, while the door is being repaired. Besides," he lied, "I need to report our findings to the department. Also, I'd like to see when Eddie will be able to join us."

Ahmed half ignored the other man. With a long black finger, he pointed toward one of the pictures. "I feel excited, Mr. Coltren. I think we really have something. Look here—a plate of food, a bottle of wine for the journey after death. And that statue in the background—it certainly appears to be made of gold."

"I thought that too," Paul nodded. "But there wasn't time to do more than photograph it. Quite a piece of craftsmanship. The chapel is rather lavish. I wonder what the burial chamber is like." Paul twisted his mouth to one side, squinted. "Behind the statue, maybe?"

Ahmed shrugged. "That could be. I am sure of one thing."

And the Arab's loose mouth went into a broad grin. "We will find it!"

He got to his feet, the stirring diffusing an unpleasant odor caused by perspiration and the need for a bath long overdue. He paused in the doorway.

"Are you going into Cairo with the professor and the girl?"

"That's my plan. I'll know better in the morning when I see them." Paul began pulling off his boots. "Good night, Ahmed."

The other man mumbled a reply and disappeared toward his own tent. Paul was left alone with his own musings, his own condemnations.

"Got to find a top Egyptologist! Ha ! *Where?* Where is there a man to be found whom one can really trust? A man who can be *sure?*

Sleep did not come. It was a dark shadow that crept down lonesome corridors, an elusive mist that he never grasped the entire night. When morning broke her rays of gold and red over the eastern horizon, the heat began bearing down also, coming insidiously, forcefully. The desert did not notice. Nor did the leathery men of the sands. But to Paul on this day it was almost too much, and for once he was ready to escape if he could. The hot wind burned his throat and dried out his eyes until it seemed an acute thing which he must deal with and overcome.

The Arabs were scarcely awake and moving when Paul started his jeep and left for the oasis. An unusual speck of life was moving across this barren waste today in the form of a Bedouin family with one lone camel. They, too, were heading toward the oasis. The woman and her child rode on the camel's awkwardly swaying back, a heap of filthy rags out of whose folds faces peered timidly. Paul waved to them and went on. Once, however, he glanced in his rearview mirror at the pitiful family.

Oppression. Yes, the Bedouin were a picture of oppression. A lingering sense of hurt passed through the American and was lost again in the locked corridor of his soul.

A feeling of peace had been upon the land until the Bedouin family had appeared. The hawk that had hung motionlessly in the sky, then glided away silently to the north, had spoken of serenity. But now, deep, deep within, the waters of his spirit had been gently disturbed again.

Carolyn was cooking hot cakes over the little camping stove, and near her on the table were syrup, oleo, and a pot of steaming coffee.

Paul met her with a cautious smile. "How can I be so fortunate? Halfway around the world, and all I have to do is drive a mile and a half or so and sit down to a cup of the world's best coffee. Better yet, with a lovely young woman sitting across from me." He stepped up to the table and poured himself a cup of coffee. Suddenly he was very grateful for the friendship of these people, thankful that he felt so at ease.

Carolyn's smile was real. Her head was tilted a little to one side as it always was when she smiled. She'd acquired a rose-hued tan since living at the oasis and her eyes shone forth like sapphires. Paul had not noticed before how lovely she was.

"And what makes you think you can make yourself so much at home?" she retorted. "After all, I made coffee last night, thinking you might come, and you didn't."

They laughed and the sounds floated out, reached for one another, and mingled.

"Where's your father?"

"Right here," a voice spoke quietly from behind. Jim was smiling his perpetual smile, his face as pink and shining as ever. "Good to have you over. You look like a man who has something on his mind."

"I do! We've found something."

"At the tomb?" Jim sat down and motioned for Paul to do likewise. "You'll eat with us, of course?"

"I certainly mean to!" He sniffed the delicious aroma of hot maple syrup. "That is, if you'll tell me how you ever keep butter in this heat."

Carolyn set a big platter of steaming hot cakes on the table. "It's oleo," she confessed quickly. "Last stick." She leaned forward and whispered, "I've been keeping it in a waterproof bag in that pool of water over there by the trees."

"Pretty sneaky," Paul murmured. "It's a wonder someone hasn't found it before now."

Jim smiled indulgently at their bantering. Now he himself seemed eager for information. "But the tomb, Paul. What did you find?"

Paul pulled the pictures out of his pocket. "I got some shots of the inside—the chapel. Before the front started to collapse."

Jim accepted the pictures. "The tomb collapsed?"

"No, just around the doorway. That's why I came over. I can take time out now to make that trip to Cairo. The crew will be building a framework about the structure and restoring what caved in, so I'm free to get away."

Jim shook his head. "And I can't! This morning I have some green heads poking through the sand." He studied the pictures and passed them on to Carolyn. "These look great, Paul. Can you read them?"

"Not really. I need an expert." Paul hesitated for a long moment. "Jim? I can trust you, can't I? Really trust you, I mean? There's not another man I'd even want to mention this to."

Jim sipped his coffee reflectively and sat back for a moment. "Paul, we have our differences. We both know that. But, as a man, I feel that I could trust you implicitly. I hope you can find it within you to trust me the same way."

"Forgive me for even asking, Jim." He ate a bite of hot cake, commented to Carolyn about being an excellent cook, then continued. "Jim, I have other pictures. I can't tell even you what they are. I surely read them wrong, but I have to know. And you'll have to believe me when I tell you that they could be so explosive that I have to be absolutely sure I can trust the person who reads them." He spread his hands. "Now why am I even telling you this? You wouldn't know of any such Egyptologist."

Jim was silent in thought. At last he shook his head and spoke. "No, Paul, I don't know. But I think I know someone in Cairo who would give you all the information you want, and I know that he's trustworthy."

"Who is he, Jim?"

"Well, he owns and operates a café in Cairo. He lived in the United States for a number of years and that's when we got to know each other well. His name is Abdel Jabari. His restaurant is called The Egyptian. He knows his country and is somewhat of an amateur archeologist himself. He is acquainted with everyone who is anyone and has answers for about anything. I believe he might be able to help you."

"Well, that sounds great!" Hurriedly Paul scribbled the man's name and the name of his restaurant on a piece of paper.

"I confess my ignorance in this field, Paul, but why can't you just wait until the tomb is restored and then you and Ahmed go in and study the pictures?"

"Maybe it's a quirk," Paul said, speaking quietly, "but I have to do it this way. I have to know, to be sure. Maybe it's for myself, I really am not sure."

"I'm wondering, Paul, about the possibility of Carolyn going into Cairo with you? We need some things—"

Paul put out a hand of protest. His lips curved slightly. "I was going to ask, myself! How about it, Carolyn? I can show you all sorts of credentials and ID cards and—"

Her laughter was droplets of water sparkling in the sunshine. "As a matter of fact, if no one else had invited me, I was going to invite myself. The thought of getting away for a day sounds absolutely delightful. And there certainly are some supplies I need to buy."

Paul drank the last drop of coffee, and reached for his helmet. He had put his hand on the table to get up when his eyes fell upon a small clothbound book near him. He didn't know why he picked up the book, except that deep inside there was still that mysterious something that made him want to fight back at the Fosters' religion. He sat back down, leaning forward.

"This Way to Happiness," he mused, more to himself than to them, though intended for their benefit. His dark eyes probed the face of the professor, which was calmly serene.

"What *is* the way, Jim?"

The older man returned that steady gaze unflinchingly. Then he spoke gently and with feeling. "Jesus said, 'I am the way, the truth, and the life.' He's the only way there is, Paul."

Hardness coupled with memory came into Paul's face. His eyes grew sultry, cynical, without feeling—yet with intense feeling. "Would you believe, Professor, that I once knew a man who chose that way? I'm not in the least sympathetic to his beliefs, but if there ever was such a thing as a Christian, Billy Williams was."

Paul was gripped with remorse the moment he'd spoken the words. Now Jim and Carolyn would ask questions and he'd have to answer them or there would be feelings again. Why couldn't he learn to keep his mouth shut? He waited for them to begin, glancing from one to the other to see who would be first and wondering why it took them so long.

"Kids used to make fun of him when they saw him coming, and they'd chant, 'Here comes William Williams, here comes William Williams!' " Paul winced at the words. Memory had not stung him so hard in long years. "They—everybody—knew how much he hated to be called that."

A troubled frown dropped over Paul's face. Again he expected someone to begin the bombardment, but no one did. He couldn't stop now; he had to pour out every drop of the story. Strange that it should strike his heart with such pain—

"Billy Williams was a bed wetter. Excuse me, Carolyn, but that's what he was." A shuddering thrill shot through him. "Billy was a skinny, ugly little kid who lived on the farm next to ours back in Idaho. Every night he wet the bed, till he was sixteen years old. The kids in town found out and Billy never had a minute's peace.

"His mom kind of tried to understand him, but his dad never did. He whipped Billy for his problem until sometimes I wondered if the kid would commit suicide just to escape. They were real poor, the Williams family—poorer than we were, and that was bad enough. Billy slept on a straw tick. Every morning the straw was wet, and every morning Billy dragged the tick outdoors, emptied the straw on the hillside and put fresh straw in it for that night. When winter came—bitter winters back there—Billy would almost freeze to death at night on that wet straw. He was always missing school because of colds.

"It's amazing that he never caught pneumonia. You'd think someone would have reported it to the authorities, but they never did."

Paul blinked his eyes, angry all over just to think about it. His mouth twitched once or twice. With precision movement, he slapped the devotional book onto the table.

"That was his life. He'd cut his toe hoeing potatoes and his father would beat him for cutting into a potato. His hair was cut a dozen different lengths. He had nothing!" Paul's face was severe and he spoke with fervor. "And one night—Billy was almost sixteen—he came to my house and told me that—that he'd found the—the *way*. He changed. Everything about him changed. That perpetual look of fear went out of his eyes. He even put on weight and his grades came up and he became a man while still a boy. The kids stopped making fun of him, they started calling him Bill."

Paul nodded to himself. "So you see, I have known one person who feels as you do."

"What happened to Billy—Bill?" Carolyn asked, keeping her voice low so the wonder of this moment would not be destroyed.

"What happened to Bill?" Paul repeated trance-like. "What happened?" He brought up the fingertips of both hands and braced his forehead against them. "Bill graduated from high school and went off to—to study the Bible somewhere. Eventually he made his way to Peru. He'd always declared that his supposed 'call' had been Peru, to the headhunters." Paul's voice changed suddenly, grew low and bitter. "And they killed him for his efforts! They didn't want him or his God. *His God!*"

"Paul—"

The archeologist swung his head up, dark eyes narrowed, and lips chiseled from granite. "Don't do it, Jim. Don't give me all this about God having a purpose. I don't buy it. Something happened to Billy, I realize that. And beyond that point, I stop thinking. He died. He *died!*" And there was no anger in his voice. There was only sadness and a kind of weariness. The profound pathos of brokenness too deep to recall further.

Paul stared away, seeing and not seeing the gently swaying palm trees, vacantly staring at the pillars of the ancient temple, not seeing their splendor. He was numb, unseeing and unfeeling. But something had broken inside of him.

He blinked against the brief moment of suffering. He knew that Jim and Carolyn were thinking of Bill's life and martyrdom, but Paul was himself again, standing very tall and straight, confident of himself.

"Say, that reminds me, is it possible that I could borrow a Bible from you just overnight? I promise to return it in the morning when I come by for you, Carolyn." He hesitated, then added quickly, "Oh, and incidentally, we'll be better off if we start about five-thirty. We'll beat some of the day's heat that way. All right?"

Carolyn handed Paul her own Bible. "That's fine, Paul. I'll be ready."

9

From time to time later on that day Paul left the dig to sit under the meager shade of his tent's awning and pore over the book of Exodus. A satisfied smile played elusively about his lips. It wasn't that he had not known what this portion of the Bible said; it was that he wanted to refresh his memory, to prove again to himself how far removed this discovery could be from what was supposed to be truth.

Ahmed returned once to fill his canteen. Seeing Paul engrossed in the book which he knew to be a Bible, he knotted his brows.

"Mr. Coltren, are you looking for religion? I'll loan you my Koran. I have one written in English."

Paul went into convulsive laughter, which he sought to subdue immediately.

"Forgive me, Ahmed, I honestly wasn't laughing at you and certainly not at your Koran. I was laughing at the ridiculous idea of me trying to find religion." Paul's face grew serious and the light in his eyes went out. "I can assure you, I'm not interested."

The Arab clucked his tongue with disapproval, but Paul's obvious contempt for all that was spiritual kept him from speaking.

"Oh, Ahmed!" Paul swung to his feet and went to the other man. "I *will* be driving into Cairo tomorrow morning early. Be back sometime late tomorrow night probably."

Ahmed gave an abrupt nod, swallowed a mouthful of warm water from his canteen, and waited for his Adam's apple to stop working before he spoke. "I'll keep the tomb guarded every minute, Mr. Coltren. Don't give it a thought."

"Don't you forget it, Ahmed!"

"I swear, by Allah!"

Paul looked at the ground almost pensively. "I'm not really looking for Arnold to come back, but he may fool us and do it anyway. Especially if he finds out I'm gone."

Ahmed screwed the cap on his canteen and let it fall at his side with a little slapping sound. "I have a rifle, Mr. Coltren. Remember? I wouldn't want to use it—"

"I know. But do what you have to."

He walked back to the dig and stood on the slope studying the tomb's facade. The doorway was still jammed with dirt, rubble, and broken stones. It would take days for complete restoration.

Sleep was deep that night. Even when Ahmed yelled at a skulking jackal outside the tent, Paul did not awaken. Only once, when a song began creeping into his dreams, did he arouse enough to turn over and unconsciously force the song away.

When his alarm went off at five o'clock he threw the netting back over his cot and dressed. The sun helmet was replaced today with a casual khaki hat and neither neckerchief nor sweatband was worn. He felt a little giddy about a trip to Cairo with Carolyn. Maybe they could even take an hour away from business to ride across the Nile in a *felucca,* an Egyptian taxi. Something worth thinking about.

It was still dark outside. A half-moon sat well up in the sky, and a shower of stars garnished the heavens. Paul thought he had never seen the sky so beautiful.

Carolyn and Professor Foster were both waiting for him. Jim came to the jeep and expressed his disappointment in not being able to make the trip with them.

"But I did give Carolyn a list of things to get," he said. "Oh, and, Paul, she knows where this restaurant is that I told you about. I want you to eat there and have a good dinner on me."

Paul shook the extended hand. "Thanks, Jim, but you've done far too much already. Besides," he grinned, "if you don't mind, I'd like to have the privilege of taking your daughter to dinner."

Jim tightened the handclasp. "She's in good hands, I know that! Good-bye—have a good time."

Paul waved a hand and drove away, cutting a new path across the desert sand. Turning to Carolyn, he said, "I hope you won't be ashamed of me. I look like the proverbial fugitive from a barber shop."

Again Paul was aware of her loveliness and femininity. A cool blue shift emphasized her smoothly tanned arms and face and lent new lights to the blue of her eyes. Her hair had been swept up on top of her head today, giving her a maturity that Paul had not seen before. Though she wore tennis shoes, a pair of pumps lay tucked in a bag at her feet for later.

"I like your hair that way."

"Thank you!" She touched it at her neck, tucked in an imaginary strand. "It's cooler this way."

"You look terrific."

Carolyn made no reply. They rode along in comfortable silence for a time, and finally the night fell back as the orange fireball came crawling laboriously over the horizon.

Once they passed through a tiny village where men and women clad in white and black worked in small fields. Some of them looked up as the jeep passed, and Carolyn pressed back against the seat with a look of consternation when she saw the yellow rivers of infection running down several faces, upon which flies by the dozen crawled and even bogged down.

"Eye diseases are common here," Paul explained. "Don't let it get you."

"Oh, Paul, it isn't that!" There was pain in her eyes—pain for their suffering. "It's that—there is so much suffering in the world. So much bruising and brokenness." She looked at him. "I'm not trying to be melodramatic, Paul. It's not in me. But people need help. And who really cares?"

For one fleeting moment his eyes narrowed with scorn. "And you care, Carolyn?"

She hesitated. "I do, Paul. I'm not from that hotbed you spoke of, that spiritual hotbed. I've looked into the eyes of a world crying for help. I've seen people reaching—little kids on a wharf in California, smoking and using drugs and trying to make believe they're men! I've had breakfast with girls in trouble and have had drug addicts call me at all hours of the day and night. I've seen some make it and I've seen some fall. It's like—it's like everyone is reaching out, groping for something that eludes them."

Paul swallowed. He'd felt he was getting to know Carolyn Foster, but now he knew that he didn't know her at all. This was a creature he had never met. This poise and passion and fervency of speech.

"What have you offered these—these social offenders that's so great?"

"I have offered them Jesus," she replied honestly. "And now I'm here in Egypt where it seems I can do nothing. Perhaps that's the greatest suffering of all, for me. Before, my life counted at least a little and I was able to reach some. But here, the language barrier, the different culture—I feel very useless to the Lord; yet the need is great."

He glanced at her sideways, his hands hard against the steering wheel. "And that's why you looked so hurt when you saw those wretched Arabs back there?"

She nodded slowly. "I have only one life, Paul. If it doesn't count for Christ, for whom will it count? He's done everything for me. I want Him to live again through me, to reach out to others through my life." She hesitated. "I'm dreaming of starting a women's Bible study in Dahshur before long, but again the language barrier. If I can find someone who will be willing to interpret for me." She moistened her lips. "Meanwhile all I can offer is a smear of ointment or a bit of Merthiolate. So little to give."

"You mustn't think that way, Carolyn. It isn't right."

She fell silent for a moment, studying her slender fingers. Quietly then, she spoke. "I have a good friend, Paul, an Anglican priest. When he had his encounter with Christ, it was on a lonely country road, and God called him into the ministry. He said, 'Lord, I don't have any money. I'm really not very smart. My grades were always low in school, so You *know* I'm not very smart. But I do have a life, Lord; I want to give You that life.' That's what I want too," Carolyn went on. "I want Him to have my life."

Paul did not reply. Rather, he welcomed the new silence that fell between them. But the now familiar song began weaving its way through his thoughts again: *One day a Stranger, a wondrous Stranger, came walking down by blue Galilee. None other spoke like this gracious Stranger, none wrought such wonderful works as He. . . . And this same Jesus still has the power to save the lost and sick to heal! Then come this moment, on Him believing—His mighty power He will reveal!"*

Paul closed his eyes tightly, opened them again. His fingers tightened yet more. But when he spoke he sounded relaxed and his voice was strangely weary.

"He is a stranger to me, Carolyn."

She half turned in her seat to look at him and her eyes were moist. "But you are not a stranger to Him, Paul, at least not in the sense that He does not know this moment who you are and where you are. A stranger to His grace, perhaps, and to His saving power. But it doesn't have to stay that way."

He frowned at her. "I'm a stranger to Him," he replied simply. "Whether or not He is a God who knows the individual, I can't say. I—I don't really know." Yet, with his own words, a slumbering memory stirred again. It was like a dream trying to move weakly into the realm of reality. But it floundered, fell back immediately, and again was as a dead thing within his heart.

"What about your mother, Carolyn?" Paul asked. "Is she—living?"

Carolyn laced her fingers. "No. She died nearly a year ago. That's why I'm staying on with Dad for a time. It hit him so hard. They were always so close, Dad and Mother."

"I'm sorry."

Cairo was ahead of them. The outskirts had many small homes, and its sandy alleys were filled with brown, barefoot children. The people were dressed in turbans and long, loose clothing.

They passed several open marketplaces where Arabs hassled over purchases. There seemed to be a good deal of activity everywhere and an incessant rumble of voices could be heard. A turbaned man on their right was offering camel rides to the tourists. His small, brown-skinned son held the lead rope of one such creature.

Paul and Carolyn exchanged glances. It seemed a day for adventure and they read one another's thoughts. Laughing, Paul stopped the jeep and, unmindful of the heat and thirst, they walked over to the awkward camels.

Delighted, the boy helped Carolyn onto the beast while Paul paid for the ride. The camel rose front end last, almost catapulting the couple through the air. Their ride was short and swaying, but it was the first break in hard work either of them had known for weeks, and it was delightful.

Cairo was an old-new city of minarets, Oriental bazaars, mosques, apartment houses, and museums. It was a city of curio shops which lined the streets and spilled their goods out onto the sidewalks. A city thronged with people in all sorts of dress.

Paul went immediately to the Department of Egyptian Antiquities and turned in the pictures he had taken at the dig, keeping only those he had secreted in his wallet. He waited until copies of them were made so that he would have a set to study on his own. Word was waiting for him there from Eddie Lambert that he was well on his way to recovery and should be able to join his friend within the next two weeks.

When a department official commented on the fact that "a section in the picture pattern seems to be missing," Paul replied only that he was sure he would be able to shoot that particular section when he regained entrance into the tomb's chapel.

Paul and Carolyn took time out to ride across the Nile in a *felucca,* a taxi boat with white lanteen sails and a huge rudder. The spray against their faces was cool and soothing after the heat of the desert, and they talked together animatedly, laughing at everything and at nothing.

Once the boat sank deeply to starboard and Carolyn slipped across the seat and beneath Paul's arm that rested along the back. They laughed again.

Time was not taken for a museum, for they had both seen them before and time was getting late. They shopped together at a large market center and then headed for "The Egyptian" and Abdel Jabari.

10

The Egyptian was detailed in authenticity. Striped curtains gave privacy to the booths and soft native music floated in from the background. Egyptian waitresses, dressed for the days of the pharaohs, served at the tables, their garments making soft little swishing noises as they moved. There was the pleasant tinkling of glasses and low conversation from all about the room. Imitation artifacts sat about the restaurant, and one entire wall was given over to hieroglyphics.

Carolyn looked at Paul expectantly.

"I like it!" he said. "The place is just right." He glanced up as the waitress approached. "I hope they have good steaks."

"They do," she assured him in a whisper. "Dad and I ate here a few weeks ago. They have American coffee too."

Both Carolyn and Paul were famished. The top sirloins, baked potatoes, and tossed salads with mounds of Roquefort dressing were all the further they read on the menus before ordering. Paul did not ask to see Mr. Jabari until they had finished their salads.

When the man entered the room, however, the American found himself totally unprepared. That the Egyptian would be suave, Paul had been certain, a man of poise and authority, a gracious man.

Mr. Jabari was all of that and more. He was like a battleship. His great feet glided silently over the sea of deep blue carpet. The massive hulk of Abdel Jabari was not all useless layers of fat, though there was a very definite frontal protrusion. He was enormous, standing at six feet five and weighing an approximate two hundred sixty pounds. His hand, extended to Paul, was a shovel, and the heel of his hand was thick and soft. Paul took in every foot of the man—imperceptibly, he hoped. Jabari was immaculate in dark suit, highly polished shoes and haji turban. Impeccable. Perfumed.

After this swift glance at strength and softness and bigness, Paul's gaze fixed upon the other man's face. It was huge, like the rest of him, and its features were very large. His nose was a hard bony structure with nostrils ending in twin flanges close to his upper lip, and his eyes were twice as black and piercing through the thick lenses of his glasses, giving an almost frightening effect.

Jabari's voice was almost melodious and Paul nearly looked around to see if someone near at hand were speaking. Ridiculous! A man the size of Jabari to have a voice like that! Yet, it went with his softness and his perfume. It was the underlying authority in the man's voice that said he could also be hard and unyielding.

"So you are Paul Coltren? It's good to meet you at last."

Paul looked over his shoulder to Carolyn, bewildered. "Mr. Jabari, I didn't know you were a wizard!"

The Egyptian threw back his great head and laughed heartily. "Don't you know? Abdel Jabari knows all but tells nothing." Still pumping Paul's hand, he reached out with his left hand and squeezed Carolyn's soft, slender hand affectionately.

"Miss Foster, I'm more than delighted to see you again. Where and how is your father?"

Carolyn responded with her own natural warmth for people. "Dad is fine, but he had to stay behind with his wheat and corn and what have you. He did send his regards, however."

"Ah, yes." Mr. Jabari nodded. Gesturing, he said, "Sit down, Mr. Coltren, sit down." And saying, he sat down too, pulling up an antiqued chair with a dark red cushion that bore two figures, a man and a woman. The man was bright pink and the woman white, which also was the method of distinguishing the man from the woman in picture writing.

Jabari leaned forward, covering nearly half the table. "You are in Cairo for supplies, I presume? But I seem to detect that there is another reason for your being here." He hesitated a moment, glanced down at the table, leaned back as the thick, dripping steaks were served, then continued with the barest inflection of pride in his voice. "You, perhaps, are in need of some advice?"

Paul stared at him silently. Who did Jabari think he was? Agresive, boldly so, and proud and—yes, and wise too. The only thing about it was the fact that Jabari really wasn't trying to show off or show any particular prowess regarding personal business. He was certainly making himself available, however, and being a bit nosy. And he was wise, no denying that. Jabari knew what was going on in his country! OK, then, how far could Paul trust him?

He sparred with words, wanting time to think. "How is it, Mr. Jabari, that you don't know why I'm here? You seem to know everything else."

"Ah, that is where my powers begin to fail." He laughed at his own confession and gave a hopeless shrug of his huge shoulders. "It could be that you, Mr. Coltren, are in need of a guiding hand. After all, you are an archeologist and your partner is still laid up in Morocco."

Carolyn cut through the tender steak. "Abdel, you sound awfully uncanny with your so-called powers, but I happen to know you don't have any!"

He laughed again, and then suddenly he was intensely serious. "All right, Mr. Coltren, I've made my little jokes. Now down to business."

"Mr. Jabari, I do need your help. Professor Foster assured me that you could be trusted to the full, and that's why I'm here." He hesitated, then plunged in. "I have discovered a tomb—perhaps a very important one." He glanced at Jabari, whose slightly bulging eyes never left the American's face. "I must have an Egyptologist—one in whom I can confide fully, without fear."

Abdel gestured. "Your foreman knows something of Egyptology. And surely the Department—" He closed his eyes and gave a grave nod of the head. "Ah, but you want someone who is totally detached from this work."

"It's that important to me," Paul said slowly.

Jabari sat back and crossed his legs, apparently in deep thought. "There is a man, not too far from your dig. He is a Greek. Oh, but wait now!" he added hastily, seeing Paul's gesture of protest. "He is a monk, and he is better skilled in Egyptology than any Egyptian of my acquaintance."

Paul felt skepticism rising within his heart. "A *monk? A Greek?*"

"Look at me," Abdel commanded. "I am Egyptian to the core. Would I tell you this if it were not so? This man is a Greek. He is in a monastery high in the cliffs—it is called Machseh. His name is Josef Zarefiris. If you want learning coupled with secrecy, this is your man." Jabari scratched at his heavy forehead, his movement filling the air with the heavy scent of perfume.

Paul spread his hands. "What would a Greek be doing in a monastery in Egypt? Especially a skilled Egyptologist?"

"It is a Greek monastery. Some of the men have found refuge there from past sins. Perhaps past crimes. It's a very strange order, totally apart from any church denomination. They call themselves 'The Righteous Ones,' though I'd hold that in question." Jabari extended a hamlike hand. "Oh, and, Mr. Coltren, be very careful of the man Arnold. For all we know, his first name may be Benedict."

Paul's first impression was to laugh, but his encounter with Arnold had been too serious. "It should be but it's not," he said. "His name is George. Sounds innocent, doesn't it?" He lifted a hand toward Jabari. "This hand had to smash old George right where it hurt the most."

Jabari's heavy brows suddenly lifted above the black rim of his glasses. "So the two of you have met? Then I need not tell you he's the kind who will refuse to fight but who will sneak up during the night and stab you in the back."

Paul laid aside his steak knife and sipped the American coffee the waitress had brought. "Mr. Jabari, if you know anything else that might be to my advantage, I'd appreciate it."

Jabari's forehead dipped into a frown and his haji turban dropped forward a half inch. "I confess that I really don't know the man's history in our country. But I know that he's a looter, a grave robber, and that he'll steal and kill too, if necessary." Jabari lifted a massive arm clothed in expensive black linen and thrust forth a finger. "I'll tell you this: I can find out about him. But most of all—both of you—beware of this man."

Paul nodded slowly. "*That* we will do! Now, tell me exactly where to find Josef Zarefiris."

11

It was frightening. Lonely. Time had sped away and the heavens had slowly pulled the deep purple curtains of night. The loud clamor of voices accompanied with arguments from windowless houses and the cries of children could be heard.

Nearer at hand, Oriental wind-bells tinkled pleasantly from sidewalk bazaars and curio shops. Wares spilled onto the narrow street. Woven straw hats, purses and whatnot rustled against each other, trying to join the song of the bells. Egyptian merchants bargained valiantly with the few remaining tourists.

For safety's sake, Carolyn had linked her arm into the inviting one Paul had offered. Once she shivered and they paused a moment before a curio shop.

"If you're frightened, we'll go back," he promised.

"Oh no! I've never seen this part of Cairo." She moved nearer Paul as a drunk Arab staggered by, brushing her shoulder in an attempt to stay on his feet. "This is something you don't learn about in college!"

"This is life, Carolyn," Paul said, speaking her name tenderly. "Raw. Rugged. *Real.*"

In the midst of the filth and squalor about the street, there suddenly came to their attention an almost smart-looking curio shop. It was unlike the other shops in that there was no Arab crying to the American in feeble English, "Mister, gifts for the lady. Beautiful imitations, mister. Come and look!" Rather, this shop sat as a beacon among all the other dirty little curio shops that lined the street. The cheap nameplate read: "The Prophet."

"Mind if we pause for just a minute, Carolyn? Then I promise we'll start home."

She smiled up at him. "Paul, I don't mind. I'm really enjoying all this. You see," she said sheepishly, "Dad's awfully protective at times. He'd never bring me here, and I really am interested."

They moved toward the dusty display window where statuettes, vases, small boats that were replicas of boats found in various tombs, and other artifacts were waiting to be sold.

"Do you ever get the feeling," Carolyn asked, "that if you look on the bottom of those statuettes you might find the words 'Made in Japan'?"

He dropped his arm, allowing his fingers to trail for a moment along hers. "Often!" he replied emphatically. He pointed to an object sitting behind and to the right of the artifacts. A moment later he said, "I see something I've got to have. Come on." Taking her hand, Paul led Carolyn into the small curio shop.

He went immediately to a various assortment of perfumes, after-shave lotions and men's cologne. Triumphantly he held up a dusty gold and black box. The gold lettering read: Oriental Jade.

"You must be out of after-shave lotion," Carolyn smiled.

"Nope. *This* is for my foreman, Ahmed. He's been working at pulling those wretched six or eight whiskers of his for about a week. You see, I promised him a few drops of my Oriental Jade when he accomplished his task." Paul threw back his head and laughed. "Can't you see his face when I present him with a whole bottle!"

"Paul, that will be too good. I wonder what his men will have to say about his new 'fragrance'?"

Paul's dark eyes were lighted and happy. "Maybe they'll go to work on their own faces!"

He was on his way to look for the proprietor when an Arab in a long, flowing garment and wearing a fez came sauntering toward them. He was brown and smiling and eager to please. "Yes, yes?" he asked. "I can help you?"

"I want this—" He hesitated, looking around over the store. "Why don't you just hold it for me for a few minutes while I look around?"

The other man gave a few rapid little nods of his head. "I will stay open! Take your time, mister. I will stay open for you."

For a place of business in this particular sector, the curio shop was fairly orderly. But the dust that covered the various objects spoke of poor trade and negligence. One long and decrepit display rack ran almost the length of the shop, right down the middle. The walls were lined with crude, handmade shelves upon which sat a few genuine pieces of jasper, alabaster, bronze, and even a statuette of gold. But the genuine pieces had been curiously interspersed with the imitations so that a novice at purchasing artifacts could easily mistake the imitation for the real. This was essentially the way smaller curio shops with smaller names made enough money to live.

Carolyn was browsing along the center rack, touching a portion of an alabaster hand. The real article. Then, tilting her blonde head in doubt, she picked up an ivory-colored statuette of some early Egyptian pharaoh.

Paul moved up beside her until their arms touched. "You must have that special sixth sense that tells you that piece isn't for real," he whispered, keeping an eye on the proprietor who was trying to appear busy behind the counter but was watching their every move. "You're right, Carolyn! It isn't real. It's a cheap imitation, as most of the articles are." He jerked his head. "I'm going to see what's back here against the wall and then I'll be ready to leave."

Paul moved to the more cluttered area against the rear wall. The dust was heavier there, but Paul shot up an eyebrow immediately. There were some good pieces back here! He moved slowly, eyeing this piece and that one. Finally he paused altogether, studying a twelve-inch-high figurine of Queen Hatshepsut, the alleged daughter of the pharaoh who rescued the baby Moses from the water. Its base was alabaster and was shaped like an artist's palette. Paul had never seen such an unusual base for a statuette. The full length was eight inches, and the entire statuette and base had been made from a single piece of alabaster. On the left side of the woman's head was a sculptor's mark, a tiny *v* with a short line going through the right side of the emblem. Paul was intrigued. That this was a genuine artifact, there could not be the slightest doubt. Reaching out, he plucked the heavy figurine from the dusty shelf. As he did so, a small white card which he saw was attached to the leg of this famed queen—ultimately to become a woman pharaoh—fell from beneath the base and dangled from a string.

"Have you found something that interests you?" Carolyn asked, moving nearer to the shelves where Paul was standing.

"Um—" Paul's long fingers caught the card, yellowed with age, and read the two words scribbled on it. As he did so an electric shock ran the entire length of his body. *George Arnold!* "George *Arnold?*"

Carolyn's eyes widened and one hand reached out automatically as though to take the statuette from Paul, but she only touched it hesitantly and then withdrew her hand and brought it to rest on her purse.

"Paul, how can it be?"

"I don't know. Tag's yellow, so it must have been here a long time, but I can't imagine that, because this is a good piece." He put a hand under her elbow and they walked toward the proprietor of the small shop.

He was smiling and delighted. "Ah, you have find something that pleases the eye?"

Paul moved a shoulder doubtfully. "The eye, yes. But I don't know about the pocketbook."

The Egyptian never lost his smile or his cunning. "The money bothers you? I make you good bargain, mister."

"Let's hear it."

The Egyptian studied for a moment, chin buried in the palm of one hand. "A good bargain I give you. Two hundred and twenty American dollars."

Paul knew it was worth it, but he also knew he couldn't pay that amount of money. Furthermore, he had a strong hunch that this old boy needed money.

"Huh-uh. That's far too much. Now I'll make you an offer. Fifty American dollars."

The face of the other man grew almost red beneath the brown-black coloring. A look of insulted pride seized his eyes and lips. "Fifty dollars?" he repeated, trying to sound sure that he had mistaken the American. "Fifty dollars! Do you know where this piece came from?"

Paul twisted his mouth to one side, held the statuette high to survey its underside. "No," he replied lazily, "I don't know where it came from. But, knowing something about George Arnold and the way he accumulates artifacts, I rather doubt that you would want to know, either, where this came from. It's a whole lot safer not knowing. Of course," he added for the sake of emphasis, "the authorities don't know either. Because—" He tenderly stroked the base of the statuette, straining his neck to examine details.

"—this piece actually should be in a museum. The British Museum, Egyptian Museum, the—"

The Egyptian's thin lips pressed still thinner. "Fifty dollars, American money. You drive a good bargain, mister—for yourself."

Carolyn's blue eyes were gently accusing, but a teasing smile played about her full mouth.

Paul pulled out his wallet and laid down some money. Hesitantly he pointed to the yellowed tag. "I guess Arnold must sell on consignment, considering the fact that his name is on this tag?" Without waiting for an answer, Paul continued. "I have the feeling that this piece hasn't been on display as long as the color of the tag would indicate, however. Surely it would have sold before all that time!" He pretended to be absorbed in getting a personal card from his wallet, but he was watching the Egyptian's every expression.

The black face changed from wariness to anger to reserve and caution. He took the American's money and nervously placed the after-shave lotion and the figurine, carefully wrapped, into a cheap brown bag.

"Here," Paul continued as casually as ever, "give Arnold my card the next time you see him. I'm sure," he said candidly, "that he'll remember me."

The other man took the card, read the word *archeologist* beneath the name and paled a bit. He gave Paul a ghostly smile and hurriedly ushered Carolyn and Paul toward the door, locking it after them.

"Paul! How could you?" Carolyn whispered. "Aren't you afraid of some kind of repercussions?"

The sandy head lifted an inch and his shoulders squared. "Not in the slightest. In fact, it's Arnold who will begin to fear repercussions. I want him to know that I know who he is, what he is, and what kind of dirty, underhanded work he's involved in. Only one thing leaves me more than just puzzled."

She accepted his arm as they walked down the narrow, dimly lit street. "And that is?"

"The age of the name tag on this statuette. It just doesn't figure."

12

The picture was one of grim desolation. Sheer and terrifying cliffs rose up on the one side, while away on the other stretched brown and barren hills and, beyond that, sand. One great building broke the landscape, though it blended in to give the impression that it was a part of the towering cliffs. Erected from enormous blocks of brown stone, the monastery presented a formidable appearance. Its entire rear side melted into and became a part of the sheer wall of rock that ended in a narrow gorge hundreds of feet below. The gorge was choked by boulders and represented further desolation through which not even a Bedouin ever ventured.

High above this torturous cliff a young man looked down. He was clad in an ankle-length robe bound at the waist by a simple ropelike cord. On his feet were sandals. His hair was dark, and the small, neatly trimmed beard lent him a definite note of distinction. It was his eyes, however, that drew the attention. They flashed black and intense, holding fires full of fear and unrest.

A desperate inner struggle caused him to stand and stare unseeingly into the awful abyss. Finally he turned, raking the fingers of both hands through his hair. A cynical smile marred his handsome face.

"So! I am a monk!" he murmured as he cocked his head sideways. "I am a monk, and in the seclusion of a monastery, I have found peace for my soul." He frowned. "I have found peace for my soul! *I have found peace for my soul!*"

Hard, dry sobs shook his chest for a moment, and he turned again to the window, dropping his head onto the crook of an elbow to hide his anguish.

Peace? What irony! Peace in this—this *cell,* with foot-thick walls, a hard cot, a too-small table and lone chair? Peace in a place where one could not trust even his fellow monks?

The gong of a bell echoed through the narrow stone corridor

and Josef's inward meditations came to a momentary halt. Stepping into the cold passageway, he filed along silently with the other monks to the dining room and slid onto a hard bench beside the table. All the monks ate here except for the superiors, who had a smaller dining room to themselves.

Josef glanced up at the walls. Even after six years of monastic life, he could not accustom himself to eating with these hideous, much-faded paintings glaring down at him. To his right was the judgment scene depicting the unrighteous being cast into hell. Straight before him, blood-chilling and grotesque, the fires of hell tormented a multitude of lost souls.

Purposely Josef tore his gaze from the faded orange flames to the shrewd face of the man entering the dining room with a large tray of lukewarm food. Somehow Josef had never been able to picture this man in the kitchen. In an underworld gang, perhaps, but not in a kitchen! Abraham was too cunning and his face was that of a hardened criminal.

Abraham— Josef mused. *The friend of God!* He wanted to laugh, but dared not so much as to allow his lips to curve with amusement.

For an instant, as though sensing Josef's thoughts, Abraham looked straight at him, but then he set down the tray of food and left the room as silently as some apparition.

"Unseasoned again! Don't they have a salt shaker in that kitchen!"

Every fork paused in midair and a disapproving silence filled the atmosphere. One seldom spoke in this gloomy place, and never at mealtime.

Josef tried to warn the younger monk with his eyes, but he failed. Such an outburst would bring a flogging such as could better be imagined than described. But then, Peter had been there but three short months. Surely that would be taken into consideration.

After the evening meal, the monks walked in single file through the maze of dimly lit passages to the gloomy chapel. Faded and morose paintings, stark and all too meaningful, were flung over the walls. Splinters of moonlight made their way through the glass-domed ceiling.

Here Josef and the other monks droned out their repetitious prayers. Then began the weird chants that were so much a part of monastic life, the singsong rituals that lasted until well after midnight.

"I can't stand it any longer!" a voice at his side whispered urgently. "I wanted to escape reality, but not like this! And you feel the same way, Josef, I know you do—I see it in your face! I'm going to leave. Why don't you come with me?"

Josef's blood chilled at the words. Escape from the monastery? One could as easily fly across the gorge at the edge of this great building. Then abruptly the cold eyes of Abraham were peering at them both, and Josef knew that Peter's words had been overheard.

Through the weary hours of night Josef tossed restlessly. At last the faint streaks of dawn crept through the curtainless window and the gong sounded. It was time for morning meditations. Then breakfast, with its bowls of cold oatmeal and cups of lukewarm tea. It was a ritual, all of it, always. There was never any deviation, never a moment of pleasure.

There was but one thing in the favor of the monks. They did have duties that kept them busy and their minds occupied. And there were studies. All of these things enabled the men to keep their bodies under subjection.

By the time lunch was served Josef was feeling tired from the loss of sleep and from the morning's work.

"You have English-speaking visitors waiting to see you," a voice informed him suddenly from behind his shoulder. "Americans. You may have an hour."

"Visitors for me?" Josef repeated wonderingly, half rising from his seat.

"That's what was told me," came the sardonic reply. "If they wish to look around, you know where to take them."

Josef nodded briefly with understanding. Then, removing his own plate and cup from the table, he gave the cord about his waist a firm tug, squared his jaw, and made his way to the small, cheerless reception room.

Josef was startled to discover that one of the visitors was a woman—a very young woman with blonde hair and very blue eyes. He turned his gaze swiftly from her to the tall young man at her side.

"I'm Josef Zarefiris."

Paul extended his hand quickly. "My name is Paul Coltren. This is Miss Foster. Four days ago, in Cairo, I met a man named Abdel Jabari. He sent me here to see you."

Josef cocked his handsome head to one side. "Oh?"

"Yes, he tells me that you're an expert Egyptologist."

Josef bowed slightly. "Mr. Jabari is extremely flattering. How can I help you, Mr. Coltren?"

Paul looked around. "Is there somewhere we can talk—privately, that is? What I would like to discuss with you is very confidential."

"Of course. It's a bit of a problem since a woman is involved, for no woman is permitted into the monastery proper. However, there is a small conference room where we can talk with privacy." He turned. "Please come with me."

Josef led the way down an airless, dimly lit passageway and into a room that was hardly bigger than the cell in which he lived. He indicated the cold, straight chairs around the small table and they all sat down.

"You have discovered something and you are bewildered about it?" Josef said with a wry smile.

"I have," Paul replied. "But I must be absolutely certain that I can trust you with the information I have."

Josef shrugged. "And how do you hope to accomplish this?"

Paul felt himself relaxing. "Well, I guess you've got me there. I really don't have a choice, do I?"

"I have been at Machseh for six years and I have lost my identity. There's nothing for me to lose and nothing to gain."

Paul looked at Josef for a long moment, pondering the meaning of the man's words.

Carolyn, silent up to this time, suddenly sat forward a little. "Josef—are we supposed to call you *Josef?*—what is the meaning of the word *Machseh?"*

Josef avoided gazing directly at Carolyn. "It means 'place of refuge.' "

Paul found an opportunity to ease the atmosphere. "And have you found it that?" he asked.

Josef's jaw went hard, his nostrils flaring. "Of course I have! I have found at Machseh everything in life that I have wanted. *Everything!"* And he didn't realize that his dark eyes betrayed him.

Paul reached for his wallet and took out the hidden pictures. "I have found a tomb," he said, "and was able to get pictures of the chapel just before we suffered a cave-in. I have numbered the pictures as I took them, cropped them where they overlapped, and this is what I have come up with. Would you take a look at them, Josef?"

The monk leaned forward hurriedly. "Yes, I will!" Then, with lowered voice, "We have but one hour, Mr. Coltren."

Silence enveloped the room. Once the sound of steady footfalls came from within the passage, but otherwise all was wrapped in complete silence. It was a quiet that neither Paul nor Carolyn really felt comfortable in. Yet, oddly, they were attracted to the bearded monk who hunched over the display of pictures, studying them from every possible angle.

Finally Josef looked up. His jaw was hard and square, his brows knit in puzzlement. "I can see what you have been thinking, Mr. Coltren, and of course we will have to have further evidence. I would like to keep the pictures with me for intensive study, and then perhaps you can return in a week or so for a possible conclusion."

"I know," Paul replied, gently gnawing the inside of his jaw. "I realize that the burial chamber will reveal a whole lot more—and yet—"

Josef nodded. "And yet— The tomb is very decisively one of two persons. Some Egyptian totally unknown at the moment, or—" He broke off, closed his eyes against the evidence of the pictures themselves, opened them again. A baby hidden in a basket in rushes along a river's edge. A boy standing with a woman of royalty, the daughter of a pharaoh. A young man watching the hard labor of the Hebrews, a man with love in his eyes.

Josef did not take his eyes from the pictures. "From what you tell me of the tomb, it could not be one of royalty. But it could possibly be the tomb of one raised in the courts of royalty. A noble, too, perhaps." He lifted his gaze slowly. "It *could* be the tomb—of *Moses!*"

13

The reaction of all three persons was one of acute shock. Even for Paul, though he had suspected it from the first. A heavy, breathless stillness crept into every crevice of the cheerless room. They almost had the feeling that ears were listening, and that what was spoken must be spoken in whispers.

"Paul!" It was Carolyn who broke the silence at last. Her eyes were wide and violet, her lips parted, her face uplifted. "You can't possibly be serious!"

He turned with a frown. "But I *am* serious, Carolyn. And the proof of such a possibility is before your own eyes."

She smiled slowly, and the look of inner peace was not in the least perturbed. "The Bible tells us clearly that no one knows where Moses' body was taken, for the Lord Himself took charge of that funeral!"

"But you forget that I—and an uncounted number just like me—do not happen to believe the Bible." Paul's words held no bitterness, no hardness. He spoke slowly, almost with a feeling of gentleness.

Carolyn's face registered incredulity. She gazed at Paul with a compassion not her own, but she did not speak.

"How about it, Josef?" Paul asked the black-robed monk.

Josef contemplated. How could he tell these people that the Bible was not included as a part of their daily routine? That their nightly devotions and rigid schedule included study from many excellent scholars, but that a real study of God's holy book was not a part of their curriculum?

Finally the monk made a futile gesture with his hands. "I—I can only give you my impression of what is before me. The hieroglyphics point to Moses, there can be no question about that."

Paul pointed with a forefinger to the pictures. "What about these smaller black markings, emblems and such?"

"The marks of higher wisdom, the skills of the magicians, of intensive training—all of which point to the man Moses." Josef sank back into his chair, pondering. "An amazing discovery, Mr. Coltren. I wonder what the world will think—"

"The world?" Carolyn whispered. "Surely—you wouldn't tell—*the world!*"

Josef stroked his beard gently. "Certainly not just yet, Miss Foster. I will compare every marking for authenticity—for solid fact! Everything will be checked until all impossibility is erased. But, you see, hieroglyphics read into each other, and the story these tell cannot be denied."

Carolyn spoke softly, with feeling. "But Moses died in the land of Moab. And God Himself buried Moses 'over against Bethpeor,' as the Bible says." She looked as if she did not at all comprehend what the men had said. "Paul, this is history!"

Paul moistened his lips. His eyes shone very dark. "It's *Bible,* Carolyn. *If* it's true that Moses died where the Bible says, then someone has evidently brought him back and buried him here in his native land. If, on the other hand, Moses never left Egypt, then the world has quite a hoax on its hands."

Carolyn shook her head slowly. "I just can't believe you're serious. Paul, surely you can recall the history of the Jews, see them in their land today, and know that God had a man to lead them."

Paul pursed his lips and looked toward the pictures. "You can make the world believe a lot of things," he said slowly. "You can give them all sorts of error and wrong thinking. You can lead them down every avenue of thinking and beliefs imaginable. But you present tangible proof to people—like these pictures—and people have to believe truth!"

Carolyn sat forward. "Oh, Paul, do you know the calamity that would come to the people of this world? Shipwreck to the faith of those who are weak and to those who are about to make decisions for Christ?"

Paul looked at her. "What would it do to you, Carolyn?"

"To me?" Her eyes grew thoughtful and a smile crept over her lips. "I have known the Lord Jesus most of my life, loved Him deeply. God has proven Himself to me by His Word too many times for me to ever doubt it—or Him. I would continue to believe what God said about Moses even though you might think you had concrete proof that Moses' body lies within that tomb."

Paul examined his nails in the glare of the one shadeless bulb hanging from the ceiling. "Well, you're right about one thing. It would shock the world."

"Is that what you want?" Carolyn asked softly.

He blinked his eyes rapidly a few times. "I want truth, Carolyn."

Josef had taken in the conversation but had not once ventured a word of agreement or disagreement. His own inner conflict was far too great to let the tomb of Moses bother him. That fact mattered little to him, actually. It was what Carolyn had said about Jesus Christ that disturbed him most.

Paul gestured. "I have something else to leave with you, Josef. A jasper cylinder that contains some papyrus that was found by my foreman during the few moments inside the chapel of the tomb. I had not seen or photographed it when we heard the rumblings of a cave-in near the door." Paul shrugged. "Ahmed does know better. Maybe he thought the whole place was going. I don't know, but anyway he broke protocol and snatched up the cylinder on his way toward the door."

Josef leaned forward, his dark eyes burning. "I am glad for it, I must admit. But, where is it?"

Paul stood up and walked to the heavy door. "In the jeep. I wasn't sure how much privacy we would have, so I left it there."

The Greek said, "By all means, leave the papyrus. It may mean a mass of business affairs, figures, personal history—the latter is what we'll hope for."

Paul had his hand on the iron door latch when there was a rapid knock on the other side. Before Josef could respond, the door opened and a brisk, businesslike monk walked inside. His flowing black robe brushed Paul inadvertently, and the sandaled feet went straight to Josef.

"There is a sandstorm coming, a bad one for this time of year. Already the desert below us has disappeared." He glanced coldly toward the Americans. "It has been suggested that your visitors remain for refreshments and a few hours' rest. Perhaps by that time the storm will have abated."

Josef bowed toward his superior and, as the monk passed

through the door, Paul hurriedly thrust the pictures into Josef's hands.

The three people returned to the gloomy reception room. Josef went to the massive door and pulled it open. Even at this height a mighty gust of wind rushed into the room, billowing Josef's robe and tossing stray strands of Carolyn's hair.

Away before them, down in the desert region, great clouds of sand filled the air. All was obscure to their vision. The road down the cliffs was totally impassable, and the road across the desert would be lost in the storm. There was nothing to do but wait until the storm was over.

"You will wait here, Mr. Coltren." Josef shut the heavy door, inclined his head toward Carolyn. "Miss Foster, I'll get you some refreshment."

Carolyn and Paul were left alone.

"I wonder what his life is really like here?" Carolyn mused. "I wonder if Josef is truly happy?"

"I doubt it." Paul went to stand beside Carolyn. "I feel like I've tricked you," he said, "in bringing you here with me, then letting you find out. Will you believe me when I tell you that this was not the case? I guess I was so excited about the possibility—you know—that I didn't think."

"Paul, I do believe you. But, if I had known, I wouldn't have come. It just seemed so natural to come, I guess. And I didn't dream—"

He reached out and put his hands on her shoulders, looking deeply into her eyes. He read honesty, sincerity. How he longed in that moment to gather her to him, to assure her that he would not for worlds deceive or hurt her in any way. Absurd thought! Yet Paul remembered that lovely moment in the *felucca* crossing the Nile, when she had slid under the shelter of his arm. Their laughter. Their joy.

He turned from her abruptly. This was madness! He'd made a discovery, a very exciting and important discovery. What did that have to do with Carolyn, anyway?

Josef returned with a tray. "There is tea," he murmured laconically. "Abraham even found some cakes which he had been keeping for visitors."

"Will you join us?" Paul questioned. "There's so much more—" But a look from Josef stopped him from continuing.

"Perhaps later?" Josef said.

"Later?"

"The storm has worsened. It looks as though you may have to stay overnight."

"Overnight?" Paul's forehead wrinkled. "Carolyn's father would be worried sick!"

Josef's black eyes gave way to a moment of tenderness. Almost of understanding. "I'm sorry about that. However, we do have quarters for overnight guests, so there is no real problem."

Paul was tense. Carolyn alone in this dungeon of a place all night?

"It will be quite safe for the girl, I assure you," Josef said calmly, as though reading Paul's thoughts.

Carolyn laid a warm hand over Paul's. Her laughter rang out, hollow and strange in the room. "If it comes to staying overnight, Paul, it'll be all right. And the storm is probably whipping through our camp, so Dad will understand perfectly why we haven't returned."

The day wore on. The storm raged below, forming new dunes and erasing old ones, covering roads, drifting against the tents that the Bedouin lived in, driving tourists into seclusion, and causing animals to hunch up against the wind and pitting sand.

Dusk fell and all hope of returning home that night was gone. Josef appeared again.

"I'm sorry that the lady is not permitted in the dining room, or I would invite you both to eat with us." His intense black eyes seemed to be trying to tell them something. Perhaps something of his loneliness, his yearnings. "Abraham will bring you trays here. Then, if you wish, Mr. Coltren, I can show you parts of the monastery. If my superior does not object, you could even sit in on evening devotions." He saw Carolyn's evident desire and added, "I am sorry, Miss Foster. Women are strictly forbidden at all such functions of monastic life."

"I'm sorry too!" she said softly. "But I do understand." Turning to Paul, she added, "You will go, won't you, Paul?"

He smiled. "So I can come back and tell you about it?" He

pursed his lips. "Yes, I think I will. I've never seen how monks make their contact with the Most High!"

Paul was not sure, however, that he had made the right choice when he sat beside Josef four hours later in the morbid chapel and heard the men droning out their prayers.

He tried to avoid looking at the awful paintings spread over the walls. He tried not to think of Carolyn, who at that very moment was on her knees in the visitors' quarters, praying to the God whom she knew intimately and lived for twenty-four hours a day.

He tried not to see the wistfulness on Josef's face, did not want to know about the longings that all too obviously lay within the man's soul. And never would Paul forget the confused yearnings on the face of the young man Peter. Paul listened to the singsong chants and his heart began to twist within him. If it had been possible, he would have turned and fled. But one did not run and hide here. One stayed and faced the inevitable, no matter what it brought.

Inner groanings became so intense that Paul was fearful lest someone detect them. Lest they become audible and Paul himself would be forced into facing his own heart.

"God!" he agonized inwardly. *"God!"*

It was the first time Paul had cried out to the Saviour in many years. Ironically, it had taken the gloom of a monastery, the longing heart of a monk, and the hideous paintings on these chapel walls to bring it about. *This is not reality! This is pretense and the worst kind of hypocrisy! God! My God, if there is reality anywhere in this world, let me find it!*

* * *

Josef paced up and down his cell-like room. The lights had been extinguished all over the monastery. Only the faint glow from a half-moon sent its glow over the land. The storm had worn itself out and was gone. It was late. By standing close to his tiny window, Josef could see the yawning gorge below. But halfway down it was thrown into shadow and lost to his view. Carolyn's words reechoed again in his mind.

I have known the Lord Jesus most of my life, loved Him deeply. God has proved Himself to me by His Word—by His Word—by His—

A faint flicker of movement some distance away caught Josef's attention. A moment later there was the faint shriek of a man in unspeakable terror. The sound died out quickly in the gorge below.

Josef's dark eyes stared from a face that was suddenly white. *Peter!* It must have been Peter! Josef covered his face with shaking hands. He'd tried to warn the younger monk several times. And now another victim had been claimed by Machseh.

" 'Place of Refuge,' " Josef groaned. "What irony!" And, lifting his tortured face to the distant stars, he whispered fervently, "My God, where will it all end? Where is the answer?"

14

For moments Josef stared downward through the pale moonlight. The sound of Peter's cry still bounced up from below, still emanated through the thick stone walls that formed his cell. Peter was gone —numbered among those whose ghastly deaths were referred to by fellow monks as "unfortunate accidents." Situated in a desolate spot such as this, the accounts of the mysterious deaths did not reach the outside world but were kept within the ranks of their sect.

After all, not even the monks ever *saw* the accidents. Even if they had, there was not a one of them who would have dared to speak.

"Poor fool," Josef whispered to the stillness. "Probably thought he could make it with visitors spending the night, and the shifting sand to blot his tracks below. He didn't realize that no one ever leaves Machseh."

A damp chill crept into his stone chamber before morning, and the one blanket was never sufficient for warmth. He lay staring into the darkness, wondering if the girl in the visitors' quarters was resting well. And the man, Paul. A strange one, Paul, a bit difficult to figure— With thoughts of the couple, a strange, bitter loneliness gripped him.

Finally Josef moved from his narrow cot, lighted a candle, hugged his blanket about him, and sat down at the little table to pore over the pictures Paul had given him.

When the fingers of dawn reached through his tiny window to paint the opposite wall with gold, Josef snuffed out the candle and made himself ready for morning prayers.

A little later he went to the kitchen to get the guest trays for Paul and Carolyn. Josef wanted to put off seeing them as long as possible, for he knew they'd be on their way as soon as they had eaten.

Abraham's cunning black eyes looked full at Josef. "Most unfortunate," he said casually, "the accident last night."

Josef suddenly remembered that it had been Abraham who had overheard Peter's whispered words in the chapel last night. Was Abraham perhaps sounding a warning to Josef? Oh, but what nonsense! At least one thing was confirmed to Josef, however. Abraham performed many duties here at the monastery that went beyond his regular schedule.

Josef found Paul and Carolyn waiting for him in the vestibule. His heartbeat quickened. "Good morning! I trust that you slept well?"

Carolyn looked up with a smile. "I did, until I was awakened by some sort of—of *cry.*" A tremor passed over her slim body. "I know it was silly of me, but I felt chilled through and through."

Josef forced a laugh. "I heard it too, and it was quite real, I assure you. I saw the shadow from my window. It was a jackal—poor creature! Wandered too close to the edge of the cliff and lost its footing. Most unusual for such an animal. I wondered if it could have been mad."

"Josef—" Carolyn glanced at Paul, saw that he was merely curious about the small black book in her hand. She studied the face of the monk, wondering if she dared. "Would—will you accept this, and read it often? I'd be very happy if you would."

Josef moistened his lips. "Thank you, but I cannot accept it," he replied stiffly.

"As a gift?"

He looked down at the small book and hesitated, suppressing the desire to snatch it from her hand. But did he dare? He felt the palms of his hands grow moist. His heart beat savagely. It was a New Testament. He wanted it. Longed for it. It was something he had never possessed. They had their ceremonies here, their rigid studies. Yet—

In one smooth motion he reached for and accepted the book. In a moment it was concealed in the folds of his long black robe. His look was one of apology, but the countenances of both Paul and Carolyn said that they understood.

An hour later he stood beside Carolyn and Paul to bid them farewell and to promise the information regarding the tomb in one week's time. He returned Paul's firm handclasp, but he only gazed at Carolyn with warm eyes.

"Josef," she was saying, "please study the Testament, for within its pages lies the secret to eternal life. It cannot be had through ceremonies but through the shed blood of Jesus Christ, God's Son."

With those words, Carolyn slipped into the jeep and soon it was headed down the steep hill leading away from the monastery. For some moments after their departure Josef stood staring at the little whirls of dust and sand caused by the tires. The words spoken by Carolyn Foster echoed through his mind.

At last he turned and walked to the edge of the gaping precipice. There was no evidence of last night's incident. In what manner it had been erased, Josef knew he would never discover. Peter was simply gone, and it would not be disclosed either by word or look from any of the monks that anything out of the ordinary had taken place.

Josef sighed deeply. His eyes narrowed with thought, and he stood for a moment, lost to his surroundings. For a moment he was back in Akharnai, Greece. He saw himself as a boy, romping on the grassy hillsides with his dog. Josef had been a loner, always. If he had his dog, he was content. His parents had been kind and good. With his mother there was the warm association of strong character, tender love, and the aroma of freshly baked bread filling the house. With his bearded father it was calloused hands, hard work and an ability to understand. Yet there was always the hunger, the searching. Questions that no one could answer. College failed to bring him the peace he craved, the inner satisfaction. He had thought to find that in the monastery, and that too, had failed.

With an inner despair, Josef turned and walked away, his head bowed.

The ironical twist was that one year after he had entered the monastery he knew he'd made a mistake. And then it was too late. For, once a man had committed himself to Machseh, there was no turning back. Once he came, he did not leave.

And, Josef knew, certainly all who had tumbled into the yawning gorge below did not die by criminal action. Others had been troubled by brooding disappointment, or had met with failure in an attempt to get away, and they had sought out the gorge as a way of escape. Some committed suicide because of fear, others because of depression, hopelessness. Some because of the giant of hate and despair that lived in their lives. Had not Josef himself contemplated such a move?

But now there was work to do. Much studying. He would discover in a short time whether the tomb really belonged to Moses. Though it seemed there could be little doubt. And the cartouche on the bricks. Was it, perhaps, the name or emblem of one of Moses' sons? For often a son finished his father's tomb. Well, he would see.

* * *

Paul drove carefully down the winding, steep road that led away from Machseh. Both he and Carolyn were silent, each occupied in thought. Carolyn spoke after a few moments, as though reading Paul's meditation.

"You won't say anything to Ahmed, will you, Paul? Or to anyone who might let the information regarding the tomb—"

Paul raised his eyebrows. "After all, Carolyn, there's always the possibility that Moses *did* die where the Bible says, and that he was brought back here for burial."

Carolyn spread her hands and surveyed her nails critically. "It's not possible, Paul."

"Why not?" he challenged as he maneuvered a turn on the road. "Just twenty years ago there were scrolls discovered in Egypt that are thought to be comparable to the Dead Sea Scrolls. And they're written in Greek! Now, how did they get here? I contend that it would be just as possible for Moses—" He paused and shrugged his shoulders. "But why go over it again? I *have* the evidence. It's not like I have to try and prove anything."

"The evidence is wrong. It implies truth, but it can't be true."

"Josef agrees with me," he countered. "And he's one of the best-known Egyptologists in the country—Greek or not!"

"Paul, it isn't for myself. I know what I believe and why. But what about new believers in Christ, and the weak in faith, and those who are on the threshold of salvation? You don't know for sure that this is Moses' tomb, but if the news of this—this discovery should get out before you know the complete truth about it, think what it would do."

Paul grimaced. "Just because we think the tomb of Moses has been found?"

"If one part of the Bible is wrong, how can the Christian believe any part of it?" She gazed at him steadily. "Please, Paul! Not even Ahmed."

"In time—"

"Then *wait* for that time!"

He looked at her, and again he had the distinct impression that he was seeing within her, knowing her as she was. A kind of thrill shot through him. He didn't want to hurt her. Not Carolyn.

"You believe the story of Moses to be a myth," she murmured softly. "Yet, what about the people of Israel today and all that the Word of God says about their future? What do you do with this?"

Paul pursed his lips. He sat very tall, almost severely handsome. "The people of Israel?" he said slowly, repeating her words. "The regathering? From the north, south, east, and west. A nation in a day? Gaining the land promised to them by God thousands of years ago. Seeing its beginning in our day—"

He stared out the open doorway of the jeep to the newly formed sand dunes. "What do I do with that?" It was as if he was talking to himself now, searching through his own mind for the answer. "I guess I don't do anything with it. Not—not anything at all."

The air was still and hot after yesterday's violent sandstorm. On the horizon a hawk hung motionless, but there was no stir of life on the ground where they traveled. Not even a hot, tired Bedouin journeyed. Only one time in the course of that morning did they see another human being, and that was when they passed a dirty hovel where a few *fellaheen* sat dipping bread in sour camel's milk.

When Paul reached his campsite at noon, the sun was a blazing fireball and the workmen were stopping for lunch. Obviously the heat was penetrating deeply today, for the men were dripping with sweat and were quiet, uncommunicative. Exhausted, they threw themselves to the ground by the tents, and only Ahmed, wiping his face against his ragged sleeve, came toward Paul. He was eager, intense. "Well, how did it go? Anything new develop?"

Paul peered at Ahmed's clean chin with a sense of personal pride. Above the raw smell of old perspiration and body odor, there would soon arise the triumphant aroma of Oriental Jade.

"I haven't found much more than I already knew," Paul hedged. "But I will know more later."

Ahmed nodded his head thoughtfully in rapid little jerks. "Do you want to see the work that we have done on the doorway? Another day or two and we should be able to go inside."

"Well, that sounds great, Ahmed!" But Paul had more enthusiasm in his voice than he felt in his heart. 'Seems like we've waited forever to really go in there and see what we've discovered. I'll be there as soon as I drive Miss Foster back to the oasis."

* * *

As he followed Ahmed toward the dig, he mused, *Why was it Paul Coltren who had to discover the tomb of Moses? My life was so nicely arranged. Knew just what I believed and why. Conflict all behind—a skeleton of my past. Hurts all buried. Faith settled into well-organized explanations. Why does it have to hurt all over again? Like—* He pushed his hands far down into his pockets and hunched his shoulders. *Like an old wound being opened. I knew the Bible wasn't true! Then why am I shocked all over again?*

He walked on through the burning caramel-colored sand to the top step, now cleared completely and leading to the tomb below. He should have taken that job in New York. There was something easy and secure in an ankle-deep carpet and a window overlooking Times Square. Should have kept his life orderly and categorized, uncomplicated. The way it was, he was becoming more deeply involved, more entangled every day, like a youngster playing with a flyback ball and paddle—never being quite certain from which direction the ball would rebound, nor which way to strike it when it did.

"Mr. Coltren?"

Paul brought his fists out of his pockets slowly and let them fall limply into hands again. "Ahmed. Sorry. Let's go see the door."

The Arab put out his hand. "Arnold was around again last night."

Paul came sharply to attention. "He *came back?* After all— But tell me about it, Ahmed."

The other man rubbed his smooth chin proudly, pretending to be in deep thought. "It was sometime after midnight. I was standing guard when he came around the corner and I swung my rifle stock and nearly caught him in the face. He yelped and took out over the dunes like the jackal he is." Ahmed's brown teeth bared in a smug grin. "I don't think he will return."

Paul thought of the statuette and placed a question mark after Ahmed's declaration. "Which direction did he take?"

"He was running toward the oasis, Mr. Coltren."

Paul's slow release of breath was soft, like the easy sigh of surf skimming over the sand at an ocean beach. But his emotions were as a crashing high tide, and all he could see was the girl with whom he had journeyed to Cairo, the girl who had accidentally slid under his arm in the *felucca,* the girl who had accompanied him to the monastery and for whom he had been keenly concerned during the night. In his imagination he saw her, and he saw Arnold, too, at the oasis, and he knew within himself that if Arnold ever dared to touch her, he would kill him!

15

The tomb's facade looked good. The blocks had been carefully restored and the scaffolding would keep them intact. The door itself was free from debris, but it would not yet swing open. The pivot was offset from the cave-in and would have to be reworked. But, all in all, progress had been made, and certainly before long Paul would be able to enter the tomb and discover for himself whether the grave had been robbed or whether the mummy—or mummies—was still present. And he would know if the hieroglyphics proved out and if it really *was* the tomb of Moses.

After yesterday's sandstorm, the heat seemed, somehow, more oppressive than ever. Perspiration poured from the workers' bodies. Paul wore both neckerchief and headband to absorb sweat. Canteens went dry quickly as the men were driven again and again to the water supply. Particles of dust and sand clung to their faces and arms. But the work still went forward.

So did Paul's thoughts. Dogging him, giving him no rest.

First, there was Carolyn. It had been one thing to be concerned over the work at the tomb and the possibility of Arnold creeping in unawares and making off with valuable artifacts. But it was quite another thing for him to hang around the oasis, if indeed he was. Any guy who would steal another man's work would think little of making advances toward a lovely girl.

Carolyn. Blonde, laughing Carolyn. Spiritual, serious Carolyn. Carolyn riding a camel and riding with him on the Nile. Paul stared into the distance of memory, holding his breath, remembering. What was wrong with him anyhow? This guy Arnold had messed up his thinking all day. Why couldn't he be a man and show himself in the open? Why did he have to steal around during the night and— *"And men loved darkness rather than light, because their deeds were evil."*

If a bomb had exploded at Paul's feet, dismembering his body, the effect would have been no greater than that a long-forgotten memory verse should burst before him.

"Mr. Coltren?" Ahmed's shining black eyes were filled with deep concern. "Do you worry about something?"

Paul moistened his lips before replying. Then, with careful deliberation he drew on a pair of working gloves. "I was just thinking about Miss Foster and her father, Ahmed," he lied. "I think I'd better go to their camp tonight and warn them again about Arnold. I just wish," he said through gritted teeth, "that he'd come around when I'm here."

The Arab nodded. "He is afraid to do that."

Paul's eyes were angry. "I know it. But how does he know when I'm here?"

"I do not know, Mr. Coltren. We do not even know how he travels, except that we did hear the engine of a jeep or some other vehicle one night."

Paul stroked a block with a delicate brush. Under the encrusted sand was another cartouche. Ahmed became busy somewhere else now, and Paul's thoughts galloped on, tripping over one another in their race.

His brain had been caught up in a whirlpool of questions. Always questions.

What about Israel? If Moses didn't lead the children of Israel out of Egypt, who did? That was the easy way, to take the train of thought that Moses had been brought back here after leading them out. Except that Paul doubted it terribly. And that would still prove a part of the Bible untrue.

But what did it matter? Was it for Carolyn? Or for Christians in general? Or—could it possibly be—for himself?

Carolyn. If anything ever happened to her—

And what about Josef? One week— By then perhaps Paul himself would have entered the tomb and would know the truth already.

The man paused, laid aside the brush he had been toying with, and wiped the perspiration from his forehead. Unstrapping his canteen, he took a small drink. Nearly out of water again.

Got to stop thinking! It was hardly conceivable that finding such a tomb had seemed so great.

"Mr. Coltren? The men have quit work, and you have had a lot of sun."

Paul looked up. "Sure, Ahmed. I hadn't realized—"

"Are you sick, Mr. Coltren?" Ahmed queried anxiously.

Paul stood to his feet. His eyes strayed toward the distant oasis. Slowly he removed his helmet and took off the sweatband. "I think I am," he said simply.

His bath was skimpy, for he was nearly out of water. He looked at the bottle of men's cologne somewhat skeptically before using it, found a suit of clean khakis, and replaced his boots with dress shoes. His helmet was left behind.

By the time he headed for the Fosters' camp, the moon hung in the inky sky and stars had begun to pop out by the millions. A breeze had swept in and the desert night was growing more comfortable.

The jeep bounced its way over the newly molded dunes, stopping at last when it reached the oasis. Paul stepped outside, sniffed, smiled, and went on. Carolyn had brewed coffee. Perhaps she had anticipated his coming.

Professor Foster met him. "Paul! We had a hunch you were going to drop over."

"The storm must have hit you hard, Jim, from the way things look."

The older man smiled. "If it hadn't been for the canvas fences around my cultivated plots, they would have been totally ruined. As it is, I pretty well know already what's going to grow in this sand."

They walked to the camp table and sat down. "I understand you and Carolyn received quite an education at the monastery."

"We did!" Paul looked toward Carolyn, clad in jeans and boots. His gaze was tender. "It's quite a life there evidently. I wouldn't like it!" Paul said grimly. "I learned that much."

Carolyn poured coffee and the three of them sat down to talk. Paul hesitated briefly before bringing Mr. Arnold into the conversation again.

"Mind you," he told them earnestly, broad brown hands wrapped around the coffee cup, "I have met this man, and I know him to be ruthless. Ironically, he's a coward, yet capable of murder. That's a little hard to explain, I realize. Jabari warned me about him in Cairo. Now Ahmed saw him heading toward the oasis. You know all the implications in that."

Jim frowned, causing dark pink lines to appear on his smooth forehead. "Yes, I do see the danger." He looked at his daughter, allowing his troubled gaze to linger upon her. "One of my guides carries a firearm, Paul. The others are reliable, honest. I can ask them to watch for this man."

Carolyn remained silent. If she was the least bit perturbed, she certainly showed no signs of it.

"I'll check in often too," Paul promised. "Just be on guard and keep Carolyn close to you, Jim."

The professor looked away through the palm trees, then toward the trickle of water, and finally toward the temple, as though even at this moment the mystical Mr. Arnold might be watching them.

Paul glanced at his watch and went to get his water container. "Want to walk with me to the spring, Carolyn?"

She came around the table quickly, her steps light. "I'd love to, Paul."

Jim slapped his knees gently and got to his feet. "And *I,*" he said, "shall see my guides and tell them to be on guard as they have never been on guard before."

Paul and Carolyn made their way to the spring. Moonlight filtered through the palm trees and paved their way with light. Carolyn's smile was contagious. Paul knelt to fill his container, and when he straightened, he found himself looking into her eyes.

Slowly he set the water on the ground. His lips moved and he smiled. They moved slowly toward the ruins of the temple.

Paul's heart was pounding. How lovely she was, how very lovely. Her face was filled with many emotions, and there were stars in her eyes. He looked down at her. Slowly his arms went out to her. Just as slowly she came into them. Once she was there, Paul gathered her close. His lips found hers and she pulled away, sobbing.

"Carolyn, darling, I love you!"

"Paul—"

"I'm sorry, Carolyn, I tried not to. I love you!"

"Paul, no!" She was crying brokenly. "Please let me go! Please, Paul, I can't! I can't love you!" And she clung to him, sobbing.

"I love you."

"I love you!"

He kissed her again, tenderly, lingeringly. They separated, looking at each other.

The moon was an enchanting torch hung in the sky to splash the desert with light. It was a night made for them, the two of them alone. Their fingers touched and linked, and they sat down on the top step of the ruins.

"I'm sorry, Carolyn," Paul whispered. "It seemed so right."

She drew her hand away slowly. "Oh, Paul, I did mean it. I love you. But—I don't dare love you. Our worlds are far apart, so very far apart."

He sighed, and the burden of life was suddenly too heavy. "I know. I know. I wish it were not so." He let his hands drop loosely between his knees. "It wasn't always so, Carolyn."

"Tell me, Paul. You've evaded so long. Please tell me what happened in your life to make you so bitter about—about the Lord Jesus Christ."

He stared away over the palm trees to the velvet backdrop of heaven. It was a long time before he spoke. He glanced at her and then away again.

"I was seventeen. My father had died and my mother was dying of cancer." He paused and was grateful that Carolyn didn't rush in with trite little phrases that he'd already heard a hundred times. "My father was a deaf-mute. He was out in the field one day with the tractor, and somehow the tractor slipped into gear after he had gone in front of it to examine a tree stump. His back was turned to the tractor, so he never knew it was coming to run over him. My mother—" he said softly. "She was the one who suffered as she died."

Paul lifted his head and its sheer masculinity was silhouetted against the sky. He squinted at the heavens for a moment, remembering the times he'd felt his mother's suffering and had run away from the house and into the barn, where he'd hide and try to stem the tide of rushing, paralyzing fear, hiding from her cries of agony.

"I will never forget my mother or her pain. When she died, neighbors came and helped take over.

"I didn't even know a preacher to preach her funeral. But Billy Williams knew one. He stayed with me, helped me through the ordeal. Billy was called Bill by everyone in town by then, and there in his little church I heard a strange man speak of my mother, and I found that I liked the man. But it wasn't what the preacher said about my mother that stirred me so; it was what he said about

Jesus Christ." His voice dropped to a hushed whisper, haunted, uneasy at mention of the name dropping from his own lips.

"Oh, Paul!" It was the first time she had spoken, and the words came with infinite tenderness and understanding. She sat on the steps with her arms wrapped about her knees and the chill breeze moving her hair about her face. "Please tell me the rest."

"The night after Mom's funeral," he said, his profile rigid and hard in the half-light. "I met the—the— I met Christ." He spoke now with great difficulty, forcing every word through stiff, resisting lips. "I—I thought I had a real experience with God. He—Christ—was so real to me that I couldn't describe it to anyone. He was so near, it seemed. My life changed rapidly, and my sole ambition was to become a minister of the gospel."

"Oh, Paul!" It was the second time she had spoken the words, but this time her lips trembled and the words came on the breath of a sob.

He turned and looked at her. Gently he picked up one of her hands and held it between both of his. "You see, Carolyn, I didn't know that my church was just one of a very few that had not gone—what they call *modern.* I didn't know that the denomination was dead and that its core only believed parts of the Bible and discarded what was not convenient."

Carolyn's fingers tightened around his, but she did not speak.

"After a few months of this so-called new life, my pastor died of a heart attack. I was eighteen and just out of high school. A new minister was assigned to the church. When I told him of my aspirations, he encouraged me to go to seminary, and suggested that I attend a church-related college in preparation for seminary. He was just out of seminary himself and ours was his first church. It sounded like the answer to a—prayer. He even helped me get a full scholarship."

There was a long, painful silence. Carolyn broke it at last. "And you did go, didn't you, Paul?"

"I did go," he replied slowly. "The teaching was not—what I had expected. Somehow God didn't seem to be real to the young people at college. The miracles in the Bible were done away with so easily, so—logically. Including Moses, with his pillar of fire, his cloud, his Red Sea experience. The whole thing. Little by little, something began to happen to me. My ideas began to change. *I* changed. Little by little—these things never happen overnight—I stopped praying. When I read the Bible, there was no expectation, for it was no longer true. My faith crumbled, and after only two years I changed my major to archeology and went off the Christian pathway. Christ's presence and reality vanished. I found myself terribly alone, and I started out to find a new life—without God."

Silver rivulets streaked Carolyn's face. "Oh, Paul, how tragic! No wonder your attitude has been so strange where spiritual matters are concerned. But, you don't have to settle for this. You can come back! Darling, you *can* come back!"

"It seems like a long way," he murmured soberly. "Too long. Too much has happened. I've changed too much. I don't even think the same anymore."

Paul sat with bowed head. His fingers clenched Carolyn's fiercely, as though fearful of letting her go. She was his only link to God, the only one he'd found in such a very long time. He was afraid to let her go.

"Paul? Do you believe that Jesus was divine? That His blood alone can cleanse the heart from sin?"

Paul shook his head wordlessly. "I don't know anymore. I'm not sure. I thought before that I'd found something real—found the answer to all of life. My heart was so full. And when the crash came, it was so brutal. The hurt—brokenness. I wouldn't ever want to do that to anyone, Carolyn!"

They glanced at one another and away, for both of them were thinking of the tomb and of Paul's desire to give to the world the gift of the tomb of Moses. Suddenly it was all different.

"But you do remember how it was when you walked with God?"

"I can't forget, that's the whole problem." Paul rose suddenly to his feet, walked to the top step and turned his back. Girls were not meant to see men cry.

The memories that pressed in tonight! But how could anyone like Carolyn ever understand what it was for faith to die? To die inside. To very slowly lose the thrill, the eagerness. To be so hurt, so bruised, that there were no words, no tears. To utter not one word in prayer!

He turned at last. The tears had been conquered successfully. " 'If the light that is in you be darkness, how great is that darkness.' " He spoke the words in a tone of awful finality.

"Paul, it doesn't have to stay that way. If you'll call out to Him, He'll hear you. If you'll just call!" He came to her and she grasped his hands. "Don't you realize that the Holy Spirit is at work in your heart right now? He's trying to win you back again, Paul."

Paul stood very tall, shoulders square, jaw hard, resisting. He laughed a hollow laugh. "We'd better get back, Carolyn. Your father will think I've made off with you for certain this time!"

"All right, Paul. I guess we had."

He paused, searching her eyes. "You'll be very careful? Don't even go to the spring alone? If that man Arnold should ever touch you—"

"I promise to be careful, Paul. But you mustn't worry."

Paul lowered his head as if to kiss her, but she drew back; so he took her hand and walked with her back to camp.

Reluctantly he said good night to the professor and started away in the jeep. His teeth were clenched. He didn't want to think. It had been the first time that he had bared his heart, the first time he'd ever spoken of his broken faith.

Faith— His had been weak apparently, but it had also been beautiful. And he had tasted. Tasted of Jesus Christ, God's Son, and of His reality. Funny— Paul had truly thought that he'd forgotten. But could one who had walked with God forget so easily? Or did the Christ of glory always dog the steps of that one, always plead—somehow—through someone—to win him back? Would it always be so? Could he never escape?

Slowly he became aware of the presence of Someone with him. In a way, it was familiar. In a way it was not. The presence of Christ which Paul had once known had been joyful, sweet, infinitely precious. This was a sweet presence with him now, true, but it was also sad. Poignantly sweet and sad. It came unbidden and it lingered all the way back to camp, and afterward. Paul's heart grew heavy with the burden of it, but he found that he no longer steeled himself against it.

16

Sometime after four o'clock in the morning Paul awakened out of sleep. He had the distinct impression that someone was in his tent. But when he opened his eyes and lay unmoving in the darkness, he sensed the same sad, almost lonely presence of Christ that had come home with him in the jeep. It was not frightening, not ghostly; rather it was a definite presence of one who lingered near his cot.

Paul lay quietly, not moving, not understanding. He remembered when he was nine years old and his mother had taken him to spend a week with his grandmother. He recalled the terrible homesickness that had come to him, the loneliness and yearning to see his parents. He knew they were not far away, but he could not see them, or touch them, and the homesickness had been awful. Sad and poignant. This was like that homesickness. The one he had known so intimately, loved so well, was standing near him. But Paul could neither see nor touch Him, and the feeling in his innermost being was so like the feeling he had had when he had stayed that week with his grandmother.

Paul lay awake for some time. A single tear escaped and ran swiftly down his hard jaw and onto his pillow, vanishing as quickly as it had come. What other presence could cause a man to weep?

The nearness of *Him!* This one altogether lovely, whom Paul could not admit was truly divine. Or could he? Who but God's own Son could come into a man's tent if He were not divine? But if He were, then it had to be the blood that cleansed from sin and brought peace to the human heart! If Christ were divine, then the Bible had to be true!

Then what about the tomb Paul had found? What about the pictures that so clearly declared the man Moses to be buried there?

The Presence lingered but a moment longer, and then, very slowly, lifted. But it left the atmosphere changed. *Charged!*

One day a Stranger—a wondrous Stranger! came walking down by blue Galilee.

Paul got out of bed, but he did not light his lantern. He walked to the door of his tent and stood gazing out into the star-filled night. That Stranger had come into his tent tonight. *That,* he could never deny. And, even though His presence had made Paul feel sad, Paul regretted that He had gone.

He looked at the stars, stepped outside and stood with the breeze hailing his heart. What was there in life apart from Jesus Christ? W*hat was there?* Emptiness! Aloneness. When a man had walked with God, what could he ever find that would satisfy?

It was some time before Paul went back to bed; but when he did, it seemed no time at all until his alarm was buzzing and dawn had come to deck the sky with color.

Men were moving about outside, and the sound of fluent Arabic floated not unpleasantly into Paul's tent. The fragrance of strong coffee, mingled with some other, more alien food odor, came to his nostrils.

Almost woodenly Paul came out from under the mosquito netting and pulled on his clothes. Again, more fervently, he wished for Eddie. Not so much because Ed was a stabilizing force—though he was that—but because he would be company, perhaps allowing Paul a time of forgetfulness. Of escape.

He left the shade of his tent and accepted a cup of thick, sweet Arabic coffee from the hand of the smiling Kamal. Paul felt himself relax from the whole situation. It was like disengaging his mind and letting it slip into neutral. He would attempt to keep this attitude all day. Just coast along and not think about the spiritual aspect of life from any angle.

Of course, there was Carolyn. Paul uncurled the metal from around the can of ham and eggs and slipped off the lid. *Carolyn.* The kiss. He would remember the kiss. Yet, he had had no right. They both knew it. He loved her too much to hurt her. Certainly, as an agnostic—or whatever he was—he would not want to bring pain into her life.

He sighed deeply and Ahmed saw his turbulence.

"Mr. Coltren? This may be our biggest day yet!"

Paul gave a toss of his sandy head and reached for his sun helmet. "Maybe so, Ahmed! I sure hope this is the day!"

Did he? Josef had seemed certain that this could be the tomb of Moses. Paul himself could see no room for doubt. Did he want to enter the recesses of the tomb and face what truly lay there? What could he tell Carolyn? What would the world say? And—the Christian world? What would be the reply of his own heart? To come face to face with the fact that the Bible could not be entirely trusted? That it was true, after all, that a part of it was untrue? If one could not trust a part of God's Word, how could one trust any part of it. Did he really want *that?*

He squared his jaw. His nose seemed to jut out a little more than usual. His eyes were fierce. Doggedly he went toward the dig. As in a trance, he heard the men begin their singsong chant, heard the spade, the pick, and the brush against the blocks. His mind had slipped into gear again and was racing along at top speed.

Like those days in college, he reflected silently. *The fight! The conflict— Out of the fight one minute; back in it the next, and never knowing quite how I got there.*

But why the fight now? The minister who had led him to Christ had always preached that the devil never bothered much with those who were not doing anything for God. Paul wasn't doing anything for God! But, was it just conceivable that the enemy was fighting to keep him from the old kind of fellowship with Jesus Christ?

"Ahmed!" Paul moved from his position deliberately. "Isn't that another cartouche? No—there by the door, about four or five blocks up?" Where was the enthusiastic tone of his voice? Had all eagerness, all thrill for this particular work fled away? Yes. Yes, Paul felt that it had. What was another cartouche anyway? They'd found several. Who cared? Who really cared anyway? Ahmed, perhaps. It would be rewarding to him and, in some measure, to the crew. Personally, Paul would like to have chucked the whole business and gone off to find himself another tomb—innocent and unimportant. A commoner's grave would suit him fine!

The American had a compelling desire this morning to tell Ahmed what he knew. Paul had a feeling, though, that the Arab knew anyhow that he was holding something back. Ahmed might be a clown whose grin was more like a leer, and he might wear baggy trousers that ballooned around his spindly legs; but Ahmed was not stupid by any means.

"There may be a whole family buried inside this tomb," Ahmed stated suddenly.

The truth of the statement swept Paul with an electric shock. To find not only Moses but his wife and sons and daughters!

"Don't you like that idea?" the Arab asked. Then, slowly, "Mr. Coltren, why are you troubled over this tomb?"

Paul clamped his teeth decisively before answering. Then, with a swiftness that startled him, he replied, "Let me ask you, Ahmed, what you think of a supposedly ancient leader by the name of Moses?"

Ahmed's eyes snapped like kindling catching hold in the old wood-burning stove on the farm in Idaho. "Moses! What could he have to do— What are you trying to say, Mr. Coltren?"

Paul slipped his canteen from its canvas pouch and took a long draught of water. "Not one thing, Ahmed. But there are a couple of things that don't add up. We'll know a lot more after we get inside this place."

The voice of Kamal sounded, beckoning to Paul, and the archeologist took the opportunity to snap the conversation with Ahmed in two. He made his way through the crew. The men were leaning on spade handles, relaxed in their long tattered garments that smelled so offensively of sweat and uncleanness. Oily strands of black hair straggled out of their turbans, giving them the appearance of slapstick comedians instead of specialists in their own field.

"All right, Mister Coltren," Kamal said huskily with an accent. "It's safe now." And he motioned with a brawny arm toward the massive door of the tomb.

Paul sucked in his breath. Done. Finished. What finality in that single word. Christ had said that word from the cross. Finished. Now he must go inside. Now he could no longer evade the inevitable. Now he must come to grips with reality.

His whole body pulsated with eagerness and fear. He reached out to examine the face of the tomb. Solid! His gaze probed and silently surveyed the door. *Safe.* He could tie a handkerchief over his nose and mouth to protect himself from the powder-fine dust and admit himself to this tomb. It gave him the sensation of playing "Time Tunnel," for certainly he was about to take a journey back through the countless ages of Egyptian history. All right. He touched his shirt pocket with its note pad and pencil, was acutely conscious of the camera bouncing against his chest, and stood back while the men put their shoulders to the door. There was the grinding of sand, the protest of centuries, as the great door turned on its pivot. The air inside the dome-shaped chapel was not as stale as it had been that first time, but the siltlike dust rose in billows.

Paul's heartbeat was the wild, senseless pounding of the baby cottontail he'd caught one day as a boy. The rabbit's fear of the unknown. He waited longer than necessary, under the pretext that the dust was yet too dangerous, fingered his shirt pocket to make sure he had his booklet, *From the World of Hierogylphics to the World of ABC's.* And, when he could wait no longer, he stepped carefully through the door and stood again within the chapel with his foreman.

Dismay that was more despair caught at him, even while there was a certain joy over having found the tomb. He stood in one spot, in the middle of the floor, while his eyes searched for him. He saw the six-foot golden statue before what appeared to be the door leading to the burial chamber. He examined the walls with the brilliant picture writing. A pharaoh. A woman bathing in the river, taking a baby from a basket concealed in the rushes. A boy standing in the palace under men of learning.

Paul turned his head, eyes closed against the evidence before him. When he looked again, a young man stood before his gaze, a man who had learned the skills of the magicians, the healing arts, a man of learning and great wisdom. Further on, however, this man turned and killed another man, an Egyptian. And on still to the scene depicting scenes of the future life. An estate, feasting on the Nile, hunting, enjoying a life of plenty.

Sick in a way he had never experienced, Paul turned from the paintings to the various niches in the walls. Two of the niches still displayed their treasures, but most of them were empty.

"There has been a grave robber here before us, after all," Ahmed announced soberly.

"So I see." Paul moved for the first time, stepping forward to one of the niches. A heavy layer of dust lay on the little platform that should have held a statuette or some other treasure. But all that was left was a lesser measure of gray-brown dust where the base of the statuette itself would have been. "Yeah, someone made it before us, after all. But, from the look of accumulated dust where the base of the statuette had been, it was a long time ago." Paul sighed heavily. "I suppose we ought to have expected that."

Ahmed made a sound like a grunt of assent and moved to examine the outline of the door behind the statue. "A fake," he said. "You can run into dead-end passages and even cul-de-sacs in these tombs. Yet, in spite of the efforts made to protect the burial chambers, they were still discovered.

Paul suddenly gasped, followed by a short cough. He pushed back his helmet and stared into one of the niches. In his dark eyes was the look of slow-dawning comprehension. "Well! I think I'm beginning to see something!"

Ahmed cocked his turbaned head. "What is it, Mr. Coltren?"

"I think I understand why Mr. Arnold has shown such interest in this tomb. *He's been here!*" With that, Paul's thoughts went racing headlong, paused, and crashed into fragments.

17

Paul strode back and forth in the confines of his tent. His body tingled with realization. His brain was filled with thoughts, questions, and ideas that all tumbled and fell together, with no clear answer for any of them.

The statuette Paul had bought from Mahmoud had a peculiar base, shaped almost like a painter's palette. The sculptor's mark on the left side of the head was a tiny mark resembling a roman *v* with a straight line crossing the right side of the emblem. *The same base and marking that were on the statuettes inside the tomb!* Not only that, but the piece Paul had purchased in Cairo had been dated around 1500 B.C., when the ruling pharaoh was thought to have been Thotmes I. Now it was established that the date of the tomb was the same. It was growing very evident that this statuette had been taken from this very tomb! That fixed the date even more accurately. If Bible history were true, this placed the period as being from Moses to the exodus. If the Bible were wrong, it was evident that this was in reality the tomb of Moses and that his life had been a complete hoax.

The statuette had exactly matched the niche in the wall of the tomb's chapel. The base perfectly matched the other statuette bases and the height was exact. Paul knew that another visit to Cairo was in order. He must return to the curio shop to ask some questions that had to be answered.

What had Arnold been doing there before Paul? How long ago had it been? The tag on the statuette had been yellowed with age. Where did that fact fit into the picture?

"No wonder Arnold wants this tomb so badly!" Paul pressed his temples with burning fingertips, grimaced his mental confusion. "When was he here—and *how?*"

He sighed and the sound was vast in the emptiness of the night about him. His delight over finding the tomb had changed to bewilderment and now to an almost holy fear.

Paul spread the pictures on the table again, then stood towering above them, face taut and severe, hands driven into his pockets, mouth twisted to one side.

There it was. Thotmes I. Then there was his daughter, Queen Hatshepsut, taking a baby from the rushes. Moses. Another man, unidentified, but a man of fairly high standing. Moses again, dressed in Egypt's finery, standing in pharaoh's court. Moses and another man. A man lying face down, evidently either dead or seriously wounded.

Paul went to the door and stared away through the darkness. *How can I face Carolyn and Jim? What shall I tell them? What can I say?*

His restless feet took him around the table. It wasn't *his* fault! It only served to substantiate the liberal teaching that God's Word was filled with myths, unfounded fables, and a myriad of contradictions. And all that did not fit into these categories could be taken care of by simple explanations which Paul did not desire to recall.

He took a deep, shuddering breath. One or two of the men must be sleepless too, for he smelled the smoke from Egyptian cigarettes. Moving again to the door, he watched the slow blue curls of smoke in the afterglow of the campfire. Unseen fingers strummed the strings of some musical instrument, sending oddly sweet strains of melody into the night. It was caressingly, strangely beautiful. An Egyptian love song.

Under this magic spell, Paul left the tent and walked toward the dunes. He saw Ahmed start toward him and hastened his steps. He didn't want to talk to Ahmed now. Nor to anyone. Not this moment, when his emotions were churning and his thoughts burning and the Hound of heaven was seeking to track him down.

Paul walked for an hour, high cheekbones taut and hard, chin jutted almost angrily. He shivered with cold, hunched his shoulders, and walked on. He told himself that never again could he come close to God. He felt nothing. In a way he wanted to. But then again, he didn't. Maybe if the significance of the tomb had remained in obscurity— But it was too late for that. If God's Spirit had been stirring his heart last night, that was one thing.

But tonight there was not much doubt left. And tomorrow—yes, by tomorrow he and Ahmed would have found the secret door. On the other side, wrapped up like a bale of yard goods, inside a magnificent sarcophagus, would be lying the Old Testament saint and patriarch, Moses!

Paul's lips turned down in a sneer. "Sure! Great old man of God! A lie, like the burning bush and the Red Sea crossing and all the rest of it!" His voice was bitter in the silence, tainted with sarcasm. "And then the world will know."

Just like that. So simple. The news could never be held back. And, some would lose faith in the Word of God.

Suddenly Paul hesitated, frowned and turned slowly back to camp. "If Arnold was in that tomb once, then—then he must know that Moses is there too. How odd I hadn't thought of that. He knows, but he's never told." Paul walked slowly, measuring every step. "But of course he knows, and that's why he'll kill if need be to get back what he lost. No wonder he's such a desperate man. He already knows what's there!" He hastened his steps now. "Well, here's one guy who doesn't intend for him to get the tomb or its contents in his control! And I think one Paul Coltren is going to make another hurried trip to Cairo just as soon as possible."

Paul saw the tiny light of a cigarette down at the dig and went down to speak to Ahmed. "Everything all right?"

The Arab nodded. "So far. You'd better get some sleep, Mr. Coltren."

Paul twisted his mouth and took a look around. "I'll do that, Ahmed. Look, wake me up about four o'clock and I'll take over. You'll need a little sleep yourself."

Ahmed nodded his turbaned head. As Paul walked away he heard Ahmed break open his Lee-Enfield rifle. Either he was double checking to see that there was a shell in the chamber, or else he was racking one in. Anyway, the Arab was ready for action.

The bittersweet presence of Christ that had touched Paul from time to time that night suddenly vanished altogether. Gone as it had come, silently, intangibly, secretly. Would it return? Paul winced at the thought. What if it never came back? Pain pierced his heart. It was better to know the poignancy of His presence than to endure life without it at all.

How strange life was, with its clever surprises and subtle memories. Paul had believed; he had suffered and withdrawn. He'd thought himself to be cured of religion. And yet now, with concrete evidence staring him in the eye, Paul knew that he had known again that blessed presence, and he remembered, remembered, remembered—and the pain pierced like an arrow striking its target.

He brought his fist down solidly upon the table. "Why does it hurt so much?" he cried to the silence. "If my faith is dead and it's really over between us, God, then why does it have to hurt so much?" And, flinging himself back onto the campstool, he folded his arms upon the table, rested his face against them, and shook visibly.

How long he trembled under the convicting power of the Holy Spirit, Paul would never know. But when finally he rose, doused the light and flung himself upon his cot, he was weary and spent. Sleep came almost immediately, but it did not last. An hour later he wakened and lay staring into the darkness.

For long moments he lay, straining for sleep that would not return. Outside the tent was a soft rustle of sound against the canvas of his tent. A moment later an unearthly yell pierced the night and the rustling stopped. A jackal had cried for its mate, and the mate had left the camp to rush into the shadows to meet with its own kind.

An Arab snored outside in the darkness near the other tent. The sound was vaguely disturbing.

Paul turned, felt in back of him to make sure the netting was in place, guarding against insects and scorpions. He punched his pillow, pushed his head against it with clenched teeth and a determined jaw. Sleep would not come.

At last he threw back the netting, shook his boots upside down before putting them on, and stepped outside in his pajamas. Soft shadows fell over the sand. A gentle breeze stirred.

Paul walked on outside. He gazed at the star-studded sky for a time, then pursed his lips and strolled at an unhurried pace toward the dig.

In the moonlight, it was impressive indeed. What would it look like when the scaffolding was taken away and the exterior was restored as at the beginning? Not like the temple at Luxor, of course, nor even some of the other greats. Probably it would not even possess the grandeur of the unknown remains of work at the oasis. No. It would be credited among Egypt's greats because of the mummy which lay within the burial ch—

Paul's thoughts came unstrung quickly, never to return. His body tensed. His forehead furrowed and his keen dark eyes strained through the half light. *What?* The shadow of a man below at the entrance of the tomb! A man had been *inside* the tomb!

Ahmed? He sucked in his breath. *What would Ahmed be doing in the tomb?*

He was poised above the dig, tense, watching. The shadowy figure wore no turban. *George Arnold? Ahmed! Where was Ahmed?*

Paul cupped his hands about his mouth. *"Ahmed!* Ahmed, get that man!"

With the cry, the figure below paused abruptly. At the same instant, as one in a trance, Ahmed came up out of his doze on the ground in a half crouch. The rifle barrel swung through the air, hesitated, and the sound of a shot split the peace of the night in two.

The shadowy figure spun, fell. Ahmed was trying desperately to spring into full wakefulness and grasp the situation at hand. The figure rose to his full height, holding his wound. Ducking into the shadows, he disappeared around the tomb, reappeared briefly, and was gone from sight.

Paul dashed down the broad steps and around to Ahmed. But the Arab was bobbing his rifle up and down in his excitement and Paul left him to his own confusion and made for the man who had caused him so much distress.

He paused, ears straining for sound, and eyes sifting all the shadows of night for a human outline. There was nothing.

Ahmed was at his side now, fully alert, thumb on the safety. "I'm sorry. I've never—"

"Forget it!" Paul snapped. "You hit him, I know it. But where did he make off to?"

18

Ahmed flashed his light around the darker areas of the tomb. "I don't know, Mr. Coltren. I never saw a man make off so fast!"

Paul whirled in an agony of impatience. His teeth were bared and his countenance was twisted in rage. "Well, look for him, will you? I'll get another light."

The loose-jointed Arab began loping around the dig, stabbing the darkness with light at random. Seeing a splotch of blood on the ground, he swooped down to investigate.

"He was hit, all right," he said wonderingly, and brought his fingers away from the ground smeared with red. They grated together with sand and the dark-faced man felt a chill go through him. His intense gaze searched the shadows, but he was convinced that Arnold was no longer in the dig.

He could not have walked all the way from Dahshur. Then he must have some kind of a vehicle parked over one of the dunes. He stood awkwardly as Paul returned.

"There's a spot of blood here, Mr. Coltren. It shouldn't be hard to follow a blood trail and find out where Arnold has been coming from when he visits the dig."

Paul snapped his light into position, examined the freshly spilled blood and looked away into the distance.

The American's strides were long and filled with purpose. "Come on," he flashed back to Ahmed. "Let's get this thing over. If he's here, we're going to find him."

Methodically, foot by foot, the men followed the trail of blood. For several yards it was a steady trail, but then it dropped away to a spot here and another one farther on.

"Here," Paul said, pointing with his powerful light, "it looks as if he may have stopped. Maybe he made a tourniquet or a makeshift compress to try and stop the bleeding."

With the dawning of another day and pale gray light sifting

through the heavens, the trail was more and more difficult to find. And finally it seemed to end completely.

Ahmed examined the inside of his jaw with his tongue. "The breeze is erasing the footprints, Mr. Coltren. And Arnold must have succeeded in getting the bleeding to stop, so—"

The Arab paused suddenly and bent to look at something.

Paul ran lightly to his side. An Arab from their campsite emerged from the tent, caught sight of the two men, and let loose with a rapid flow of Arabic.

Ahmed straightened long enough to reply, whereupon several men started toward them. Most of them were cinching their trousers as they ran.

"Tell them not to come too close," Paul cautioned. "It looks like we've picked up Arnold's trail again, and we don't want any more footprints around here."

Ahmed relayed the message, and the men gathered behind the two men and stood gazing at the earth in great curiosity. They sounded like so many magpies, so intermingled was the chatter among themselves.

Paul touched the sand and then stood to his feet. "Blood, all right. And it looks like he was having a lot of trouble." He walked a few feet. "Here, Ahmed. Our man fell again. The sand has really been disturbed, as if he'd had a struggle getting back on his feet."

The men moved forward slowly. The footprints grew more and more uneven. About here Arnold had been having much difficulty. He must be just ahead of them. Probably just over the next sand dune they would find his unconscious form. Or—dead.

"The wind, Mr. Coltren!" Ahmed cried softly. "We must find him soon or the wind will take away all prints."

Paul gave a low whistle. "Our search ends right here." Kneeling once more, he stroked his fingertips over the sand. "See these impressions, Ahmed? He had his jeep parked here, because the footprints end and the jeep treads begin. The wind rubbed away the treads that brought Arnold here and started clean new ones when he left." He looked back toward camp. "I'd say a good three-quarters of a mile from the dig, walked in—somehow made it back after being wounded."

The Arab nodded his grizzly head. "We can still follow him."

"Where do you think he went?" Paul questioned.

The other man laughed shortly. "To a doctor!"

Paul gazed toward the oasis, glad that Arnold had not been there, anyway. "To a doctor *where,* Ahmed?"

Ahmed shrugged. "Well, a doctor has been brought to the little village of Suma between here and Dahshur. They've had an outbreak of cerebral malaria. Maybe he'd try to see that doctor." A second later, however, the turbaned head shook negatively. "No, because policemen will have the village blocked off, and at this point I don't think Mr. Arnold will want to talk with policemen."

"Where, then?"

"Maybe El Giza. It's easier to lose oneself in a bigger place."

"Right." Paul pulled his brows in close. "Tell you what, since you know your people and country better than I, you take the jeep and see if you can find this guy. I don't think he'll be able to bother us for a while, but I'd like to know where he is. I'll keep busy at the dig until you return."

Ahmed nodded slowly. His piercing eyes searched through the empty desert around their camp. "I'll try to find him, Mr. Coltren." His jaw clamped decisively. "I certainly will try."

A few minutes later Paul stood listening to the grinding gears of his jeep. He winced once at the clanging, whining sound and hoped fervently that Ahmed would not ruin or wreck the vehicle before he got back. And then the lumbering jeep rolled out of sight and Paul turned back to his tent.

There was a gnawing feeling in the pit of his stomach over the loss of sleep, and a cup of hot, too-strong coffee didn't help any. He forced down a heated tin of scrambled eggs and bacon, toasted a piece of real bread, and, after dressing, started back for the excavation site.

Standing on the first step, he studied what had once been a rather magnificent structure. "I only wish the New York office could see this one," he muttered to himself. "Or the department in Cairo." His nostrils flared. "Or Eddie!"

Well, Eddie would be here on the scene in just a few days now. He was bound to be up and around, and in a short time he and Paul would complete this job together. Only one thing wrong with wishing Eddie was here. He was an atheist—or so he said. He'd do everything in his power to drive all the facts home in order to prove to the world that this was Moses' tomb. *Not that it would matter!* Paul snorted to himself. It was but a matter of time until a news release would carry to the world the message that *the Bible was not entirely true!*

On that note, Paul's thoughts became suspended, detached, incapable of further notice. The door turned smoothly on its timeless pivot, and Paul went inside.

The air was much better now, though the fine dust was still disturbed easily, rising in small puffs that took his breath. He paused, pulled his neckerchief up over his nose and mouth, and began to poke about. Tapping. Thumping the walls. Examining the hieroglyphics for a crevice, a crack, no matter how minute. He found nothing. Again he went to the gold statue, stood before it with a sense of awe. But the door behind it was clearly fake.

With the use of the magnifying glass, Paul could see that the crevice had been cut into the stone only about an inch and was meant to deceive. He scanned the entire outline of the door and was on his knees beside the statue when he detected a crack. A crack within the lines of the supposed door. He brought the glass closer, following the small line carefully.

"Sure!" He sat back on his heels, chagrin and surprise stamped upon his brown face. "Of course! What a clever way to hide a door. Just put it inside another door, and make it just large enough for a man to crawl through!"

Still marveling at the ingenuity of the ancient Egyptians, Paul examined the small door more closely. Then, reaching for a small tool, he inserted its blade into the crevice. He could move it! Move it all the way around. And, as the blade moved, the crack widened slightly. Evidently it had been filled in expertly with mortar until nothing was left for the human eye to detect.

Paul sat back again, breathless with excitement. He wished he could call in some of the crew members to finish the task—to see if this door, too, turned on a pivot, or if it was simply a stone wedged into position.

However, the crew members were skilled only in their particular outdoor task of digging, hauling away sand, sifting for relics and other such menial tasks. Only a few of the men would be capable in this matter, and Paul felt reluctant to let them know about the door or to peer into the burial chamber.

Turning his gaze inward to his heart, Paul had to admit that he wanted to clear the opening even without Ahmed. He had to get inside the chamber without curious eyes gazing at him from the doorway.

He worked slowly, brushing away mortar with an old toothbrush, picking out bits of it with a small dental tool. At last the definite outline appeared which he measured to be two and a half feet square. He pondered silently. It was impossible to move the block of stone forward, for there was no room for leverage.

Finally, sitting back and getting a firm position, he planted the soles of his boots against the stone and pushed solidly. His muscles strained, and the stone slowly began to give under the steady pressure. He pushed again, and the block fell back. Paul scrambled quickly toward the great door to see if the sound had been detected. It hadn't. The steady chorus of picks and shovels, along with the steady stream of Arabic, absorbed every other sound.

A new rush of stale air met Paul. His face was stern, almost stoic, and impatience rose up and streamed like fire through his veins. He felt like he was walking on rotten eggs in iron shoes. One wrong move could prove deadly. For two or more centuries this tomb had been hidden from the world, with the one exception of discovery and entry by Arnold. Even so, it seemed clear that the man had never been inside the burial chamber.

Paul hesitated, fought within himself. The need to see what was on the other side of this opening was insatiable. Yet, all his training spoke to him in the negative. He had been taught to go in with someone else. To take no chance, no matter how slight. To be sure of his every move!

The archeologist felt sweat streaming from his body, leaving even his trousers sucking damply at his legs. All of his intense nature drew him toward the opening and he got to his hands and knees and peered inside. He *had* to know. He had to know before Ahmed and all the others. He had to be sure.

Three mummies, wrapped in untold yards of cloth, lay just inside the opening. Someone *had* been inside! That struck Paul with perplexity, for it was clear that Arnold had not found this doorway. It was too undisturbed. There must be another entrance into the burial chamber that Paul had not detected; then Arnold, once inside the chamber, probably had found this door and decided to get the mummies out the shortest way possible.

"Well planned," Paul mused softly to himself. "Somehow George got inside this tomb—evidently a long time ago—robbed it himself and made a heap of extra money on the side, and was about to drag these mummies to a curio shop somewhere. *Then* he probably planned to bring in the officials to see what he had discovered. Very clever indeed! Only, somewhere along the line something happened that rocked his plans and caused him to close down all operations.

"I can't imagine anything big enough for that."

Paul pressed past training into the back of his mind and eased his long body through the opening. No sense fighting it; he had to know. Eyes burning from the fine dust, he stood to his full height and began looking about, careful not to touch anything.

In a case like this, one could touch an object, heretofore perishable, and up till now perfectly preserved, and it would fall into a heap of dust. Only objects made of gold and other metals were truly preserved.

On a low table had been set fowl, fish, bread, and water for a breathtaking journey through the skies. Not far away were various statuettes and other valuables. Apparently Arnold had taken just enough to make it seem that the tomb had already been raided, yet leaving it a vitally important tomb for any museum.

Covering the walls were large figures with small black writings and symbols above them. One of the paintings was Osiris, ancient god of the dead, wrapped in mummy cloths. Lying at his feet were two brass pieces, the crook and the scourge, his emblems.

With a breath so deep that Paul was left heady and numbed, he turned to the great stone coffin—the sarcophagus. He sought frantically to still the wild beating in his chest, the river of perspiration, the repeated flexing of his muscles. The sickness in the pit of his stomach.

It came as a surprise that there was no top on the coffin. It was made of quartzite and had been chipped in several places. Other than that, however, it was intact. The mummy itself rested beneath its golden coffin image, a rather weirdly painted face and body which fit over the mummy.

Several hieroglyphics were still evident on the chipped stone.

Paul dropped to his knees and pulled the worn booklet from his pocket. Meticulously he searched it out. He knew it would be a name. There—he had it worked out. No doubt about it; the name was *Moses.*

A tight, pale line wrapped around Paul's mouth. His clothing, soaked with sweat, clung to his body. A great wave of some indefinite emotion built up within until he seemed on the verge of collapse. The paintings before him portrayed Moses meeting the god of the dead. Moses! The deceiver. The fraud. Moses, a figurehead in devising a hoax that had deceived the world. At least the Christian world. The other emblems and symbols meant nothing to Paul.

Maybe you're wrong.

Paul whirled, but he had known there would be no one there. No, it was his own imagination now, rising up against him, trying to replace a figment of faith for stark unbelief.

He placed both hands upon the coffin and forced himself to look inside, into the painted gold face. "Would to God that I had been wrong!" he declared to the silence. It was too much. Everything. He could neither comprehend nor absorb.

The archeologist shook himself. What *was* the matter with him? And suddenly he knew that he was not alone. The same Christ who had been present with the Father at creation was there. The same Jesus who had walked the lonely shores of Galilee and gone into the black desert night to pray was there with him. Looking, always looking, for men who would forsake all to follow Him.

Maybe you're wrong.

The words came as a great inner impression upon the soul. It was like the same inner direction Paul had known—or thought he'd known—years ago.

His jaw tightened to the straining point and his brown eyes closed. "God, I want to be wrong! You know I do!" His head dropped to his chest. "It's that—so many things have been explained away. The burning bush. The pillar of fire—the miracles."

The sandy head lifted and he looked straight ahead. Would God deceive also, as Moses had? Would God allow a portion of His Word to be untrue? Would—? He shook his head. He had walked with Jesus Christ, known the cleansing of His blood. This was basic. Far better to stick with basics at this point. A lot of things in life had been forgotten, but the memory of his walk with Christ remained.

Paul's face strained toward the ceiling, up, up. "My God!" he cried at last in agony of soul. "My God, I don't believe that You would deceive me. But, if You could—even if You could—there is no life without You. It's been—so empty without You, God."

And the presence that had lingered so near came nearer yet, and the years with their bitterness and memories were washed away. It seemed to Paul in that moment that the Saviour held him suspended in His mighty arms and cleansed him, purified him, loved him.

"Mr. Coltren?"

It was a voice of bewilderment, and Paul turned very slowly from that rapturous moment to the opening leading into the burial chamber.

Reluctantly Paul turned and went to face Ahmed. "Did you find anything?" he asked, waving an arm. "I certainly have."

The Arab's bronze face was a mixture of anxiety and fear. "Carolyn Foster. Mr. Coltren, she is gone."

19

Paul's face turned ashen. Incredulity struck its most vicious blow. The emotion of a moment ago was suddenly mixed with other emotions: fear, consternation, love, the need to protect—God's instinct in man.

Paul came out through the opening and stood trembling under the impact of the Arab's words. "What are you talking about?"

"Miss Foster has disappeared," Ahmed said, speaking more forcibly now. "She's gone!"

Paul came close to Ahmed. His fear was being charged with anger. "What do you mean—*gone?*" he whispered harshly. "Make sense, man." All the time he knew it was bad. So bad that Ahmed was oblivious to the new discovery, so bad that Paul's whole being was zeroing in on Ahmed's words.

Ahmed gestured wildly. "I went to Dahshur, but the sickness had hit the outskirts of the city and policemen were everywhere, roping off and guarding that part of the city."

"I want to know about Carolyn," Paul said through clenched teeth.

"She is with Mr. Arnold," the Arab said softly, trying to soften the blow.

Paul's jaw sagged. His dark eyes mirrored the naked terror of his heart. His hands clenched into hard, determined fists. "How do you know that?"

"The police at Dahshur saw them together. They were in the jeep, trying to find a doctor. The police wouldn't let them pass but told them to find another doctor—one who wasn't busy with what threatened to be an epidemic of cerebral malaria."

Paul heard his voice rising. "But how do you know it was Arnold and Carolyn?"

"The description was too perfect," the Arab returned tightly. "I went to the Foster camp after that to see for myself and talked to the workmen. The guide and Mr. Foster went to Cairo on business early this morning in the guide's jeep. Mr. Foster sent his daughter over here in his jeep until they returned." Ahmed hesitated briefly. "It was very early, Mr. Coltren."

"Then you mean," Paul responded slowly, "that Arnold made his escape not in *his* jeep but in Jim Foster's? And forced Carolyn to drive him to a doctor for help?"

"That is what it looks like, Mr. Coltren."

They were walking slowly toward Paul's tent, but Paul's mind was snapping at ideas like fire snaps at dry kindling. "Did you get any kind of a lead from Dahshur? From the policemen?"

"None," the other man replied. "But I know they could not have gone to the village beyond Dahshur, for that's the place where this sickness began."

"Arnold would have to be careful," Paul pondered aloud. "He wouldn't want to tell a doctor how he got such a wound." He looked at Ahmed. "Maybe he'd go to Cairo. A bigger city, more doctors. He seems to know his way about there anyway." He rose and swung around the table, paused and looked toward the dig. "Makes it all fall into the realm of the ridiculous right now."

"We should begin searching for her right away," Ahmed suggested.

"Where?" Paul snapped. "In Cairo? We'd never stand a chance! But maybe we would!" he interrupted himself hurriedly. "Maybe we would. Abdel Jabari might have seen Jim." He straightened and his keen eyes traced an invisible road to Cairo. "Yes, if there's a man in Egypt who can tell me how to find Carolyn, this man can."

"That sounds fine, whoever the man is. Now what about the dig? Kamal—"

Paul darted around the table, laid his hand down hard, palm first. "You stay here with the dig, Ahmed. This is something I have to take care of by myself."

It seemed to Paul in the minutes that followed that the discovery of the body of Moses was the more unimportant find of his career. The discovery he had made in finding Carolyn Foster was much more important. And beyond that, even beyond that, was the discovery that Jesus Christ still loved him and cared for him after all the years of bitter denial.

It didn't occur to Paul one time to blame God for what had happened to the girl he loved. The grace that sustained him now seemed as natural as breathing, and Paul knew as he had never known that his encounter with God this morning was a once-and-forever thing. Even if it truly was the patriarch Moses who lay in that great sarcophagus, it could make no difference.

"Carolyn! Carolyn!" She had been a light that had penetrated into his darkness—uncompromising, lovely. Then she had been his beloved. Only for a moment of time, it was true. But her eyes had spoken of her love for him, even though her lips had not. And he had held her, kissed her, whispered of his own love.

Now her name brought pain and sadness and fear. What if Arnold *had* harmed her? What if he wasn't as badly wounded as it had first appeared? After all, the blood had stopped just before the appearance of the jeep tracks. Where would this madman take her? What would he do with her after finding a doctor to care for his wound? It hardly seemed conceivable that he would simply turn her loose again.

He picked up his sun helmet and strode purposefully toward the jeep. Going back near the spot where he and Ahmed had tracked Arnold this morning, Paul explored every inch of sand. But all tread marks had been meticulously erased by the wandering desert breezes. It was impossible to track the Foster jeep to its destination. The trackless sand lay in caramel ripples, hiding its secrets as it had always hidden them, leaving man with his mortality baffled and wondering.

With new humility, Paul asked God to direct him in his search for Carolyn.

He stopped at the oasis to see whether Jim had returned. He hadn't. The two Arab workmen lounging beneath the palm trees made gestures that they were alone.

Paul stood irresolutely. Such a short time ago he had stood with Carolyn on the palace steps yonder, held her close to him, whispered to her of his love, felt the glory of her lips against his.

Carolyn, beloved!

"The girl," Paul said. "Miss Foster. Do you know anything of her whereabouts?" He stood over them, silently entreating them to reply, but he knew in his heart that they could not understand him.

He tried again. "Jim? Mr. Foster. When—when will he be back?" He pointed toward the sun, hoping to get across his meaning.

One of the Arabs began to show some comprehension. He laid his hands, pressed together, beneath his head. The professor would be late getting back. Well, that was something.

Paul nodded and turned away. That settled it. He was going to Cairo. Sure, it was true that they might not be there. Maybe George Arnold had taken her to some lonely outpost to see if she couldn't patch the wound herself. There was no assurance that he had forced her to go to Cairo at all. Nevertheless, Paul was going there. There was a good possibility that Jim had seen Mr. Jabari, and that, at least, was a start.

20

A low fire burned before Paul's camp. Near its flame hunched a man of thirty-one. His eyes were dark with emotion. A kind of dread intermingled with profound peace. His hands hung loosely together. His face was lifted and his forehead shone like polished bronze against the firelight. He carried a full day's growth of beard, and he looked like a great, brown animal tensed to spring. Yet, there was peace.

The frenzied pace of the day was over. Paul had feared to go to the police just yet. First he had wanted to make contact with Abdel Jabari. Then he wanted to see the professor and discover whether Carolyn was with him.

The distance to Cairo had been covered with hair-raising rapidity. Paul had spent but scant moments in The Egyptian. Abdel Jabari, who could doubtless either have given him an answer of sorts or at least have found an answer through someone else, was out of the city on business. Paul knew no one else in Cairo except a few gentlemen at the Department of Egyptian Antiquities, and certainly he could confide in no one there.

In fact, being a stranger to the country, he dared trust no one for fear he would place Carolyn in even greater danger than she might already be in. His only hope lay within the scope of possibility that she was with her father. Arnold would have been taken to a doctor, or to a hospital *somewhere*. Then Carolyn would have found her father and—

His thoughts went jangling downward into a black chasm. Arnold was not in a hospital, at least not in Cairo, for he had checked every last one. And he had checked with doctor after doctor. Most of them did not speak English, but he had written out the name neatly on a scratch pad and the doctors had shaken their heads firmly. No Mr. Arnold had been there. Paul had demonstrated that Arnold had been shot, that he'd been wounded by a bullet.

Nothing. Finally he had parked his jeep at the curb in a dirty little sector of the city. And he had walked down dingy, littered, smelly alleys. Down sandy streets where a camel loitered beside a well, and where children played their childish games, as they did the world over. A few times Paul had paused to talk with the children, to try and describe both Arnold and Carolyn. But the children spoke no English and they looked at him wide-eyed, as though suspicious that the man was demented.

After that Paul had paid a visit to The Prophet, the same shop where he had bought the after-shave lotion for Ahmed. But the proprietor insisted staunchly that, though he had had dealings with Arnold in the past, he knew absolutely nothing of the man's whereabouts at this time.

And at last Paul had had to turn back. Jim, strangely, had not returned and Paul sat tensely waiting for the swinging lights of the jeep coming over the dunes.

When the cry of a jackal sounded through the night, Paul's heart told him foolishly that it was Carolyn crying out for help. For a moment the world went spinning about his head.

"Carolyn?" He looked up into the blue-black canopy of heaven and gazed back into the winking eyes of the stars. There were no tears now. The tears had been for God. There were no angels singing in the chapel of his soul. They had been from God. Neither was there any conflict between him and the Saviour. He felt solid about that.

"Where is she, God?" he whispered. "What has happened to her? Do You—*care* that I love her?"

Anguish crushed him. There was a breaking inside. To lose Carolyn—

He shook his head against the overwhelming pain. She'd shown him the path back to God, made him see that it was not all over. Rather, that it could be a sweet, fresh beginning.

Paul opened dry lips and spoke through a tight throat. "And this same Jesus . . . still has the power!" He couldn't do it. He tried but he couldn't continue the words. Not now. Not when everything was pain and suffering and love. Why must pain and suffering be all wrapped up in love and in loving? Painful to love Carolyn, yet precious too. Love for Christ had brought him suffering and pain as a young man, yet he had never been able to forget the wonder, the thrill and the joy of it. Running, yet always remembering. Always thirsting for Him who alone could satisfy.

In the hours when darkness lay like a shroud over the world, and the moon had hidden its brilliance in that place between night and day, Paul saw the distant lights of a jeep swaying uncertainly over the sand.

Ahmed, who had stayed with Paul all night, in the background, never speaking, never being obvious, now slipped inside the tent and went to bed.

Paul trembled, and beads of perspiration broke out over his forehead. Only one set of lights. Not two. A new surge of energy swept through him and he swung into his jeep and started toward the oasis. His hands shook against the steering wheel and his eyes strained through the darkness.

"She'll be there," he told himself firmly. "It'll be all right." But he spoke with an assurance he did not feel. An insipid misery gripped his whole being. Fool that he was, sitting there all night in the desert when she—when *Carolyn*—could be— *No!* He set his jaw firmly. He dared not panic now.

His mind went on in a hazy kind of disconnected thoughts. If she were not there, then they would have to get the police. Paul himself would abandon all to search for her. He would not rest until she was in his arms again.

He trembled at the memory of holding her. One time. Just one time. There on the steps of the ancient palace, under the stars, he had held her. He had thought he could never let her go. But he had. He'd had to because it was all a part of God's great plan for his life. How his arms ached to hold her again, fold her so close that he could breathe in the fragrance of her hair and listen to the harmony of heart beating with heart.

Paul stopped his vehicle just short of the Foster's tent and got quickly out. Jim had not yet gone inside. He looked exhausted.

"Hello, Paul. Where's Carolyn?"

Paul stopped, staring through the semidarkness at the man. He felt the strength leave his body, felt his legs grow numb with both weakness and the fullness of shock. Now that he was here and Carolyn was not with her father, what did he say? How could he tell the professor?

"Carolyn—" Paul broke off immediately, sat down on a campstool with a dizzying sensation spreading through his body. "Well, let's start at the beginning, sir."

Jim set the coffeepot on the camp stove. Then he turned wearily and sat down opposite from Paul. "Isn't Carolyn with you, Paul? She didn't go off exploring on her own, did she?" He ran on before the younger man could reply. "We'd have been home last night, but my guide's jeep had two flats. Can you beat that? And then, right in the middle of the—" He broke off and a grim line slowly encircled his mouth. "What's happened to my daughter, Paul?" he asked quietly.

"Jim, I don't know for certain." Paul felt new strength rising from within. It was as though he had tapped the source of some great energizing force that would hold both him and Carolyn's father firm and steady until the blonde-haired girl was found. "This character, Arnold, had the audacity to turn up again. Ahmed shot him last night by the tomb, and when he was trying to get away, he must have met Carolyn while she was on her way to our camp. We've figured out that he forced her to go with him. He was wounded—badly, we think. Probably she took him to some doctor in an obscure place for treatment. But where she is, I don't know."

Jim listened as one in a trance. Clearly, he did not comprehend Paul's story. But at last he bowed his head in his hands and slowly the truth became real to him. Finally he looked up slowly. "How long ago was this?"

Paul looked at the sky. The darkness had slowly given way to dawn. "It was almost exactly twenty-four hours ago."

"No trace of her since that time?"

"None, Jim. I've been to Cairo, asked questions, wandered down alleys, inquired of doctors and hospitals, talked to every Bedouin I've seen. I even visited a curio shop and the Egyptian Restaurant, but the only man who could offer a clue was a guard outside Dahshur, who saw Carolyn in the jeep with a man. But where he has forced her to go from there, no one seems to know."

Paul paced to the stove and brought back the coffeepot. His stomach was beginning to do flips from going without food. "I had hoped," continued the archeologist, "to find Carolyn with you in Cairo. I'm sure I overestimated Arnold showing that kind of compassion."

Jim looked thin and tired. His white hair was lying askew over his head. The inner strength, however, did not diminish. "All right," he replied calmly, "are we to call the police?"

Paul fingered his cup and welcomed the big slice of fresh cheese Jim handed him. "We may have to. But first, I wonder if we shouldn't try to contact Jabari again. They told me he should be back in Cairo today. He seems to have uncanny ways of gathering information and appears to know a great deal of the unusual happenings in his country. He may know something."

Jim looked down at his veined hands, relaxed together on the table. "Paul, I'd like to pray for my daughter. I—I wish you would join me."

"I will join you!" Paul returned eagerly. "You know, Jim, since this morning—it's really quite a story—I have the privilege of prayer again, and of knowing that He hears me."

Jim's gray eyes became warm and full of meaning, but he said nothing. Long afterward the men sat together making their plans and finally strengthening themselves with food and a fresh pot of coffee.

Paul felt a real concern for Jim Foster. He was not a young man, and he didn't have the physical stamina for this type of thing. Two days and a night without sleep, emotional strain and stress, mental agony. It all added up.

As for himself, Paul had an undergirding, a fathomless peace never before experienced. He didn't know when the peace came, but it was there, lastingly real and vital. The hope that had been a phantom was growing every minute.

The hope, however, dimmed with the passing of the day. The heat bore down on them all the way to Cairo and the sand was blowing, beating the flesh with its pellets and causing the eyes to grow red and irritated.

By the time they reached Cairo, weariness was gnawing at their bodies and a kind of hopelessness was poised, ready to swoop down with all its despair and futility to embed itself in their hearts.

Paul set his jaw and resisted it. From the side view he caught of Jim's face, he was doing the same. The two men had but one thought, one aim, one desire. Carolyn was gone. They had to find her!

The Egyptian was partially filled with customers when the two men entered the restaurant. They were met just inside the heavy door by a hostess.

Jim ignored her invitation to be seated. "Abdel Jabari," he said rapidly.

The girl's smile faded into bewilderment that two Americans would ask for Mr. Jabari. Nevertheless, she vanished down a dim passageway that evidently led to Abdel's private office. Music, weird and mystic, rose and fell in the background.

Paul paced. He might have gone down the corridor after the Arab girl, except that Mr. Jabari himself emerged from some unnoticed doorway and was suddenly and mysteriously standing at Jim's side. His hand was extended and he was smiling around an ill-smelling cigarette.

"Jim! My friend! And Paul, we meet again. What a pleasant surprise!" Abdel had removed his cigarette and was smiling from ear to ear. "You will have lunch with me? I'll give you the best st—" He broke off abruptly. "Where is the lovely Miss Foster today?" His eyes, enormous under the thick lenses, suddenly became even larger. "You surely have not left her behind?"

Paul's heart dropped. Then Mr. Jabari knew nothing of Carolyn! One more hope dashed.

Abdel saw their countenances change and his own face began to mirror concern. "Where *is* Carolyn, Jim?"

Jim stood erect and square-shouldered. Thin blue veins could be seen in his temples, throbbing and pulsating. But his eyes were calm and his hands steady. "We don't know. You remember a certain Mr. George Arnold? We have reason to believe he has forced her to take him to a doctor or a hospital somewhere. We have no idea where."

Mr. Jabari's thick lips parted in surprise. "Why? Has he been wounded?"

"At the dig," Paul said, speaking for the first time. "He's been coming around regularly, and last night—" He hesitated, pondered. "I guess it was night before last, time has gone so fast. Carolyn was on her way to my camp and Arnold obviously stopped her and made her take him away in the jeep."

Mr. Jabari's dark eyes picked the Americans apart. Then, with his peculiar suddenness, he said, "Come into my private office where we can talk." With the liquid grace of a jungle cat, the massive hulk glided down a thickly carpeted corridor.

In a plush office with a large window overlooking a private garden with towering date palms, lush grass and myriads of flowers, a crystal waterfall in miniature flowed lazily along through a flower-strewn path and finally lost its way under a little footbridge. It appeared to be an office for musings and for leisurely work and for dreams.

Mr. Jabari seated himself at a huge mahogany desk and swiveled around to face his friends. His great soft hands were linked tightly together, the only evidence of his inner disturbance.

"George Arnold," he said quietly in perfect English, "is a very unscrupulous man. He lost his reputation as an archeologist twenty years ago while working here in Egypt for the British Museum. He picked up pieces ahead of time and sold them here and there for sizable pocket money. He was not only fired by the museum but thrown out of our country. But he's had difficulties in other countries since then and keeps continually on the move. From time to time he's changed his name, but never succeeds in concealing his identity for long because he can't seem to change his *modus operandi*. Finally, using his own name, he came back here—up to his usual tricks by watching the digs and picking up trinkets."

The Egyptian was speaking very rapidly, his gaze steadily absorbing the carpet at his feet. "And now he has Carolyn. He may perhaps be a subdued man since he's wounded, Jim." He looked up now, sucked in his lower lip. "However, there are ways of finding things out without going to the police, which could be dangerous at the moment."

"Do you have any ideas?" Paul probed, his own gaze stony and unflinching.

Jabari thumped his heavy fist on his knee, shoved his body upward, and strode about the room. "I have some men," he evaded. "They can find out where the girl is." He looked around with an air of temporary superiority. "Quicker than the police can, and without drawing attention to what they are doing. Where will you be?"

Paul jerked a thumb. "At The Prophet over on the Street of Fatima. I want to pay Mr. Mahmoud Saleh another visit!"

21

The two men parked the jeep near the city's business center and walked to the lonelier sector of Cairo to a narrow, filthy street where dark-faced people with turbans and veils passed up and down in a steady flow of humanity. Eyes, dark and suspicious, scanned the two Americans, then looked hurriedly away. It was as though they had entered a world that was inhabited almost totally by spirits of darkness and gloom. Wares, already covered by dust and dirty from the touch of many hands, spilled onto the narrow street, and boys passing by on rickety bicycles threw out their hands to clutch at colorful head scarves blowing gently in the breeze.

"Exactly where are we going, Paul?" Jim asked at last.

"To a curio shop." He lifted an eyebrow at his friend. "One whose business affairs are not always unquestionable. The owner of the shop is an acquaintance of Mr. George Arnold. And, Jim, if he knows anything, he'd better tell it."

Jim's face was bathed in peace. He walked easily with arms swinging and hands relaxed, his body never having known the tenseness caused by a personality like Paul's that demanded almost more than a man could give.

"You love Carolyn very much, Paul?"

Paul's face did soften then and his bony profile grew gentle and reminiscent. "Love her? Yes, I do, Jim—very, very much."

Jim looked down at the narrow, cracked sidewalk as they walked. "Does she know?"

"She knows," Paul replied with a half smile. "I told her when I really had no right to invade her life with such knowledge, except —that I know she loves me too." His dark eyes were tender with feeling. "We both love her, Jim; that's why we have to find her."

" 'Be careful for nothing; but in every thing by prayer and supplication with thanksgiving let your requests be made known unto God.' "

"Yes," Paul reflected, and the glow of a great light broke forth in his soul as the Word was made real to him again. " 'And the peace of God, which passeth all understanding, shall keep your hearts and minds through Christ Jesus.' "

Jim looked at him curiously. "You know that passage of Scripture, Paul! I mean, you really know it."

"I knew it as a young man. And it, as well as the whole Bible, was snatched away from me. I was too weak in Christ to stand, and I fell hard. You see, Jim, it was the reality of your faith and Carolyn's that played such a part in my coming back to God." Paul hesitated in front of a dirty glass window filled with everything from aspirins and men's cologne to an alabaster hand, either the genuine article or a clever imitation. "This is the end of our walk, Jim." And he opened the door with its little brass bell for the older man.

The turbaned head of the little proprietor turned slowly from his position behind the dust-laden shelves. A look of consternation crossed his small dark face, masked quickly by charm and acknowledgment. "Mister Coltren!" he smiled. "So nice to see you again! Something I can show you?"

"Something you can tell me, Mahmoud. Same question as before. Have you seen George Arnold?"

The other man spread his arms and his white sleeves hung full and loose. "I tell you before. Arnold does not concern me. Many years ago he come to me with pieces—like the one you bought—but now I do not know of him."

"Somehow I don't buy that," Paul replied evenly.

"He is in some trouble?" Mahmoud asked. "He is wanted by the police?"

Paul changed his tactics. He perched his elbows on a counter and dropped his voice to a confidential tone. "I need to find him desperately. If I can make contact with him very soon, there may be no trouble at all. As his friend, Mahmoud, if you know of his whereabouts, you must tell me."

Now the Egyptian, too, became cautious in his speech and spoke to the American in a stage whisper. He was so intense that his fingers were locked securely together near Paul's elbows, and when he spoke he looked straight into the other man's eyes.

"Mister Arnold is a thief!" He spat out the last word with distaste. "He robs from other men, even from his own dig! He bring things to me—and to others." He added the word *others* quickly lest Paul be left with the idea that only Mahmoud had had dealings with Arnold. "That statuette was the last thing he bring to me." He spread his hands again. "All is over. No more. I swear by Allah. Where Arnold is now, I do not know. I swear."

Paul took a deep breath and turned away just in time to see an Arab enter the little shop. For one moment their eyes locked, and in that moment Paul knew that Jabari had sent the man.

Mahmoud departed to attend to business affairs, but the stranger made gestures that he wanted to browse for a moment. The fluent language broke off and Mahmoud went to the back shelf and began straightening the wild clutter.

Paul motioned to Jim, who followed him to look at imitation artifacts that lined a shelf nearer the front. Almost immediately the Arab came softly up from behind. Paul linked his fingers loosely behind his back and felt the small piece of paper that was pressed into them. The Arab smiled, sidestepped and was gone.

Paul's chest constricted and he held his breath. Slowly and with deliberation he brought the piece of paper around so he could unfold it. His fingers trembled as he read the scrawled words.

"Carolyn Foster left a small village southeast of Cairo one hour ago. She is alone and driving slowly. Apparently she is unharmed. You should be able to overtake her without difficulty."

Paul's breath exploded from his throat. "Jim, take a look at this!" And he thrust the paper, dirty now and double-creased in places from being crammed into the Arab's pocket, into the professor's hands.

As the younger man dashed for the jeep, Jim scanned the words in hesitation. Then a grin broke over his face and he ran and slid into the vehicle beside his friend.

"Thank God!" he cried joyfully. "Oh, thank God!"

"My first answer to prayer, I think!" Paul exclaimed. He wound the jeep through the filthy streets and eventually out of the city. "And she *is* all right!" His throat felt big inside, almost swollen with emotion, and he said no more.

He passed a camel caravan, broke into the open, away from houses and playing children, and pressed the accelerator down to the floorboard. His heart was singing a glad song. He wasn't certain what it was, but it was full of joy and it thrilled and enraptured his soul. Carolyn was all right and on her way back to camp. And she was alone.

The western horizon was beckoning to the sun and, in unresisting submission, the brilliant disc of light was drawing ever nearer to the desert sands. A half hour later it sank quietly, giving way to the lesser light of night, a light, however, which was frail again, a mere sliver of gold that decked the eastern sky. Purple curtains began to enclose the landscape, and soon a dozen stars were visible. After that they popped out so easily and so spontaneously that, before the eye could respond to and comprehend the twinkling light of one star, a half dozen more had been lured into the black dome of heaven. *And Carolyn was safe!*

Both Paul and Jim knew the way well now and did not stay to the roads. At Dahshur, however, when they were certain of overtaking Carolyn, they were at a loss. Paul stopped the jeep.

"Does Carolyn know the way to camp well enough to leave the main road?" he asked. "We don't want to miss her. Unless of course, she's already reached camp ahead of us."

Jim leaned forward. "We'll have to leave the road in a few minutes to reach camp. Maybe—" He broke off, his gray eyes searching the darkened area. "Paul, isn't that a jeep down the road a way?"

Paul flicked on his brighter headlights. Leaning forward over the steering wheel, he peered into the distance. Very slowly he started his own vehicle. His heart gave a leap. "It sure is! And it's a wagon, which means it belongs to you!"

Other thoughts hung hazy and motionless as Paul pulled his vehicle alongside the jeep station wagon. He plunged from the car and raced to Carolyn's side. There was a look of quiet radiance on her face, though her eyes were shadowed with dark rings. When Paul opened the car door, she slipped into his arms as though it was the most natural thing she had ever done.

Strong arms held her tightly and a hand pressed her head to his hard shoulder. "Darling! Oh, Carolyn, darling. Thank God you're safe!"

Carolyn felt herself drawing from his strength, and the light of a great joy was in her eyes. Somehow, in a way she did not know or understand, this was good and right. Then she released her grasp of Paul and went into the arms of her father, who had been standing silently all this time, watching misty-eyed as another man swept into his daughter's life where until now he had been the only man.

It was at that moment Paul glimpsed a man lying on the back seat of the station wagon.

22

Paul sucked in his breath, hard. Every muscle and nerve was alerted for action. His blood ran hot while his body grew clammy with cold perspiration. "Carolyn!" he whispered hoarsely.

Carolyn twisted slightly to look back at him.

"The man in the jeep!" he continued. "Who is he, Carolyn?"

Without any ado, Jim stepped between Carolyn and the jeep. With automatic movements, he flooded his light full in the man's face. Despite his appearance of gentleness, Jim was not a cowardly man, and he was in full command of the situation.

Carolyn stood tall and triumphant. "Look a little closer, Paul. Don't you know who it is?" There was a certain authority in her tone that Paul had not noticed before. "He was almost dead when I found him."

Paul stared at her in amazement. Did she know what she was saying? Hadn't all his warnings meant anything to her?

"Mr. Coltren!" The voice calling to him from the rear seat was weak from strain and injury. "Paul. Paul, forgive me for causing you so much worry."

Paul stared. Stark bewilderment fell over his face. As one flipping the pages of a book in rapid succession, so his mind began turning over the events of the past days. Mahmoud? Arnold? No, it wasn't Arnold! Then? The Egyptian! The strange, knowing Abdel Jabari. The visit to the monastery— The picture suddenly came into clear focus at last. But how—?

"Josef Zarefiris! What are you doing *here?* With Carolyn? I don't understand at all."

"The monastery," the other man tried to explain. "I—escaped. God was with me. Had to—find you!" He tried to sit up. "Someone shot me."

Paul was dazed by the entire situation. "You! You, Josef?

But it was Arnold. We were sure it was Arnold! And we—we thought he had you, Carolyn, and had taken you off somewhere."

"Oh, Paul!" Then, quickly sensing that her father was standing alone and baffled, she turned to him. "Dad! I'm sorry I worried you. I found Josef there on the desert and bleeding badly, and you had just left so I was sure of catching up with you and letting you take him to a doctor for help. But I didn't find you! I gave up after a time and realized that I couldn't take him back to Paul, because he would never have lived the way he was losing blood. But it's a long story and Josef must not be discovered."

"And you're all right, Carolyn? We thought, when we saw the wagon here—"

She squeezed her father's hand. "I'm fine, Dad, just a little tired. I stopped because I wasn't sure where to turn off for our camp. I'm glad you came!"

Jim dropped her hand and nodded to Paul. "I'll drive your friend to your camp. Why don't you let Carolyn ride with you?"

Thanks, Paul said silently. *Thanks for understanding.*

Paul started away over the softly rolling dunes, acutely aware that Carolyn was at his side. His arms throbbed to hold her and a great fire was kindled inside of him that he deliberately placed under subjection. He loved her. He loved her! Did she know and understand? Would she respond? His own heart gave him the answer.

"So it wasn't Arnold after all. We thought it was Arnold all the time, and it was only the monk of Machseh. What absolute irony." Paul spoke casually as though having a conversation with himself.

"Then Josef was shot because you thought he was Mr. Arnold?"

"That's right. And now I wonder if Arnold really had anything to do with this, after all." There were many things that Paul longed to say to Carolyn, but he restrained himself. She was tired now and needed to rest. He would wait until the time was right and then open his whole heart to her.

"Where was Josef hit?"

"In his thigh. The wound was actually superficial, but he lost a lot of blood." Carolyn studied Paul's profile in the dim light, and a thrill of electricity shot through her. Their love could not be. Could it? With difficulty she returned to the subject. "What Josef needs now, Paul, is rest until his strength returns."

"I'm sorry about this whole thing," the man mused. "Sorry you had to go through it too."

She reached out involuntarily to touch his hand, and he caught it and held it in his grasp.

"It wasn't such a trial, Paul," she said quietly. "It never is when we can touch another life, help someone."

His heart gave a leap of gladness and the song started up again. It had nothing to do with Carolyn, yet paradoxically it had everything to do with her.

One day a Stranger! And all that God was or had ever been to Paul Coltren came tumbling over him and through him in sweetest reality. Christ was real! *He was real.*

"Carolyn?"

Her hand lay in his still, tenderly clinging, exchanging communications silently, hand in hand and heart to heart.

"Paul." She looked at him expectantly.

"I've come again to Someone I thought I had lost years ago. I met Him in the burial chamber at the dig—standing beside what all evidence declares to be the tomb of Moses."

She half turned in her seat and there was a quick embrace. "Oh, darling, I knew it was coming, but how wonderful that it has already happened!"

They stopped at Paul's camp, and the archeologist slid out from under the wheel, glad when Ahmed stepped briskly to him. The Arab saw Carolyn get into the other vehicle and he turned his broad grin full on Paul.

"I'm glad she's safe, Mr. Coltren!"

"So am I. But listen to me carefully now. The man we shot was not Arnold." The Arab's gaze widened and his mouth dropped. Paul put out a hand of caution. "I don't *know* where Arnold fits into this thing. Ahmed, the man you shot is in Foster's jeep there, and no one—do you understand?—no one—is to know he's in camp."

"Why not, Mr. Coltren?"

"Because he is the monk I visited recently, and now he has escaped and come to us. If he were discovered by the monastery, he'd really lose his life. Besides," Paul added as an afterthought, "he may have information for us concerning the tomb. He's the best Egyptologist around here."

A gleam of understanding entered Ahmed's liquid eyes. "Yes. Yes, I see. Then Arnold was not here after all?" He squared his scrawny shoulders. "How badly was this man hurt?"

"Badly enough," Paul replied abruptly. "Give us a hand, Ahmed."

The Arab checked to be sure all the crew was asleep, and then they moved Josef onto the spare bed in Paul's tent. Even now the monk was handsome with his hard, angular face and black beard. And the civilian shirt and trousers gave him a dash he'd lacked before. Paul wondered absently where he got them.

"All right, Mr. Coltren? Is there anything I can do before I leave?"

"Thanks, Ahmed, this is fine. But don't tell one person."

"I swear by Allah," promised the other man.

Ahmed was wearing a wrapperlike *galabieh,* long and flowing, and was as a wraith passing from the tent. Paul secured the tent flap behind the Arab.

"Would you like some water?" Paul queried. "Food?" He was beginning to feel the marks of nervous energy and stifled it immediately, forcing himself to move slowly and in a more relaxed way.

"I would," Josef confessed. "But you must be exhausted and—"

"No more than you and the Fosters. Only Arnold has escaped weariness. He's the one we thought had been wounded, you know." He searched through the box beneath his cot. "Beef and noodles? Ham and eggs? Or canned soup? Chick—"

Josef held up a hand of protest, but when he tried to chuckle, it died suddenly in a moan. "The beef, Paul. Beef will be just fine."

Paul stood over the Greek as he opened the can. "You don't look like much of a monk in a checkered shirt and brown trousers."

Josef's bushy black brows went up. "I discarded the robe first, in the rock gorge behind the monastery."

Paul placed the food over canned heat and gave a low whistle. "I know you have quite a story to tell, but it will have to wait until we've both had some sleep." He removed the tin from the heat, reached for a fork, and sat down while Josef ate. "You'll need a greater disguise than clothing can give you, Josef. Shaving off your beard should be a good start, don't you think? Just in case any fellow monks should come this way looking for you?"

"That's the biggest giveaway I have—this beard. Yes, if you'll loan me your razor, I'll go to work on it in the morning."

There was no more talk that night. Josef gratefully finished the beef and noodles and drank a tall glass of water that had been freshly boiled. So Paul and Josef slept.

It was but a few hours, however, until morning flooded the desert with light and all the creatures of darkness silently secluded themselves. Sunlight filtered into the tent and beckoned the American to wakefulness. Paul was somewhat startled to see another man occupying the other cot; but then he remembered and fell back against his pillow with a sigh. How would the Greek ever endure the heat of this tent until he was able to be up and about?

Paul seriously contemplated going back to sleep, but the sound of the zippered tent door being opened and the smiling face of Ahmed pushing through did away with all such ideas.

"Mr. Coltren? If you want to sleep for a few more hours, we'll just keep busy sifting and depositing the sand." He nodded his dirty turban toward Josef. "Does he have the information about the tomb? Because, if he doesn't come up with some other answers, we have an unpleasant surprise for the world."

Paul's countenance fell. *The world.* The Christian world. He'd been so busy over other matters that he had nearly forgotten that. He'd come safely over the burial chamber of Moses at last, by the mercy of God. But—what about others? Millions of others.

"Well, Ahmed, I guess that's something we'll have to pray over." He rose and flexed his arms. "You know something, Ahmed? God's Word *is* true. Not even the throngs of an unbelieving world can change that. I think I remember something along that line that goes like this: 'For what if some did not believe? Shall their unbelief make the faithfulness of God without effect?' "*

Ahmed looked at the American strangely. "That is from your Bible?"

"It is."

The Arab nodded slowly, pulled in his lips tightly, and turned away.

As Paul dressed, Josef began to stir. When first he opened his eyes there was that same bewilderment Paul had had when waking.

*Romans 3:3, margin.

Then, seeing someone familiar, Josef relaxed with a smile. *"Safe!* What a comfortable word! Do you really know its meaning, Paul?"

Paul sat down to pull on his boots. "I'm sure it doesn't mean to me what it must mean to you, Josef." He stood and reached for two packets of powdered coffee. He kept forgetting to buy a can of real ground coffee in Cairo. "Will you feel up to talking about the tomb today?"

"I'm sure I will, Paul. By the way, I brought the jasper tube with the papyri, also a couple of books that were necessary to keep with me." Josef sat up with difficulty. "Don't forget to tell me where your razor is and I'll see what I can do with this beard."

"Right!"

"And Paul?"

"Yeah?"

"If that tomb doesn't come up with a lot more than the pictures, we have a big problem on our hands."

Paul's jaw hardened and his eyes narrowed with a kind of tenacity. He would find truth, the substance that every archeologist sought. His countenance was a mixture of both coldness and compassion, but the cry of his heart was strong—and only God understood it.

23

The two men sat across the tiny table from one another within the confines of the tent. Such a sense of fellowship existed between them that Paul could only feel amazed, especially when he recalled the dreary ceremony he had attended with Josef at Machseh.

Josef sat carefully, his injured leg extended to its full length. "Would you mind if I start at the very beginning? Otherwise I'd feel as if I were jumping right into the middle of the story."

Paul had heated canned scrambled eggs, bacon, and rolls, and he discovered that they were not half as bad when he could share them with someone. The coffee was black, robust and strengthening.

"Start wherever you like. It just feels good to have this opportunity to rest."

Josef did not speak for a moment. It was almost as though he was so used to eating in silence that he could not break the habit. This, however, was not the case. Forehead furrowed, his face white without the black beard, looking extremely Westernized in khakis and boots, no one would ever have taken second notice of him. Except, of course, for the missing beard. He'd have to get some sun right away to rid his face of the telltale white. He was deep in meditation and, when he finally spoke, his voice was deeply reflective.

"I remember at thirteen, having such a strange hunger, searching, in my heart. I plunged into my studies, read everything I could find about ancient Egypt. Always this country had fascinated me, and when finally I was in college I majored in ancient history. The study of hieroglyphics was a wonder to me, for I specialized in the history of Egypt.

"But I never escaped the hunger. Sometimes I went to a beautiful little fountain in my town of Akharnai, where a great statue of the Virgin Mary stood. It was said that those who believed and plunged themselves into that water would be healed of physical infirmities. I had no infirmities, but I had a spiritual infirmity, a need. Sometimes, when no one was about, I would go into that fountain with my clothes on. I thought that surely God would give peace to my heart! All searching, however, was without avail, or so it seemed.

"At last I entered Machseh. There I would find peace! Imagine, if you can, what it was like to discover that the men who rebelled against the rigid ceremonies and rules mysteriously disappeared at night, never to be heard of again. To find that some of the men were criminals! I was more alone than ever, Paul. *Aloneness.* Such hunger at times gripped my soul that I agonized alone in my cell. No one knew my torment. No one in that dreary place cared. Not until Carolyn Foster came with you to see me. You remember, perhaps, that she left a little book, the New Testament, in my hand.

"Alone at night I pored over the pages of the little book. Slowly, very slowly, a pale light shone within me. The more I read, the brighter that light became. At last I came to the place where it tells of Calvary and the death of Jesus Christ. Slowly I came to understand that, if I would 'receive' Him, as Saint John wrote, I would possess eternal life." Josef's countenance radiated the inner light of which he spoke. "It had been a wasted life of works without the true knowledge of the cross. Paul!" The Greek leaned forward eagerly. "Perhaps I was very crude in my transaction with God, but I—I just told Him how I felt, that I needed Him. I know He heard me! I know it!"

Paul's heartbeat was one of empathy. "I know it, too, Josef."

"Right after this I felt some inner compulsion to leave. *Escape* is the right word. Many others had tried and failed, so who was I to succeed in such a dangerous getaway? But I had to try.

"Really, it seems so vague now," the monk said quietly. "I had overheard Abraham in the kitchen telling the cook that they would have to remain in the kitchen late that night because a truck was bringing up flour, sugar, produce, and other badly needed items. The shipment had been detained because of a blowout.

"The idea came immediately, for I knew that truck well. It had a tailgate, not a full door. I dressed for chapel as usual. It was quite dark and I lingered behind for a moment. But I heard the truck struggle up that last steep incline. Mentally, I guessed it would take twenty minutes to unload the merchandise. Trembling and with a quivering kind of pain in my throat, I passed from my cell and began to make my way very slowly down the darkened corridor. There was but a pale light glowing from one end.

"Outside in the night, I found a place to hide beside the road where masses of great oleanders grow." Josef smiled at Paul, and for the first time Paul saw the Greek's wit. "That's where I really learned how to pray! A few minutes later the truck turned around, the driver waved to the two retreating monks, and headed straight for me. With a wild dash for that safety chain on the tailgate, I threw my body inside, quaked when the driver slowed to see whether he had hit something, changed his mind, and kept going." He sipped his coffee while a smile played in his eyes. "It seemed so extremely impossible then. I've seen too much. Peter—others. But I had to come. And the simplicity of it struck me there in the rear of that vehicle and I sat and laughed."

"You came near Dahshur, then?"

"Yes. The truck stopped for something in Dahshur and I disembarked there. You had told me where your camp was, Paul, but it still took a day and a night to find it. I would have never made it without the gallon of water I brought with me."

Paul pressed his lips and nodded. "God was with you."

Josef stroked the white-black outline of his missing beard. "Yes, definitely. Well, from that point, then. I stumbled to the entrance of the tomb while searching for you. I had had no thought of going into the dig." He spread big, bony hands. "No need to take that up again. We both know I was shot." He fingered his cup and looked up at Paul, who had not realized before how large Josef's facial features were, nor how bony his whole body was. His brows, heavy and black, hung close to his thoughtful black eyes, and his shoulders were hunched over the table. Without long sleeves, his arms appeared muscular and Paul wondered if he had gardened part time or done some other physical work at the monastery. He was much more handsome than himself, thought Paul. A nudge of jealousy asked him if Carolyn would have noticed.

"I ran doubled over," Josef continued, his voice deep and strangely soft. "I didn't know which way to go and thought surely

I had been wrong in thinking this to be your dig. Knew too, that even if it was, I couldn't call to you because of perhaps being discovered as a refugee from Machseh. So I ran and the pain was like hot steel in my thigh. I must have lost a lot of blood, because I continually felt so weak and dizzy." He paused, stared unseeing out the door of the tent. "And then the jeep came and I saw Miss Foster. She was an angel whom God had sent to me. It was just gray dawn and I was lying in a great pool of blood, not able to run any farther. She helped get me into the back of the jeep and said she could catch her father in a few minutes—that he'd know exactly what to do and where to take me. We both knew that if we didn't find a doctor quickly it would be fatal. At the same time, we knew that for me to be taken by spies sent out from the monastery would also be fatal."

"But she didn't catch up with her father."

"She did not," Josef replied. "He had evidently taken another route and we could not sort out all the various tracks to decide which were his. Besides, the breeze erased them all in a very short time. And we could not come back to you, for we had gone too far. I would have died if she had tried it." A slow smile came over his whole face. "Once we tried to laugh over the fact that we could call you on the phone."

Paul waited in silence. How bravely Carolyn had stood up under such pressure. Such a divine undergirding God must have granted her. And, of course it was true: she had had no way to let him or her father know of her whereabouts.

"We passed a small village once that had just been smitten with its first case of cerebral malaria, and a doctor was just driving away. There was only one thing to do now, and that was to trust this doctor. We explained to him what had happened. Rather, Carolyn did. I was fading and wakening by turns by then. He took us to his home, a little village on the Nile. I was thoroughly disoriented by that time. But the doctor got the bullet out. He didn't ask a question and seemed not to care who we were." Josef was lying down again now, still suffering from physical weakness. "You know the rest. Carolyn took wonderful care of me. But she grew tired, too, Paul. She has great endurance, but she is, after all, a woman. And, Paul? It goes without saying how sorry I am to have kept her away and to have caused you and her father so much worry."

Paul waved an arm. "Well, after all, we thought it was someone else who had been shot and then forced Carolyn to go away with him."

"I would never do that, Paul. Don't you know," he joked feebly, "that monks are not supposed to be attracted to pretty women?" He hesitated, then added more seriously. "Besides that, Paul, she belongs to you."

Paul gazed into the other man's eyes until it was as if they looked into one another's souls. "Thank you, Josef." But his expression told the monk that he knew Josef, too, could care for Carolyn and that he trusted God would make it up to him.

24

Since that night, Paul's love for Carolyn deepened into fullest bloom. It was the rich-hued velvet of a rose petal. It was delicate perfume that dazed and dazzled the senses and filled the heart with ecstasy. It was early dawn and loneliness and sunset and she was not there. It was the rare reaching out of soul and spirit to feel her nearness.

Yet, Paul dared not leave the camp at the present time, not even to see his beloved. Josef must not be discovered just yet, though at times he did go outside the tent when the crew was at work. Continually he pored over the delicate bits of papyri, studied the pictures, and waited for the day when he could study inside the tomb. And all his mysterious methods and studies left Paul the more amazed and silenced in the presence of a professional.

The American found it increasingly strange and delightful to have a Christian companion, and the men often spent time together in prayer and in searching the Word of God. Josef was a clear, sharp, and perceptive thinker and learned with great ease. His strength was returning to him rapidly, and there were times now when he and Paul went for short walks after dark.

Caution was of the utmost importance, and even small things, such as having coffee ready for Paul when he came from work, was impossible. Coffee was fragrant and the Egyptians would be able to smell it. Great care was taken especially when the two men spoke to one another. Yet, despite the necessity to speak softly, they entered into this joyous fellowship.

Josef had taken on enough of a tan to blend in with his naturally olive complexion and thus hide the whiteness of face that said he had had a beard.

One night the two men walked close to the oasis and gazed across the smooth dunes to the distant lantern hanging by the Foster camp. Paul strained to catch a glimpse of Carolyn, but she was not in sight. Inside he tingled and trembled. He longed for her touch, yearned to hold her in his arms, heart against heart, throbbing the timeless love song, yet sensing above all else the immeasurable love of Christ who had made their love possible.

Josef touched Paul's arm. "Why don't you go on—spend a few minutes with her? I don't mind waiting."

Paul felt everything in his heart and mind hesitate. He looked from the bright light ahead to the dimmer glow of their flashlight, then to the oasis again. Just a few—

"Come on, Josef, let's go back. She understands why I haven't come." He put on an air of indifference. "Besides, there are scorpions in the sand, and jackals over those dunes! And," he emphasized, "you're too valuable to lose."

Josef fell silent for a time. Then, "Paul, it has occurred to me that I might pose to be your Ed Lambert. Not a person here would know the difference. Even if someone from the monastery searched this area, it would be hard for them to know me without my beard and in civilian clothing."

Paul kept step with his friend, but there was a vague sickness in the pit of his stomach over the words just spoken. Not, however, that all Josef said was not true.

"But you know, Paul," Josef continued, "I cannot do it. I'm not sure what the reason is, for I could lie easily enough at the monastery. Do you suppose, Paul, that—it's because Christ—well, comes and makes us over?"

Paul thrust his hands into his pockets and wondered at the lightness of his steps. A song, like the opening of a delicate flower, burst within his heart. A guy had to admit the goodness of God in preparing Christians to help each other. "I think that's it exactly, Josef!"

"Do you think, Paul, that it would taste of a lie to say that I am here to study the funeral texts and some papyri concerning the tomb?"

Paul pondered, drawing up his shoulders from the cold air. "I don't think so, Josef. That certainly is a major reason for your being here, and then you could have liberty to come and go as you please." Paul stopped and looked at Josef squarely. "I need *desperately* to know whatever it is you can tell me about this tomb. I've got to get you inside so you can see and study."

Josef nodded slowly and walked on. "I understand that, Paul, but all I can say at this point is that all indications point to the fact that this tomb did indeed belong to Moses."

Paul swallowed. Compassion shone from his eyes, not for himself or for Carolyn and her father, but for a world that was seeking desperately for that place in God where there was rest and peace. For a world that wasn't even aware of her searching.

"Would it make a great deal of difference?"

Paul stared at his friend. "Can you imagine the effect on America if an H-bomb were dropped in the middle of New York City? The confusion. The falling away of those—" Paul looked at Josef and did not continue.

Yes, he thought, *the pulse of religious Christianity would be almost annihilated, while true born-again Christians—though they might for a time suffer great conflict—would come through, with some of them scarred. Not to mention the stark drop in new conversions.*

They walked back to the tent in silence. While Josef went directly to his cot, Paul called Ahmed aside for a moment's conversation.

"Ahmed—about Josef. He's the only man I know at the moment who can give us any information on the tomb. Can you explain this to the crew so he can begin coming and going as he wants to?"

Ahmed pursed his lips. "I can and I will; but it will be more difficult now."

Paul looked at him intently. "What do you mean? *Now?"*

"An hour ago, while you and Josef were gone, we had visitors. I'm convinced they were from the monastery."

Paul started. "Tonight? What did they say? What did they look like?"

Ahmed waved him aside. "They were bearded—a short little man with small, shining eyes, and a taller man. They wore Western clothing, but their manner and speech was that of another world." Ahmed weighed his words carefully. "I was suspicious when they drove up and I turned them over to Kamal without telling him why. Naturally, not knowing of Josef's presence here, Kamal was outraged from the first. They demanded a full description of you and accused Kamal of hiding word of another man, a Greek. Then, about the time they headed for your tent, apparently intending to investigate on their own, Kamal grabbed his rifle and went after them." Ahmed grinned. "That discouraged them and they got into their car and left."

"Do you think they'll come back?"

"I doubt it. Kamal was very convincing. After all, not knowing anything, he thought he was telling the truth."

Paul nodded. "We thought someone would show sooner or later. They don't let the men leave Machseh easily." He started to move away. "You will take care of Josef's presence here, then, so far as the crew is concerned?"

"I'm sure the men will accept him without question."

"But no lies," Paul cautioned sternly.

"I will not lie. I swear by Allah." The Arab smelled so weirdly of cologne and body odor that Paul turned his face away for a moment. "After all," Ahmed went on, "the fact that he is here to help us is solid truth. And a wise man does not tell *all* that he knows."

And, with that remark, Ahmed sauntered away, leaving a trail of Oriental Jade moving slowly behind him. Paul hoped fervently that the Arab would not become generous and start sharing it with the other men!

Josef and Paul secured the tent so no one could see in. They would open the window and door later on. For now, they sat across from one another sharing a pot of coffee.

At the end of the table the papyri had been spread out carefully and a piece of glass borrowed from Mr. Foster's crude "hotbed" placed over the fragments. They had been rearranged until Josef was finally satisfied that they were in the only possible order, and he'd spent many hours scanning the pieces with a magnifying glass. The pictures also were placed in order.

"Josef?"

The Greek looked up. "Yes, Paul?"

"We had company tonight."

Josef's big hands tensed automatically. "Company? Who?"

"We can't be sure, but from the descriptions, I'd say one of them was Abraham." Paul laced his fingers together and studied them. "They were, of course, looking for you."

There was a fleeting anxiety that crossed Josef's dark countenance. "Yes. I knew they'd come looking for me sooner or later. Tell me about it."

"Well, they didn't hang around long. Kamal handled them and, of course, he didn't know you were here so he was pretty convincing. I don't think we need to worry, though we'll certainly keep our eyes alert. They've got a lot more digs to check out before returning here."

Josef pursed his lips and sighed. "That's true." He fumbled with some papers. "All right, Paul, let's get to work, shall we?"

"Right!"

"Actually, Paul, I need to get into that tomb. There is so much I need to see for myself before coming to a definite conclusion. There may be certain hieroglyphics that can change everything. The funeral texts will surely bring to light exactly what we want. The name on the coffin—"

"I told you," Paul stated quietly. "The name is Moses."

Josef looked troubled. "Same as these papyri. They're simply personal letters—fragments of them— You see here, Paul? The heading is *oses* because part of the address is gone. And over there—that's a business account and the signature is *Moses*."

Paul took up the magnifying glass and scanned the account. "But, Josef, wasn't there another letter before the name?"

"It looks that way, but there is no proof." The Greek sighed wearily and limped about the tent.

Paul stood very straight and tall. "The man Moses would have had much larger business accounts, wouldn't he?"

Josef folded his lower lip over his upper one for a moment. "Why? I've studied the history of Egypt most of my life. There's no question but that the man Moses lived here at one time. That's not the question. And if truth were still involved in the fact that he spent years on the desert, that would certainly account for the fact that he wasn't as wealthy as he had once been."

Paul reluctantly agreed. "Yeah. You're right, of course. But there has to be a way somehow to prove that the tomb didn't belong to the Moses we know about."

"One thing we agree on. The world will never know until we have exhausted all possibilities." The monk looked at Paul solemnly. "I marvel that you met the Saviour in that burial chamber, when you really thought you were looking down at the body of Moses."

"I had to, Josef, I had to! He came to me there. And I knew that if I could believe Him there, I would never fall again. It was so-called evidence stacked up against me that caused me to turn away from Him before." He turned away and smiled to hide the fountain of joy within his soul. "This Jesus is one who takes nothing, yet demands everything. But He puts it into the heart to give all."

"And gladly so," Josef replied, though he did not understand all that Paul was telling him.

"That's why Moses ended up in the wilderness instead of in Pharaoh's courts. Becoming, perhaps in time, an heir to the throne and Egypt's ruler. Yet, he esteemed 'the reproach of Christ greater riches than the treasures in Egypt'—of which there are many!"

In the distance they heard a camel roar loudly, sounding alarmingly like the roar of a mountain lion. Then silence fell, broken intermittently by the lonely jackal's cry. And there was silence in Paul Coltren's soul, mixed with tender longings for the woman he loved.

The lantern was extinguished and the tent windows and door flaps tied up to allow a flow of cold air. There was no moonlight, but the stars were bright and flashing. Even the dome of heaven was warm and friendly.

By the following morning Ahmed had informed the crew that one Josef Zarefiris, a Greek Egyptologist, was with them and they trusted he could lend them some valuable help regarding the tomb.

"Then it's not going to jolt them when Josef comes to the dig?" Paul asked, peering into Ahmed's face, studying his every expression.

"That's right, Mr. Coltren. They have not even asked where he came from." He gestured, indicating that the crew members were none too bright. "If they do, I'll simply tell them that you brought him here."

Paul stood a moment longer, sun throwing his face into full shadow, and his right arm outreached with his hand supporting his body weight against an aluminum tent support. But the sound of a throbbing engine turned his gaze and brought it to rest upon Carolyn sitting in a jeep with her father.

A pulsating of heart and mind gripped him, and he went forward to meet her, a strong man who had suffered long, but who had come forth with love and compassion he had never thought to know.

Gently he took her hands, lifted her down. For a long, precious moment she lay nestled against him, breathing unevenly. Their lips touched and she clung to him briefly and went out of his arms. The light in her eyes was one that spoke to him of love and togetherness and God.

The early morning light had thrown a backdrop of shadows and sounds that were eerie, dreadful, and beautiful over the area. It was as inspiring to the occasional artist who came here as it was foreboding to the wanderer who found himself without water. It was over this lonely sand that the small party made its way to the tomb. They were met there by Josef, who greeted the Fosters with genuine warmth.

Ahmed and Paul opened the great, tall door. The air was much better than in the beginning, smelling only of time and mystery and earthbound values of material things.

"May we see inside?" Carolyn's voice carried a twinge of thirst for adventure.

"You can take a quick look, but it's not ready for—please forgive the term, darling—for tourists yet. Josef is going in today to begin extensive study on the various emblems and texts inside the burial chamber."

The Greek had brought a thick note pad and a pocketful of pencils. He passed through the doorway and on into the burial chamber. The light of a great mystery permeated his very soul.

Jim peered through the doorway, and Paul put Carolyn in front of him so she could get a clear view of the chapel.

Once her face twisted up to his in amazement. "Oh, Paul, it was never that I disbelieved you, but—to see the—the evidence for myself seems so incredible. The baby hidden in rushes—the woman bathing, surrounded by handmaidens. The man that Moses killed for a fellow Hebrew!" For a fleeting moment several mixed emotions raced through her mind, but they did not show on her face. "Paul? What does Josef say?"

Deep concern mirrored in his dark eyes. "He says much of the papyri is missing. Mostly they are letters and business accounts anyway, and the only whole signature that appears is *Moses*."

Jim straightened and frowned, his pink forehead rapidly growing red without his helmet. "I'd say you have to be joking, Paul, except that I know you wouldn't."

Carolyn stiffened in Paul's arms, and she felt glad in that moment that he could not see her face. "What do you think, Paul?" she asked softly. "From a personal viewpoint, that is?"

Paul breathed in the sweet cleanness of her hair. "I don't know, Carolyn. Look in front of you. A person could know practically nothing about archeology but be intimately acquainted with the Bible and know at once that the young Hebrew standing there in the courts of Pharaoh was the boy Moses. One can see that he is being taught the various healing arts and skills of the magicians."

"No wonder he knew what the magicians could do and what their limit was." Carolyn stepped down and her fingers linked loosely with Paul's. "And what gods they worshiped too. Imagine the frogs appearing in their kneading troughs and in their beds!"

Paul gestured. "Do you see over there how the figures have turned, so that now they read into each other? Clearly the man facing Moses is a noble with a young boy at his side. But read on and you see that the noble has had a demotion and is now only a taskmaster—a rather unhappy one, from the look on his face."

Carolyn suddenly gasped. "What is that picture, Paul? Moses killing the Egyptian? But—"

Paul shook his head. "Nothing adds up, Carolyn, except the fact that Moses is receiving laud and glory throughout this tomb. This would never be so if Moses were not buried here."

"Paul—" Her eyes were large and anxious as she gazed up at him.

"Don't give me a thought, Carolyn. This is nothing new to me; I've already been through it."

"No, darling, it's not you. But unless God grants us a miracle, the world—"

Paul turned her and gripped both her hands. "I've been through that, too. I wish I'd never seen this place!" His brows drew together in a frown, but there was peace on his face. "I wish another sandstorm would come and seal it forever." He smiled at his own words. "That's pretty juvenile, isn't it, but that's what I wish. I'd like to blow the whole thing."

"Paul, I know, I know!"

He breathed deeply, pulled her closer. "I love you."

"And I love you!"

"Paul!" The muffled voice came from within the burial chamber. "Paul, can you come here a minute?"

Their handclasp broke as Paul strode through the chapel and toward the small opening that led into the burial chamber.

Paul crept through the opening to Josef. "Something the matter, Josef?"

The monk looked extremely sober. His attention was directed to one corner of the room, and, going forward, he paused and knelt beside a strange dark object.

Paul's stare riveted upon the same spot, and some unseen sentinel within his subconscious stood, alerted. "There's been a cave-in here, Josef! This chamber was formed of a double layer of blocks, and one of those blocks obviously has dropped, along with a lot of mortar and small stones." He began to scan the place hurriedly. "And several of the statuettes have been removed! Josef—"

"Come nearer, Paul," the Greek said quietly.

Paul felt every shock absorber in his mind and body receive the full blow. The dark object was a boot—with a foot still in it. A man was buried under the rubble.

25

Paul had come upon gory, even grotesque, scenes before, but there was something about that foot that left him with a feeling of the unreal. Perhaps because, deep in his heart, he knew that foot belonged to George Arnold.

It came to the men as fantasy that the odor of the dead lay within the confines of the searing heat. The man probably had been dead three days at least, Paul calculated. Suddenly he realized that with the passing of George Arnold would pass also the fear of further pilfering and, what was far greater, the one man on earth who could give away the secret of the tomb.

Beyond a doubt the man had come on a night when Kamal was standing guard. Paul had never approved of him as a guard. He strayed from his rifle and dozed on occasion. Evidently Arnold, thinking to make one last steal, had escaped the Arab's eye. Little had he known that it would be in this place that fate would deal him her last blow.

"Seems like God took care of him without any help," Paul murmured, his mouth twisted to one side.

Josef nodded, slowly examining his inner lips with his tongue. "Let's see what we have, Paul." He stooped and headed for a large block. "Question is, what do we do with him after we dig him out?"

"Wrap him up like a mummy and have Ahmed get him to the American Embassy in Cairo, if we can prove he is Arnold. They'll take it from there. They work so closely with the actual laws of the country that they'll know exactly what to do."

Together the men pulled handerchiefs over their noses and mouths and began their gruesome task. Ahmed, who came in to say that Jim and Carolyn had returned to the oasis, was given a brief rundown on the recent occurrence. His leering mouth became quite drawn and sober as he set to work with the Americans. It wasn't five minutes until the Arab had the other leg bared, revealing a snug-fitting silver identification chain. On the flat nameplate were words.

Paul pressed fingers against his nose to shield them from the obnoxious odor and read aloud, "Mr. George Arnold—1444 West Uchlid Street—Philadelphia, Pennsylvania."

In another ten minutes the man was uncovered, his body twisted in a bizarre fashion, and his face bearing an expression of shock, as though he anticipated the cave-in but could do nothing to prevent it or to escape it. His mouth and eyes were open, his arms thrown up as if in protection. His body was in a state of decomposition so that it was very difficult to breathe. The men rose and turned toward the badly chipped coffin and on out through the chapel and into the bright sunshine.

Later the three men returned to wrap the body and drag the weight of it outdoors. There it was loaded into the back of the jeep and Ahmed started for Cairo with it. Paul stood watching the disappearing vehicle and wondering if he should have taken the body to Cairo himself, except that the Arab had assured him over and over that he had encountered such situations before.

The crew took care of its own needs. The smell of *kisra* and *rayib* met the nostrils of the two other men, and though the odor was distasteful to them, they could see the Arabs were obviously finding the wheat cakes and vegetables very palatable.

With hearts burdened, Paul and Josef ate their lunch after brewing a pot of coffee. They hunched toward one another to talk.

"There was really no time to study in that small burial chamber," Josef spoke wonderingly. "The smell was so bad, and I kept telling myself that it was the dust and the years; but when I saw that foot I changed my mind quickly enough. But all that I *was* able to gather was more glory to the man Moses. And, of course, I did see the name on that coffin." Josef was silently meditative. "Was there ever another, previous, cave-in in that chamber?"

"Not to my knowledge. Why, Josef?"

"Nothing, probably. Only, that coffin must have had some rough treatment at one time."

Paul sipped his coffee. "Oh, you mean because of the niches in the granite? But a couple of the statuettes are the same way. Even the bowl on the table has a small wedge missing from the rim." He studied the dregs in the bottom of his cup, hesitated, and tossed them to the ground. "I guess I'd be able to see the possibility of a former cave-in, all right. Maybe that's the condition Arnold found it in twenty years ago. He cleaned it up, realized what he had, saw the opportunity of selling a few pieces on the side, and then suddenly the whole thing was ended when the sandstorm completely buried the tomb, leaving not even a trace or a clue as to its exact location."

Josef nodded, lights dancing in his dark eyes. "Then you believe that we'll have to admit eventually that this is of a truth the tomb of Moses?"

Paul spread his hands and shrugged. "I don't have the key to that puzzle. This is more in your line, Josef, and if all you can get is the corresponding name in that papyri, then, what more can we do?"

Josef gently bit the corner of his lower lip. "Paul? Now think very carefully. Is there no place—absolutely no place—that you know where we might obtain just a shred of something more to go on?"

The other man pressed weary hands to his face. "Jabari has nothing more to offer, or he would have contacted us. The only other place I can think of is that little curio shop on the Street of Fatima. You remember, the place where I found the statuette that had been taken from the chapel? That was the link that told me Arnold had been here twenty years ago."

Josef looked up slowly, his eyes narrowed. "Ah, yes! I had momentarily forgotten. Do you think—?"

Paul spoke through clenched teeth. "I've always thought Mahmoud knew more than he would tell. Perhaps now that Arnold is dead, he'll level with me."

"Then you have to find out," Josef agreed. "When can you leave for Cairo?"

"As soon as Ahmed returns with the jeep."

Josef nodded. "Then we'll spend every minute till then studying some of the more difficult emblems and symbols inside the burial chamber."

"I'll help in any way I can," Paul said, falling into step with the Greek.

By now two of the workmen had cleared away the rubble, and with the rubble had gone the stench also. Supports were used to brace the ceiling, and the surrounding areas appeared perfectly safe.

Josef prowled from chapel to burial chamber, but all past conclusions remained the same. "Rifai—" the monk mused, pausing to look at the inside block where the cartouche had been carefully engraved. "Same as on the outside blocks. But who is Rifai?"

"Is there any possibility of tracing him back through history?"

Josef stood with his chin perched on a finger and thumb. "If only I had my books from the monastery! He has to fall into history somewhere just to have been so close to Moses!" His eyes burned as from a fever. He searched the ceiling for a clue to this mystery. "Did Moses have a son named Rifai? For very clearly this Rifai followed the same God that Moses followed. This is everywhere indicated."

"Not according to Bible history." Paul paced the chapel too, then followed the Greek again into the burial chamber. His eyes scanned the figure of a woman. He knew she was a woman because there was an egg beside her and because her skin was light. Men were always red in picture writing. This was Moses' wife, perhaps, or a beloved daughter.

The eyes of the archeologist roamed downward, coming to rest upon the mummy wrapped alone in its position, somberly silent at his feet. He wondered how many mummies Arnold had made off with twenty years ago.

" 'God is not a man, that he should lie; neither the son of man, that he should repent:' " he murmured, " 'hath he said, and shall he not do it? Or hath he spoken, and shall he not make it good?' "

There was a stirring within Paul's heart. Previously the Word of God had always been his trouble—to believe it as fact or as myth or as illustration? Yet here—here by the tomb of the man thought to be Moses—Paul had given his life back to God. And with this there was the return of peace. He could not explain faith in the presence of what seemed to be a lie; he only knew that Christ was real, acutely real to him again. And somehow, God's Word *was* true.

Josef had slowed his pace. He stood staring quietly at the great gold statue, chin leaning hard on the palm of one hand. His gaze, however, was more or less vacant, and his large feet were planted widely apart.

Paul touched the other man's sleeve. "Let's forget everything till morning. You'll be too exhausted to take charge of things here, and I'd really like to have some time to look around. If there's an answer or explanation," he said grimly, "I mean to find it."

Paul heard Ahmed drive in during the night, but he slept on until morning. By the time he was dressed and had drunk a couple of cups of coffee, the sun had bedecked the eastern horizon in fairest colors that soon overspread the sky and gave promise of the glassy fireball that would soon arise to smite the land with heat.

The American cast a longing glance toward the oasis and pressed back the desire to ask Carolyn to accompany him. Even her presence must not take his time today, for then he would be unable to give himself totally to the emergency at hand.

Arnold had met with violent death. In a way, one might say that he had committed suicide. He was no longer a problem. In the hands of the American Embassy now, his body would be taken care of accordingly.

There was only the tomb and the great, overwhelming need to find a way to prove that this was not the tomb of Moses. How? Where?

Paul drove with as much speed as possible, but the road was badly rutted and the maximum speed was about fifty miles an hour. Would Jabari have any further information? If not, could Paul find information? But then, Paul was bordering on the dangerous. Before it had simply been a looter; now there would be questions. Questions about the looter that Paul could not possibly answer.

No, he'd have to be a loner on this one. He tightened the seat belt and stepped up the pace a little. Strangely, Paul was relaxed, and the muscles of his face no longer fell into the perpetual frown of his yesterdays. This was God's affair. Surely He would move to vindicate His own Word. Looking at it that way made things a lot less anxious. He slowed down near Saqqara as a roving Bedouin with three camels loaded with goat hides crossed in front of him and disappeared into the vast reaches of nothingness.

Cairo lay mystic and silent in the morning light; silent, that is, until a wayfarer came into its business hubbub. Then it became a land of contrast, the old ever mingling with the new. Black men with turbans and flowing garments, veiled women with long skirts, Westernized businessmen in tailored suits and fezes. Bicycles were in constant conflict with cars and other traffic, while small boys with more dirt showing than skin pigment dashed hither and yon, pleading for a penny or walking in one's shadow, begging to shine shoes.

Paul deftly skirted the worst of the traffic and headed for the lonely narrow streets and inferior shops of the Street of Fatima. As before, he parked a few blocks away and made his way down the street. Groups of suspicious men watched them. Women avoided him as though he carried a death plague upon his person, and children walked far around him, watching with great, curious dark eyes. A few coins thrown their way were a mistake the moment he let them fly; but it was done and the man smiled quickly as the barefoot children scrambled for them. They started after him, crying for more, but he hastened his steps and gestured to them in the negative.

Finally he had passed from the residential part of the street to the business section. Rotting vegetables lay a foot away and hungry dogs smelled at them hopefully. But when Paul stopped before the sagging door of The Prophet, a dirty white sign had been tacked to the door. He stared at the words in dismay, written first in Arabic and then in badly scrawled English.

The American hunched forward, deciphering them. "Stor is clos to dey."

Paul brought his tall frame upward. His nostrils flared with disgust even while his heart seemed to pause in beating out its message of life. His hands automatically curled into hard fists and the frown bit into his forehead again. Irresolution took hold of him, and all the bony structure of his face became hard and prominent.

"Closed?" He uttered the single word aloud. It was without meaning. "Closed. Closed. The store is closed." His breath began with a snort. He tried the doorknob. Through the crack between the door casing and the wall Paul saw a chain lock also. Locked up tight! When things were so vital! When he could withhold evidence no longer! When Eddie was due to arrive most any day! Eddie, who was a near atheist. Paul was unaware that he had moaned aloud until small brown hands took hold of his coat and began tugging insistently. Paul turned with both impatience and alarm.

Two Arab boys of perhaps eight years confronted him with angry eyes. Clearly Paul was being accused, not only of trying to break into the shop, but of being an American who was trying to break into the shop.

Paul grinned and brought himself down to their eye level. "You're mistaken, fellows. I'm not trying to force my way in there. I have to see the store owner."

They stared unblinkingly. Finally one of the barefoot children asked Paul a question in Arabic. Paul spread his hands, letting them know that he was ignorant of the language. With this, they both let loose with such a flow of denunciation that Paul was fearful of the attention they were apt to draw.

Hurriedly he dug into his pocket and brought out a few coins. Their faces were transformed immediately, so much so that their scorn of only a moment ago turned swiftly to smiles and charm and friendship.

When they would have reached for them, however, he closed his hand. "Mahmoud Saleh," he mouthed slowly. "Mr. Mahmoud Saleh," and he opened his hand again, briefly, exposing the alluring coins.

"Mahmoud Saleh!" they chorused excitedly, proving how bright they could become at the sight of money. Taking the man's hands, a boy on either side, they would have bolted down the street with him, except that Paul's strength held them to his pace. For he still had to be careful not to attract too much attention, and certainly it was not the norm for two little Arab boys to be pulling an American down the narrow street this way.

At length the small guides suddenly paused and looked at Paul expectantly. Their looks asked the question, What if we show you where Mahmoud Saleh lives? How do we know you'll really give us the money?

Paul's dark eyes stared back, but there was no trace of expression. He simply opened his hand, split half of the coins between them and gestured that they would get the rest when he was ushered to Mr. Saleh's door.

It was but a moment, therefore, until the Arab boys led him to a little block house that was slightly more pretentious than the others that surrounded it. The shorter boy stood before the door and knocked loudly. It obviously occurred to him suddenly that if the Arab were not home they might not get the rest of the money, and so he pounded harder than before.

The results were immediate. Mahmoud pulled open the door with a look of impatience that was pointed first at the boys, then grew more severe when he saw the archeologist. Mr. Saleh pulled himself up straight and his lips fell into a thin, even line. He looked impeccable in his snowy turban and Western-cut suit. Paul was amazed at the change.

"I have no business with you today." And Mahmoud started to shut the door.

Paul got his foot in the door. "For fifty dollars?" he asked swiftly.

"I got nothing to sell you today, mister." He tried to shut the door. "Go on. Go before I get ver' angry."

The tugging began on Paul's coat again and he turned just enough to press the coins into the hand of the nearest Arab youth. "Be sure you divide it evenly!" he shouted as they darted away.

"Mister Coltren, please, not today. Not for any price today."

"Why not?" Paul demanded.

Mahmoud was indeed becoming angry. A slow dark red was appearing in his face. "This is an Arab home," he said slowly, "and you are a foreigner. I do not wish to do business with you anymore."

Paul hesitated. He could not force his way into this home. But neither could he give up when the truth of the Word of God was at stake. His chin jutted with determination and the look in his dark eyes was one of absolute assurance of what he had to do. "I have news of George Arnold for you," he said, forcing a calmness into his voice.

"What can Arnold mean to me?" But there was a certain wariness now, like a mountain lion facing at last the open end of a rifle barrel.

"He's brought you stolen merchandise in the past month." Paul wondered at his audacity, the authority by which he spoke. He was frightened at his own words.

Mahmoud's lips were stiff when he spoke. "Mister Coltren, I do not understand you. What is it you want?"

Paul felt courage stand up tall inside of him. He was in charge of the conversation now, and he knew it. "I want anything you have—*anything,* you understand?—that came out of the same tomb as that statuette I bought from your shop. I don't care how small or meaningless it may be, I want anything else you have."

"By Allah, I swear," the Arab said pathetically, almost regretfully, "all was sold many years ago. The only piece left I sell to you, Mister Coltren. I swear!"

"Did you know that Arnold is dead?"

A glimmer of something akin to gladness came to Mahmoud's ebony eyes. Perhaps it was because now he would not have to sell stolen artifacts. But small shops were glad to get any items. Who could tell the reason?

"You have nothing? Nothing at all? Not even for a hundred American dollars?"

"It is Mahmoud's loss," he replied woefully. "My son—my only son—gets married today. Could make big feast—" He sighed and started to shut the door again, when suddenly he swung it open and barged outside to face Paul.

"You tell me one hundred dollar for *anything?"*

Excitement gripped Paul. "Yes. Why?"

"Twenty years ago, when Arnold betray his own work and have to leave Egypt, he bring to shop a tool chest. Ask me to keep for him till he come back. But, this trip he never ask for it."

Paul's pulses raced through his head excitedly. "Where is that chest?"

Mahmoud gestured toward the squalor through which Paul had so recently passed. "In shop. I open once and find statuette." He smiled to himself. "I—not see his name on bottom of statue or—"

"But what else did you find?" Paul demanded quickly. "What else was in the box?"

Mahmoud hesitated, moistened his lips which had resumed their natural color. "Well—hard to be sure."

Paul heaved a sigh and allowed the question to go without an answer. Besides, what seemed terribly unimportant to Mahmoud might be extremely important to either him or Josef.

"Can we go after the tool chest now?" Paul shivered with unsuppressed eagerness.

Mahmoud glanced back toward the sound of voices and the rattling of dishes. "Yes. We go now!"

26

It had cooled rapidly by nightfall, leaving a chill on the desert air that made it comfortable for Paul and Josef to be inside the tent. All the flaps were tied down and the door was zippered securely. With an air of secrecy born of necessity, they padded the tool chest against sound, and pried off the metal lid. The chest was about eighteen inches deep and twelve inches square. The weight of it told the men that it was far from being empty.

Josef held the chest tightly while Paul pried through a small crack near the lock with a screwdriver. The key, Mahmoud said, had been lost, but Paul believed that the man had only misplaced it and did not wish to bother searching at that point—not with a marriage coming off and a hundred American dollars outstretched!

The lid gave with a surprising abruptness, leaving a twisted lock and a torn piece of metal.

Josef took the blanket from around the box slowly, as though fearful of their findings and reluctant to open the chest now that it was accessible to them.

Paul felt a momentary clenching of his stomach. His big hard hands went around the chest deliberately, however, and he placed it on the table top. Josef, slighter of frame than Paul and a couple of inches shorter, stood gazing at his friend. They read fear in each other's eyes for an instant, and then, together, they pulled back the lid of the tool chest and looked inside.

Utter dismay fell upon their countenances. A hundred dollars out of Paul's own pocket for—*this?*

Josef stuffed his hands into his pockets and took a swift turn about in the confined area. "Well, we seem to have a knack for continually building up optimism, only to have it destroyed over and over." He gave a pointed sweep of his hand toward the chest, as though the fault lay with it somehow. "Nothing!"

Paul felt the same emotions churning through his own soul. Aimlessly he picked up a knife from within the chest and laid it to one side. Next he plucked up a whisk broom and placed it beside the knife. Other than these, the chest contained fragments of granite, name cards from artifacts Arnold had brought to Mahmoud, and what appeared to be sweepings of gravel as fine as sand. An old toothbrush and a fine dental instrument, all implements of the archeologist, were snugged in with the sand.

With a pair of fine tweezers, Paul removed a bit of granite from the box and placed it upon a piece of cloth. The men examined it from every angle and Josef scrutinized it with a magnifying glass. "A perfect blank," he commented, standing erect. "Granite sweepings. It's odd that he would keep them."

Paul hunched his shoulders, feeling acute disappointment move in his stomach. This tool chest was their last opportunity, the only shred of hope. Eddie would arrive in four days and gladly complete the task of declaring to the world the discovery of Moses' tomb. What a proclamation that would be. Eddie always did things in a big way; he'd flaunt this before the eyes of the world, lift the laud and glory of it upon all the winds that blew, and the tragic message would go forth. And exceeding great wonderings would take place within the hearts of men.

Despair and hopelessness would replace faith. Paul gritted his teeth. No wonder it was always to destroy faith that Satan fought. What was there without it? A Moses who failed, an Abraham who never trusted God to raise Isaac from the dead, a Paul who never became a Christian. And the chapter would close there for many, many of God's children who had sought to walk closely to the riven side.

He unzipped the door and searched the starry sky. *God, don't You care?* his heart cried. And the solemn answer came back in another question from two thousand years before: "Carest Thou not that we perish?" Paul thought back to the words Jesus had spoken when He had entered the boat: *"Let us pass over to the other side."* His Word. *His Word.* It was always true!

With an alacrity he had not felt, Paul shut the door and came back to the table. Deliberately, one small chip at a time, he picked out the pieces of granite and laid them on the cloth. "Come on, Josef, if there's a secret here, we are going to find it."

Josef put a small magnifying glass to his right eye, picked up some tweezers, and began to study every tiny piece. "I'm using my own analytical mind instead of archeological technique right now," he confessed, "but I'm sure these pieces came from that tomb down there."

"So am I. We know the coffin had been chipped and—" The bridge of his nose suddenly came to rest on a thumb and forefinger as he grasped at knowledge. "Maybe Arnold chipped it on purpose. He could have aged the chipped places with chemicals."

Josef was lost in thought. "He surely could," he said at last. "And I'm wondering something more than that. Give me a couple of minutes here."

While Paul waited to see if there were any findings, he carefully turned the pages of an old book he had persuaded Mahmoud into throwing into the bargain. Paul felt good about that. If the findings in the chest were a total loss, at least he had a book called—what was it called? He turned it over. Oh, yes, *Nobles, Their Fame, Deeds, and Lineage.* Not that it would help if this was Moses' burying place.

It was 12:45 A.M., and the ticking of Paul's alarm clock plucked off the minutes with precision. The sounds—tick, tick, tick—were alarmingly loud in the stillness, but after a few minutes they were lost in the traffic of the mind.

Moses. He wasn't a noble, yet this was a noble's grave. Paul went back to the chill night air that flooded his lungs and mind. He wasn't thinking. He knew that whoever had finished building the tomb, one Rifai, had only completed what had already been started. And a noble had started the work. Evidently the pressure against his mind the past weeks had been more intense than he'd realized.

"Paul."

The harsh whisper brought his tall frame about sharply. "Yes."

Josef was bent over the bits of granite, eyepiece still in place, hands knotted against the table, the veins in his temples throbbing with excitement. "Come here."

It was 1:00. Paul scooted his campstool close and took up a magnifying glass. He studied Josef's strong profile a moment before examining the scrap the Greek held in the tweezers. "Wh—? I'm afraid I don't see much, Josef."

Josef pointed with a tool nearly as fine as a toothpick. "Right—

there! It's slight, but look closely, Paul, for it's the tail of a hieroglyphic."

Paul brought his eye closer to the glass. "Are you certain? Can you tell which hieroglyphic it would be?" He reached out to steady Josef's hand. He looked for a long time, then laid aside the glass. "You're right. It is there. Faint, to be sure, but definitely an impression—"

They looked to each other for the answer. Finally Josef spoke. "It's been a long day for you, Paul. Why not go on to bed? I'll wake you if I come upon anything of devastating importance." He emphasized the last two words with a grin.

But Paul shook his head stubbornly. "I'm staying up with you. After all that this tomb has put me through, I'm not fading out now. It seems to me," Paul concluded contemplatively, "that I can see Arnold taking a few strategic blows at that granite coffin—leaving no telltale impressions or indentations—just shallow pits in the granite. I'll wager he even swept up the small particles and dumped them all into the tool chest."

"Um-hum. If, for instance," said Josef, taking on Paul's surmisings, "old boy Arnold managed to extricate a few letters, say, before the name *Moses*. After all, Paul, Moses was a very popular name in those particular days. Think of Thutmose—or Thotmes—*or* Thothmes—all the same man, and his name ended with the word *Moses,* depending upon how one wished to spell it."

Paul perused the fragments of papyrus, held down by the square of glass, and noted that here also a piece was missing just before the name *Moses*. He nodded absently at Josef's statement. "That's true. And there's nothing illogical about this train of thought. Time period is right too."

"Right! 1450 B.C., eighteenth dynasty. Then there was Rameses, whose famed temples and other vast works stand today. He, too, bore the name *Moses* within his name, though spelled m-e-s-e-s." Josef's voice deepened with authority. "On that basis, I believe we have every right to think there may be other letters before that word Moses on the coffin."

It was 3 A.M. A half letter had been carefully glued together. The breakdown was tedious in the extreme, and both men were fighting the drag of pressure.

At 3:30 Paul made fresh coffee and replaced stained paper cups with clean ones. Josef took aspirin for a headache, his sensitive olive hands pressing at his temples.

Paul's attempted chuckle shattered and fell like chips of granite against the metal table. How absurd! They were trying to do the work of long weeks in a single night. It was ridiculous. Impossible.

The table had been unfolded days ago to its full length of twelve feet. The papyrus took up a good amount of the table. Piles of notes, records, forms, and other data lay nearby, while carefully recorded and classified fragments from artifacts were arranged in another space. Then there was a wig, lined with plaster of paris and sprayed all over with liquid plastic because of its condition when discovered. Pictures, dozens that would soon grow into hundreds, lay with the records.

Paul looked at it all numbly. At that moment it was difficult to concentrate on anything. But finally he took up the tweezers again and swung his gaze from his cot to the work before him.

Along with finer particles, there were also many small chips to be carefully inspected. After a half hour Paul gained a surge of strength, his second wind perhaps, and continued in the strength of it.

Using a magnifying glass and tweezers, Paul examined a slightly larger piece of stone. "Josef? Take a look at this."

Josef took it gently and studied it for a moment. "It's a dash, Paul." He got up and took it even nearer the light. "Yes—it *is* a dash!"

Paul's sandy brows came down close between his eyes. "A dash? That's for an unknown vowel, if I recall my Egyptian—ancient Egyptian, that is—writings correctly."

"That's right." Josef's black eyes shone with unveiled excitement. "A lot of Egyptian names skipped like that, a letter and a vowel and so on. The reason was that everyone had his own pet idea of what vowels should be used. That's one thing that has made it so hard for men like you and me."

They worked with more enthusiasm than before. The clock ticked off the minutes. A quarter to five. They had a whole letter. *S*. The dash went snug against it. Another letter was slowly translated. *K*.

"We're onto something!" Josef remarked breathlessly. He looked up with a solemn grin. "I think we're going to have a present for the world. The challenge to greater faith in God's Word."

Paul laughed with joy. "I believe it. I believe it!"

It was 6:30 when all the letters were found. But such small particles were missing that it was impossible to discover exactly which letter was next, or what the proper order of letters should be.

Josef sighed audibly and flexed his arm and shoulder muscles. "Let's take a look in that book over there, Paul."

Paul looked doubtful. "All right. Let's see, we have letters *S, K, H*—and a couple of dashes. Shouldn't be too hard, if the man's name is in here. Trouble is, we've got to remember that this man was not a noble at the time of his death. He was only a taskmaster. He may not even be mentioned here."

Josef sank back with a look of triumph. "There's another letter: *T*. With the dashes, we could attempt a hundred arrangements with the letters and still come up with everything but the right name."

Paul began flipping pages. Methodically he started with *H,* and then put with it every combination of *S, K,* and *T,* plus dashes, that he could think of. Nothing.

Dawn was gently lifting the veil of darkness. Yellow candle drippings had formed small pools on the table and would have to be scraped off when hardened. Outside, the crew had emerged from sleep and wanted to get some working time in while it was still cool. It seemed only a short interval before the cry sounded, a long cry like a hard urgent whiplash, and the chant broke forth. *"Salli ala elnabi! Salli ala elnabi!"*

"I don't believe it," Josef whispered.

"I do." Paul dropped to his cot and propped his head on his pillow. "Let's try *T*." But his nervous system was solemnly resisting all further attempts to concentrate, and his mind was a hard ball of tangled yarn. He passed a hand over his face, was aware of a stubble of beard, pressed the large book against his chest, glanced at Josef's closed eyes, and took heed of his heavy, even breathing. Paul sighed deeply and slept.

27

The tent was in a gloomy half-light. The Coleman lantern had gone out hours before and hung cold and dead in the rear of the tent. Candle stubs sat in hardened tallow lakes. The only real light came in narrow shafts through crevices around the canvas windows, still closed from the night before. An insect buzzed fretfully from cot to cot, finally seizing upon a few crumbs of fruitcake left in its original tin. Silence enclosed everything.

Not quite. Murmuring somewhere in Paul's subconscious were voices, but they were foreign and distant and it made no difference to him. Or did it? He opened his eyes sharply, lay as though stunned for several moments, trying to connect, to orient himself. Without moving, his eyes searched the tent. Then abruptly he untensed and closed his eyes.

He tested himself mentally to see whether he was rested. Tentatively he flexed his arm and leg muscles. He wanted desperately to sigh, but common sense told him that he'd already been doing too much of that, and that deep sighing only washed more and more carbon dioxide out of the bloodstream and made one more exhausted in the end.

He felt dirty. His clothing was wrinkled, hair unbrushed and disheveled, sandpaper covered his face. But his vision was clear and his senses rested. He looked at his watch. Two-thirty. He felt no surprise, except that Ahmed had not wakened them.

Paul swung his legs over the side of the cot and pulled himself upward. "Ahmed probably saw our light and decided to let us sleep," he mumbled.

"What did you say?"

The muffled voice came from the other cot, but Paul made no reply. Fumbling with some canned heat, he started some water boiling for coffee and a shave.

Josef moved slowly from his sleeping position. There was no

jesting today. Time was at a premium. Energy must be conserved. The Greek silently rolled up the canvas flaps and tied them, allowing brilliant light to shine through the windows. Then he opened cans of scrambled eggs and ham and passed them to Paul to be heated.

They bathed in scant amounts of water, shaved, found clean clothes, and sat down to eat without a word passing between them. Paul poked a quarter of a hot biscuit into his mouth, drank a half cup of black coffee, and reached behind him for the book that had fallen during the day.

"T," he said simply.

Josef reached for a scrap of paper. "All right, let's try for *TH.*"

Paul finished his food, put the tin to one side and opened the book. "Here's Tendad, Tamat—quite a number of men listed along here. Wait— Here's—" Paul half rose to his feet, only to sink back a moment later. "Almost got hung up on that one, Josef. T—h—smeses. But the *k* is missing. Besides that, he's from 1600 B.C."

The men went through the *t*'s at an exhausting pace. No revelation burst before them. No clue enhanced their vision. The *t*'s, so far as this book was concerned, were finished.

The *s*'s then. Josef tackled that section methodically while Paul paid a visit to Ahmed and then took a few minutes out for some badly needed exercise.

Alone and without his helmet, Paul felt the thrill of new enthusiasm flow through his veins. He trotted lightly over the newly sifted sand, wondering at the velvet-gold ripples, as though this part of the desert had never been disturbed. But the broiling sunrays were too hot for jogging and he paused to turn his gaze away to the rocky cliffs which held back the desert. Again he was aware of an excitement stirring within him.

" 'I will lift up mine eyes unto the hills,' " he murmured, " 'from whence cometh my help.' " His voice deepened and he stood straight and strong. "God, give us Your help today for Your own glory. Let the world know there's not a blotch against Your Word."

When he returned to the tent, he found Josef bending over the table, book before him. Something about the Greek spoke of anticipation, expectancy. He did not look up but simply put out a hand and motioned for Paul to come closer.

"Got something, Josef?"

"You want to hear? Listen. 'S—t—khmoses! (Occasionally spelled Setakhmeses, but usually left with dashes.) Noble who lived sometime about 1400 B.C., was important to Pharaoh as steward over the palace courts. Thought to have been caught receiving favors of visiting guests and misusing palace funds, S—t—khmoses was demoted to taskmaster. A wife, Ketah. Son, Rifai.' "

Paul sat on the stool with hands dropped loosely between his knees. "Wow! That's it, Josef! That's what we've been looking for, man!"

"Would you like to hear the rest?" the Greek asked with a rather wry smile.

"There's more?" Paul demanded eagerly. "Well, come on, let's have it."

" 'S—t—khmoses disappeared shortly after his new position and is thought to have killed himself. Rifai, a renegade after his own rights, denounced all the gods of Egypt, finished his father's tomb and vanished from history.' "

Josef passed the book to his friend, who devoured it with sharp interest. He scanned the two short paragraphs over and over, thankful that someone a couple of hundred years back had found ancient copies like unto this book and had sat down to record the nobles again, lest all of them disappear without a trace.

"Thank God," Paul said with deep feeling.

"Yes. Thank God."

Paul's mind went racing ahead. Eddie was coming. There was hard work at hand. The final reconstruction of this name must be finished first—a task that could take several days. This job was preeminent. It must be finished before the appearance of Eddie or anyone else.

"All the decipherings and all the picture writings are beginning to make sense now. With what history tells us, we know for certain now that the man being murdered in the picture is none other than our S—t—khmoses, a hated taskmaster, apparently a very cruel one, being killed by none other than Moses himself."

"All the glory being given to Moses, making it look as though it were really his tomb, when in reality Rifai had denounced the gods of Egypt to follow Moses and his God."

Paul began slowly to piece together another thought. "I wonder if he knew that by rejecting his gods and soaring to spiritual realities with his ideal he could have plunged the world into a most awful darkness?"

Josef contemplated silently. "I doubt very much whether one can ever say for certain." But the implication of it was great and it lay between them like a fearful memory whose depths would never be unfolded to a godless world.

A sudden lightness took hold of the men. Now there was no problem in the funeral texts and other writings within the tomb that alluded to the greatness and glory of the man buried in that tomb. Evidently the one-time noble had written the texts himself, looking forward to the glory of his earthly life as well as the life thereafter. For certainly none of the writings gave way to any fear that he might be demoted. And, happily looking forward to the afterlife, he had prepared well for his hoped-for eternity.

"He evidently didn't live long after becoming a taskmaster," Josef said slowly, as though seeing into Paul's thoughts.

"My conclusion exactly." He moved toward the door, flexing and unflexing his fingers. "Do you suppose that S—t—khmoses or Setakhmeses, whichever it is, was a bad father?"

Josef didn't answer. He was working meticulously, never moving his gaze from the growing piece of rose-hued quartz. There were already indications that it was going to be distinctly smooth and would take on again the same high polish as the rest of the sarcophagus.

The men worked alternately, for fitting in the particles of granite at this point took far too much concentration for one man to stay at it very long.

Once Josef picked up a Bible and turned to the book of Deuteronomy. He felt less like a monk every day, and the memory of monastic life was as a dream in another world. Finding what he was searching for, he read aloud, " 'So Moses the servant of the LORD, died there in the land of Moab, according—' Get this, Paul: '*—according to the Word* of the LORD. And *he* buried him [Moses] in a valley in the land of Moab, over against Bethpeor: but no man knoweth of his sepulchre unto this day.' Listen to this, down here at the end, Paul: 'And there arose not a prophet since in Israel like unto Moses, whom the LORD knew face to face.' "*

*Deuteronomy 34:5-6.

And Paul, having once known this portion of Scripture well, listened with heart aflame, as though just hearing it for the first time.

Josef laid aside the Bible and came to take up the work. "Do you think it's possible for a man today to know God like that?"

Paul hesitated. "Well, Josef, I'd say it would take much time, a lot of Bible, and a lot of prayer. I believe man can know God to the degree with which he truly desires and seeks to know Him."

Josef nodded slowly. "I mean to know Him a whole lot better than I do now."

"And I," Paul rejoined solemnly. "And I."

An hour ticked past. Paul went to the dig and surveyed the work. There was a continual clearing away. It was not so much now that there was a speck of antiquity discovered in these sands; rather, it was the desert moving aside to allow the bit of forgotten splendor to be seen.

Splendor. Yes, it was a mark of beauty, the simplicity of majesty. Paul would recommend that a restoration crew be sent in when he went to pick up Eddie. All crumbled parts would be so perfectly reconstructed and restored that no one would know the work had been done. Colors would be matched to perfection. The restoration to the burial chamber and the porch outside with its broken pillar would be so skillfully reconstructed that even to the professional eye the tomb would be as it was in its beginning.

It was 6:30, still light, when the men went to the dig bearing the precious lettering S—t—hk. Nevertheless, they carried powerful lights and a small bellows with which to blow out every sand or dust particle from the chipped coffin.

The golden statue of the man in the chapel met them as usual, smiling and hospitable. Inside the burial chamber other objects caught their view. The table which had been spread with food for the man's journey. A white alabaster makeup box with small jars, a jewel case, eye makeup, statuettes.

It was dim in this room. The body of the woman, Ketah, lay exactly where it had always been. On the wall behind her was her picture. There was a man at her side and a boy—Rifai—who looked away from his father to another man. There was the mark of longing on the youth's face. The same look that he bore in the chapel's picture of one man rising up and murdering another.

Moses—the man Moses—who had slain the taskmaster because he was cruel to the Hebrews. All this coincided now with the additional information in the big yellowed book whose pages had turned brittle with age.

"All the glory to Moses," Paul muttered through his teeth. "From the first picture to the last. And only four little letters to make up the difference."

"It all comes so clear now. If Setakhmoses—we'll choose our vowels too—was steward over the courts of Pharaoh, that means that Rafai would have been very familiar with the courts and the grounds also."

Paul looked up from his kneeling position at the coffin. "You mean, since Moses grew up in those courts that he probably had many encounters with the boy?"

"Certainly! Would he not, then, have told Rifai about his belief in the true God?"

Paul comprehended quickly. "You may have the answer, Josef. For Moses' mother, we can be sure, was faithful in teaching Moses about *the* God during the time she had him with her. We know this is so, or it would never have been said that Moses esteemed the reproach of Christ greater riches than the treasures of Egypt. Faith surely entered into the heart of Rifai, then, for him to forsake the gods of Egypt and follow after Moses."

Paul was working with a fine dental tool, dislodging a last particle of sand. Four hands worked as one during the next tense moments. The insert was perfect. No one could ever doubt but that the writings were in perfect position.

"Some of those other chips will fit these other nicks too, I'll wager," Paul grinned. "And when it's finished even the sarcophagus will be perfectly restored to its original condition."

* * *

Carolyn was waiting under the awning of Paul's tent. Tiny sand flurries settled upon her shoes, changing them from white to gold. Paul had never seen her so lovely. She was music and sunshine and a soft summer night. She was love and laughter and a bubbling brook.

It seemed incredible that this desolation and heat and nothingness would not immediately consume such a touch of beauty. The American's heart melted with gratitude that God would have so cared for him as to send Carolyn to this bleak land to give him the message of the cross once again.

He paused a few feet from her, embracing her without a touch. The delicate fragrance of perfume pressed close and then eluded him oddly.

He looked at the green and gold collar that hugged her neck. "No one but you could wear the accent of India with such grace— except perhaps Nehru himself. And then it would lack the feminine charm."

Their voices blended in laughter. Their embrace was easy, natural; it was home for them both. For a moment or two he held her, and the warm, tender security of love exchanged and flowed together.

Carolyn walked slowly toward the jeep alone, got inside and made herself comfortable. Paul brought an attaché case from the tent, filled with maps, survey forms, data on the political, economical, and cultural evidence gathered from both tomb and papyri. There were now more than two hundred pictures and more pages of notes than Paul cared to recount.

It was Josef's last day with Paul and both men felt the loss keenly. No longer a monk, Josef was dressed in a light-weight pinstripe suit donated by Jim Foster, and waiting for him at The Egyptian were his papers. Mr. Jabari had pulled a few strings in order for Josef to fly to the United States, but his passport was in perfect order and Josef was eager now to take up his new life. Jabari had a job waiting for Josef when he arrived in the United States. It was with the Arrowhead Archeological Foundation, a firm who sent out small parties in search of Indian ruins, old pueblo dwellings, cave dwellings, and ancient picture writings. But both Paul and Josef wondered if they might not be brought together at some future date to again work to bring history to light in this part of a darkened world.

Jim, who could not accompany them to Cairo because of his own experiments, Ahmed, and members of the crew shook hands with the Greek, for he had won the friendship and confidence of them all.

Paul and Carolyn would pick up Eddie this same afternoon, and he and Paul would carry on with the work until they were completely finished, a matter of at least several weeks.

The jeep rolled lazily through the sand. No one spoke for several moments. Then Josef said, "It's pretty well rolled up, Paul."

"Thanks to your help."

"Do you think the whole story will ever leak out?" Josef asked, more to himself than to Paul.

Paul glanced at Carolyn, loved her with his eyes, then to Josef, who was a brother in Christ walking down the warm corridors of his soul. A song formed within his heart. "One day a Stranger, a wondrous Stranger, came walking down by blue Galilee! . . . And this same Jesus still has the power, to save the lost and sick to heal!"

This Jesus! *This Jesus. And Moses esteemed the reproach of Christ greater—* How the world needed this very same Jesus.